AMERICAN EMERALD

DAVID SNOW

BY THE SAME AUTHOR
Someone Has Taken My Place
Universal Scams & Fraud Detection
The Special Investigation (Screenplay)
www.davidsnowwriter.com
ISBN: 0995467609
ISBN 13: 9780995467606

DEDICATION & NOTE FROM THE AUTHOR

T his book is dedicated to all American, British, Irish Soldiers and other members of the military including their families, who put themselves in harm's way, so that we can continue to enjoy what we should never take for granted; our Freedom and Peace.

In particular, I remember Sgt. Daniel Tallouzi of the United States Army and the courageous efforts of his mother Mary, who works tirelessly with the Wounded Warrior Project. Daniel Tallouzi died of wounds sustained in Iraq in 2009. He was 25 years of age. It is so important that we, not just American's recognise Daniel and the sacrifice of so many in the pursuit of freedom.

In addition, the British and Irish Forces and in particular the many Irish men who served with great pride in all the wars, but most notably World War 2 and the liberation of Europe. My Grandfather Joseph Snow and Great Grandfather Joseph Brooks, who both served with pride in the British military.

We must show our appreciation and gratitude by supporting the soldiers on their return to our shores. Get behind charities such as the American Gary Sinise Foundation – *"serving honor and need,"* – https://www.garysinisefoundation.org/

The Wounded Warrior Project https://www.woundedwarriorproject.org/

or The British Help for Heroes charity http://www.helpforheroes.org.uk/

'You don't have to support the war to support the soldiers.'

Additionally the Irish charity A Little Lifetime Foundation provides support to bereaved parents of babies who die at the time of birth. A very worthwhile charity

http://www.alittlelifetime.ie/

If you have received a discounted or free copy of this book, please pay it forward and consider making a donation to one of the above charities.

Thanks to Mary Tallouzi of the United States Wounded Warrior Project and my friend and colleague Brian Wilson, for the US military research and technical assistance.

A particular note of thanks to my former English teacher, Alec McAllister, who made the subject of English interesting and never gave up on any student. An inspirational teacher to all students who attended his Music and English classes.

US Army Sgt. Daniel Tallouzi

"We are forever indebted to those who have given their lives that we might be free"

U.S. President Ronald Reagan

CHAPTER 1
DONEGAL IRELAND

ߺߒ

I t was a soft day in the townland of Termon, Donegal, with a misty rain and fog covering the lowlands and beautiful green-covered mountains shining through the mist. Termon is a small and quaint village on the outskirts of Letterkenny in Donegal County, Ireland. Late in June, the weather was warm and pleasant but still chilly at night. Daniel Flynn, the son of Martin and Rose Flynn, was a fine, young, strapping man, 6' 2' tall with the muscular upper body of a rugby player. Daniel was a handsome man, with dark hair, piercing blue eyes, and the whitest teeth. Having just turned twenty years of age, he had lived all his life on the island of Ireland. He had visions and big dreams of a great and mighty future on the other side of the Atlantic Ocean. Daniel was not going to waste his time with university in Ireland; he was planning on moving to America, to follow his dream and his destiny.

Like so many past Irish generations, Daniel had planned to save up enough money from helping out at his Dad's six-bedroom hotel pub and on his uncle's farm to buy himself a plane ticket to America, join the U.S. Army, learn a skill or trade, and then to simply take it from there. One advantage Daniel had in being accepted in America was that his mother Rose had been born in America. Although she had only lived in America as a child for a couple of years before returning to Ireland, this gave Daniel a distinct advantage, at least in his own head. He also had two aunts living in Philadelphia, Ann and Nora, whom he had met only once when he was about seven years of age, but Ann's late American husband had left a real impression on the young Daniel. His mind had been focused from that moment on travelling to America.

Daniel walked along the narrow country road. Well, with respect to Termon, this was a main road, but in comparison to city roads or motorways, this was a country road.

'Well, Danny, how's she cutting?' asked young Michael Flynn, who was out digging his father's field.

'Hello, Mickey, she's cutting mighty fine. Are you going to the party tonight?'

'Wouldn't miss it for the world, Danny. I will see you there. And you never know, young Naomi O'Brien might be there,' said Michael in a flirtatious tone.

'Well, she won't be looking at you, Mick, especially if Joe is there in his new convertible BMW,' said Daniel.

'Ah, feck off, Danny. Someone's going to have to sort that bastard out. He's getting all the ladies around here. What chance have we got, boy?'

'He is welcome to them, Mickey. I am off to the United States of America to find my lady and fortune,' responded Daniel.

'Well, you have no fucking chance if you can't compete with Joe McGuirk here. Sure, isn't there thousands of rich yanks like Joe McGuirk over there?'

Daniel smiled as he continued walking towards his house. 'We will see, Mickey.'

'Ah… Good luck, Danny boy. Will I pick you up later? I have me Ma's car?' shouted Mickey.

'Thanks, Mickey, that would be great. Best make it about 8:30pm.'

Joe McGuirk was the local lad who had it all. He had a good education from Trinity Law School in Dublin but had done nothing with it. He worked in his Dad's Law Firm in Letterkenny as a lawyer. However, he had plenty of money and had done well from the Celtic Tiger economic boom. That is, he was one of the lucky few. He had sold his seven houses before the economy went bang, making a tidy nest egg for himself. That being said, he enjoyed flaunting his wealth, having spent over fifty thousand euro on his new BMW convertible complete with leather interior.

Daniel entered his parent's house, which was to the rear of the hotel pub. There was nothing else within a four-mile radius of the hotel, other than mountains, sheep, and a couple of farm houses. The bright yellow neon light of the hotel glittered the words 'Flynn's Hotel' into the misty night sky. The sign had done wonders over the years to fuel Daniel's imagination of the neon lights of American big cities such as New York or Los Angeles.

'Hi, Ma,' said Daniel to his mother, who was emptying the washing machine.

'Ah, Daniel my boy, will you go into the bar and help your Father? That bloody drunk owl Billy is shouting abuse again.'

Dan walked into the bar, which was also the restaurant of the small hotel. At best, it would hold no more than twenty-five to thirty people, although on a busy night like tonight, a Saturday, over thirty people could pack themselves into the small bar. Daniel's Dad was trying to talk sense into the local man, Billy, who had been abusing some British tourists.

'You're only a hungry shower of bastards,' bellowed Billy at the British couple, who appeared to be highly offended.

The other people in the bar remained seated, with the few regulars sitting at the bar staring into their pints of Guinness. They had become accustomed to the local man known as 'auld Billy.'

'I am very sorry about this,' said Martin, Daniel's father, to the British gentleman.

'Oh, that's quite all right,' responded the British man.

'That's an English Bastard, Danny. Get him out,' shouted Billy.

'Come on, Billy, I'll bring you into the kitchen for some of me Ma's apple pie,' replied Daniel.

Daniel and his father jostled Billy into the kitchen of their home, where he continued to shout abuse, but nobody was listening to him.

'English rotten bastards. Get them out and, wait a minute... yes bastards, where is me pint of Guinness gone?' asked Billy

'Sit down here now, you big drunk lump,' said Martin as he lifted Billy into the armchair located beside the television.

'Daniel, will you go into the bar and look after that English man? Give him a drink on the house whilst I try and sober up owl Billy.'

'English bastard,' shouted Billy.

'Sure. Da,' replied Daniel. He walked back into the bar and up to the British man.

'I am very sorry, sir. Now, can I get you a drink?' asked Daniel.

'That's quite alright, I have had worse. May I have a glass of Guinness and a Bacardi and Coke for my wife?' asked the British man.

'Certainly. Are you over on holidays?' asked Daniel.

'Sort of. I am doing some research on my Irish roots,' responded the Englishman.

Daniel poured a large Bacardi and a glass of Guinness for the Englishman.

'That's a bit unusual, an Englishman looking for his roots… in Ireland.'

'My dear fellow, I served in the British forces, Royal Irish Regiment, which is made up of fine fellows of Irish descent.'

'Shush now,' responded Daniel

'I know the war is over, but there are a few people in this area who would not be so welcoming to a British soldier.'

Daniel handed the drinks to the British man. 'They are on the house.'

'Thank you, very much, but there really is no need.'

'No, please, have a drink on us. You're most welcome here any time,' responded Daniel.

'That really is kind of you,' said the Englishman as he put out his hand to shake Daniel's.

Daniel shook his hand. 'What is your relative's name that you're looking for?'

'Oh, yes, my name is Terry O'Neill. That's Major Terry O'Neill,' he whispered. 'My Mother was Teresa O'Neill from this very townland.'

Daniel thought for a moment then continued: 'There is a Francis O'Neill who lives at the end of the lane on the right, about two miles out the road. I am sure she can help you.'

'Thank you, sir, thank you. But you know my name. May I ask yours?'

'It's Daniel Flynn.'

'Well, Daniel Flynn, thank you kindly for the drinks.'

The Englishman went and sat with his wife in front of a large open fireplace, which had been fitted with an artificial electric fire.

'Would that be Sean O'Neill's boy,' asked one of the men drinking at the bar.

'I don't know, but he is a true British Gentlemen, that's for sure,' responded Daniel.

Daniel's Dad Martin walked back into the bar. 'Daniel, will you give us a hand to put Billy in the car? I'll have to bring him home. He is completely locked drunk tonight.'

Daniel and Martin carried Billy out to the car park and tried to put him into the back of Martin's car.

'Stop, lads, stop! I have my own transport with me.'

'Billy, you're not driving in that drunk state. If Sgt. O'Brien catches you in that state, you will be barred from driving for life,' said Martin.

'Who said anything about driving? Sure, haven't I got Albert with me?'

'Ah, will you stop. Who is Albert, now? An imaginary friend who is going to drive you home?' said Martin.

'No, Albert is my horse. He is over by the wall. Albert! Albert!' shouted Billy, and he let out a couple of whistles.

Out from behind a wall walked a small grey donkey.

'That's not a horse, it's a donkey,' said Martin.

'Yes, a donkey to you, but a transportation vehicle to me, without an engine, which means I can drive him home without breaking the law. Now lift me up onto him.'

Martin and Daniel pushed and pushed at owl Billy until he was sitting on the Donkey.

'Thanks, lads. Good luck to ya,' shouted Billy as the donkey walked away.

Daniel and his Dad walked back towards the bar.

'You see what drinking does to you, son? Keep away from beer, 'tis evil and will destroy your life.'

'Don't worry, Dad. I don't mind selling it, but drink is not for me. By the way, could you give me a loan of €20 as I am heading over to the parish hall for the party tonight?'

'Are you still saving your money for America, son?'

'Yes, Dad. I change my money once a month into dollars, and I am just a little short.'

'You're a good lad. Here you are,' said Martin as he handed over a fresh, crisp €20 note from his wallet.

'Thanks, Da. Can you handle the bar on your own tonight?'

'Of course I can, son. Go on now and have some fun.'

Dan turned to walk away when his Dad grabbed his right arm and said, 'Dan, are you still leaving next Friday?'

There was a quiver in his father's voice, something Dan had never heard before, as his dad normally hid his emotions.

'Dad, you know I am. Sure, I have my flight booked.'

'Son?'

Another word his Dad never called him. It was normally Dan or Daniel when he was in trouble. 'Yes, Dad?'

'You know, son, I am very proud of you, and Ireland's loss is America's gain. I am going to talk to your Mam tonight and give her the news.'

'What, Dad, you mean you haven't told her yet?'

'I just couldn't find the right moment, son. This is going to really upset her. Look, you go out tonight, and I will tell her.'

'Dad, you have known for the past two months.'

'I know, son, I know. Look, I promise you, I will tell her tonight.'

'Da, do you want me to tell her?'

'No, son, I will tell her. This is going to be really hard for her, but please, leave it to me?'

'OK, Da.'

CHAPTER 2

D aniel's mother, Rose welcomed Mickey into the house: 'Michael,
come in. He will be ready in a minute.'

'Daniel, Michael is down here. Are you ready?' shouted Daniel's mum.

Daniel came running down the stairs in his new blue jeans, black
boots, and shirt.

'Well, would you look at the head on that,' said Michael.

'You boys have a good night, and don't be bringing home any funny
girls, Daniel. I am far too young to become a granny.'

'Ok, Mam, see ya later,' said Daniel as he kissed his mum goodbye.

'What the hell, Mickey? We're not going in that banger?' asked Daniel.

'It's a 1990 Ford Escort XR3i with a 1.6 litre engine and a Pioneer
stereo.'

'It's a bucket of shit, Mickey.'

'Well, if you want to walk, Danny boy…'

'Ah, come on, let's go.'

Mickey drove down the lane from Flynn's bar and hotel.

'Wait till you hear the sounds man,' said Mickey with excitement as he switched on the car CD player. 'Staying Alive' by the Bee Gees blasted from the stereo.

'The Bee Gees, Mickey? Are you fuckin serious?'

'Yea, Dan, class music. Trying to get tickets to see Barry Gibb in Dublin in September.'

'Well, Mickey, the car is a heap of rubbish, but at least the stereo is good. Not so sure about your choice of music. Is it not a bit 1970s?'

Mickey drove the short distance to the St. Colmcille's parish hall, where there was a party arranged to raise funds for the local GAA.

'Evening lads,' said Garda O'Brien as he stopped the car.

'Hi, Seamus. Are you not supposed to be checking for drink driving after the party?' asked Mickey.

'Less of the Seamus, its Sgt. O'Brien to you now; I see your road tax is out at the end of the month, Michael.'

'It is, Sgt. O'Brien… em, is Naomi here tonight?'

'You keep your filthy eyes off my daughter, ya scoundrel, ya. Now park that bucket of shit over there beside Joe's lovely new BMW.'

Daniel was embarrassed to park beside Joe's sparkling red BMW, which was polished and shiny like a new coin.

'Stop looking at it, Dan. Come on, will ya.'

Daniel and Mickey entered the parish hall. It was a typical Irish party, with a DJ from Dublin playing all the latest hits in the corner. The local ladies were sitting on one side of the room, and the men were staring into their pints of Guinness while looking at the women like a pack of lions waiting to attack a group of deer. They just needed a little false courage from the pints of Guinness.

'Are you having a drink, Mickey?'

'Yea, the usual, please, Dan.'

Michael walked over to the barman, pushing past a group of young men who were all out chasing women, hopeful of securing a date from a young Irish girl.

'Pint of Guinness and a Coke,' shouted Daniel over the music, which was blasting from the speakers. Daniel returned to Mickey with the drinks, and they stood chatting together while eyeing up a couple of the local girls.

'So, Dan, are you still heading to America?'

'I sure am. I applied to the US army, and I have been accepted.'

'Are you fuckin mad, Dan? The US Army. Sure, ya will end up in Afghanistan or Iraq.'

'So... somebody has to go to keep to us safe from the nuts.'

'When are you going, Dan?' asked Mickey, with a sad and solemn look on his face.

'Next Friday, Mickey.'

'Next Friday. Sure, that's only a couple of days away.'

'I know, Mickey. I bought my ticket with Delta Airlines, and I am flying to Atlanta on Saturday, leaving for Dublin on Friday.'

'Jeepers, Dan, what does your Mam think?'

'Well, I kind of haven't told her yet. I told my Dad, but I don't think he has taken it in at all.'

'Dan, your Mam is not going to be happy with this news.'

'I know, Mickey. She has always known my plan to go to America, but she will not be happy when she hears I am joining the army.'

Mickey looked into his drink, took a gasp of air, and then patted Dan on his right shoulder, saying, 'Well, fair play to you, Dan. I will miss ya around here, but its more Donegal women for me when you're gone.'

'Oh, well, here he comes. Look at the head on him. 'Tis Joe McGuirk with two women. Well… would ya look at that bastard in his white trousers. Who does he think he is… Don Johnson from Miami Vice?' suggested Mickey.

'Ah, sure, leave him to it, Mickey, there's plenty of other birds in here.' Mickey really had a dislike for Joe going back many years.

'Ah, how ya, lads?' said Joe.

'All right, Joe!' responded Dan

'Somebody parked a bucket of shit beside my BMW.'

'You're a dirty bastard, Joe. Now fuck off with your red BMW,' said Mickey.

'Glass of Cider for me, two white wines for my lady friends, and give Mickey a glass of Coke and a packet of crisps for his troubles,' shouted Joe to the bartender. The two girls under Joe's arms laughed in the direction of Mickey.

'I am gonna kill him,' said Mickey. He reached out to punch or grapple at Joe, and Joe drew back his right arm as if to strike out at Mickey.

Dan put himself in the middle of them. 'Ah, lads, settle down, will ya. Come on, now.' Dan put his arm around Mickey and ushered him away from the bar.

Joe shouted after them, 'I will see you later, Mickey… you chicken shit.'

Without warning, Mickey jumped away from Dan and dived across the room, landing a punch square on Joe's face. Instantly, Joe's nose exploded, with red blood running down his face and onto his woollen cricket jumper.

Dan quickly grabbed at Mickey. 'Get off him, Mickey, leave him alone,' said Dan. However, as he was leaning over, trying to pull his friend off Joe, he felt a sudden pain in his head as one of the women with Joe smashed a Budweiser bottle over Dan's head. Feeling dazed, Dan looked up only to feel the kick of the same woman landing perfectly on his left eye. Dazed and bleeding, he felt Mickey pulling at him as Sgt. O'Brien in his full Garda uniform walked into the hall. Seeing the commotion and blood on Dan's face, and Joe trying to pick himself up off the floor, Sgt. O'Brien told the DJ to switch off the music.

'I fuckin knew yis bastards would be fighting. Didn't I warn you?' said Sgt. O'Brien as he grabbed Dan and Mickey and threw them out of the hall. Dan landed flat on his back in the car park, his head bleeding onto his face and his eye already starting to bulge and shine. This time Mickey stood over Dan, pulling him to his feet. 'Some kicking you got by that chick!'

'Shut up, will ya,' said Dan as he wiped the blood from his face.

'Come on, Dan. Sure, I will buy you a burger and chips in Fran's chippy.'

Mickey drove the short distance to Fran's chip shop with Dan holding an old jumper against his head to stop the bleeding.

'Do you want me to take ya to Letterkenny Hospital? Looks like a nasty cut.'

'No, I am fine. That wagon just caught me off guard.'

'I will sort that Joe McGuirk if it's the last thing I do. Come on, the grub is on me, Dan.'

Dan and Mickey walked into Fran's chip shop, which was a greasy, stale-looking place with a foul smell of sweat, the kind of smell you get in a toilet that has not been cleaned in years. Mickey put a coin in the jukebox, which had seen better days.

'Not another Bee Gees song... How many years old is Tragedy?' asked Dan

'We are a bloody tragedy, Dan, especially our love lives. What chance have we got in picking up any ladies?' asked Mickey.

'Well, it won't be a problem for me as I am off on Friday.'

'In one way, Dan, you are lucky, but I hope your luck doesn't run out when you're in Iraq!'

'Give us two large chips and burgers, Fran, and two cokes,' requested Mickey.

'What are you going to do when I am gone, Mickey?'

'I am going to try my luck with Naomi O'Brien, maybe settle down with a couple of kids, and sure, I will get my Dad's farm.'

'Mickey, your only nineteen. Do you not want to see the world first?'

'Ah, no. Sure, like I have all I need here in Ireland, and you know 'tis my home.'

Fran came over with the food. 'Who's paying for these burgers? Well, the Holy God, what the hell happened to you, Dan Flynn? Did you have a run in with Mike Tyson or something?' she asked.

'Yea, something like that, Fran.'

'I will get you some ice, lad.'

'Say, Mickey, you know the way you like this Naomi O'Brien girl?' smirked Dan.

'Oh, yes, a fine bit of stuff, a real babe. The things I would like to do to her,' replied Mickey

'And what would those things be?' asked Sgt. O'Brien, who was standing behind Mickey.

'Oh, sorry, Sgt. O'Brien, I... was... just,' shrieked Mickey.

'You put a hand on my daughter, and it will be the last thing you do, young Mickey Flynn.'

'Sorry, Sgt., we were just going.'

As Mickey and Dan left the diner, Mickey said, 'A dirty trick, Dan. Ya could have told me he was standing behind me.'

'Honestly, Mickey, I didn't see him standing there.'

'Hi, Boys.' It was Naomi, sitting in the front of her Dad's Ford Mondeo police car.

'Hi, Naomi. Early night then,' smiled Mickey as he waved over to Naomi.

'Yes, do you want a lift home, boys? My Dad will drop you off.'

'Hey, Mickey, I dare you. It will really piss of the Sgt.,' whispered Dan.

'No… but thanks, Naomi. I have me Mam's car with me tonight.'

'Me Mam's car, how corny does that sound, Mr. Bee Gee Staying Alive?' laughed Dan.

'Fuck off. Come on, let's go… more of a Tragedy tonight, Danny boy.'

'That's true Mickey, that's true.'

CHAPTER 3

cℓℓ℘

'Come on now, Dan, rise and shine,' said Dan's father as he pulled back the curtains, letting the bright sun in the window, lighting up Dan's bedroom.

'Ah, Dad,' responded Dan.

'Don't ah Dad me now, son. Come on, I need you to run the bar today. I am taking your mum into town to tell her your news. Well, look at the head on you. That's some shiner. Who were you fighting?'

'Don't ask, Dad. I need a shower. I will be down in an hour.'

'You have twenty minutes, son, now get a move on.'

Dan climbed out of the bed and looked in the mirror at his black and blue eye and battered face. At least his head had stopped bleeding. He stood dazed as he switched on the shower in his bathroom. Dan walked over to the window and peered out at the sun, which was rising over the beautiful green-grassed mountains. *I guess America will be all cities and grey buildings*, he thought to himself. He felt excited, but with an eerie feeling in the pit of his stomach as if he were about to sit an important exam.

'Good morning, son. I see you have been fighting again,' said Dan's Mum as he walked into the kitchen. 'There's tea in the pot and bacon in the oven. We will be back later this afternoon.'

'What about the guests. Will they not need breakfast?' asked Dan.

'All checked out, and Betty has been and gone, so the rooms are all done,' responded Dan's Mum.

Dan's Dad said, 'Dan, it's after 10 am. You just open the bar at 11. No doubt Billy will be back to keep you company. Oh! and stay away from Father O'Shea. We told him you were sick, but he heard about you and that McGuirk lad fighting last night.'

'Swell, Dad, swell!'

'See ya later, son. There's a couple due to check it today, said they will be here about 1 pm, a Joe and Sandy Evans. I think they're from Canada,' said Dan's Dad as he walked out of the kitchen towards the car with Dan's Mum.

'Oh, my head aches,' moaned Dan as he searched the kitchen press for some pain killers. Then he sat at the table drinking tea and talking to the dog while holding his head in his hands.

Within what felt like only a few minutes, there was a knocking or banging on the front timber door of the pub and hotel. Dan walked towards the pub door, saying, 'Will you hold your horses! I will be with you in a minute.' Dan opened the front door only to see Billy standing at the door, holding some twine that was attached to the neck of his donkey.

'Well, the holy... look at that for a shiner. I hope she was worth it. Come on now, open up, lad, and give me a drink.'

'Sure, it's not 11 o'clock, Billy?' shrieked Dan.

'Be God, your right, Dan, it's 10 after 11.'

Dan looked at his watch, which stated that the time was 11:14 am.

'OK, Billy, come on,' responded Dan as he opened the large timber front doors to the pub.

'You're a Gent and a scholar, young Dan Flynn,' said Billy as he turned and whispered something in the ear of his donkey. As if by magic, the donkey turned and walked to the rear of the pub, into the car parking area.

Dan shook his head in disbelief as Billy pushed him out of the way and walked into the bar.

'A Pint of Guinness, Dan, and a double shot of Jameson whiskey. Make sure it's Jameson. Don't be cheating me with any of that foreign Scotch whiskey.'

'Give me a minute, Billy. I will have to switch on the bar pumps.'

Dan walked away from Billy, leaving him in the bar on his own while he went to the keg storage area to switch on the pump. When he returned, Billy was sitting at the bar with an empty whiskey glass in front of him.

'Well, I see you got your whiskey, Billy.'

'What, that's a terrible, terrible thing to say to an old man like me, and this the Sabbath day. Do you know to accuse a man of stealing...'

'Billy, relax, man. Jameson wasn't it? And a Guinness?'

'Ah, you're a decent man, young Dan, a decent man.'

Dan pulled a nice creamy pint of Guinness and a double shot of Jameson whiskey without using a measure so it appeared more like a treble then a double. Dan and Billy made small talk while Dan opened the bar curtains and got the bar ready for the few regulars who would drop in for a few pints after midday mass. On occasion, a few of the local

Protestants would also drop in for a coffee and a scone after their service, so Dan switched on the coffee machine to prepare the fresh coffee.

'Does me eye look bad, Billy?'

'Not as bad as I thought it was going to look,' responded Billy.

'What do you mean? Who said it to you?'

'Ah, sure I got 10 o'clock Mass, and Fr. O'Shea told me you got a right beating from Joe McGuirk.'

Dan was annoyed at Joe spreading this rumour but was happier that it was supposed to be Joe that beat him up and not one of his many girlfriends.

'You know, I was surprised, Dan, as Joe McGuirk is only a little lad. Sure, you could have squashed him with one punch.'

'Don't believe all that you hear, Billy, but thanks for the compliment. Here, have a refill on me.'

Dan filled up Billy's glass with whiskey.

'You're a decent man, Dan, a decent man.'

'Billy, give me a shout if anybody comes in. I need to power up the cooker for the lunches.'

'Work away, Dan. The drink is safe with me.'

Dan smirked as he walked into the kitchen, leaving the local alcoholic in charge of the drink. Dan had put some of his mother's foundation makeup on his face in an effort to conceal his eye and bruises, and to be fair, it didn't look that bad.

'Dan, Dan, boy, we have a visitor'

Dan walked back into the bar, glancing at Billy, who was still sitting at the bar staring into his pint of Guinness. The bright sunlight shone into the bar area, and Dan could just about make out the outline of a person standing in the sunlight. It was then that she stepped forward out of the sunlight and into Dan's vision. Dan stopped and glared at the woman. He was in shock, completely frozen as his eyes feasted on the vision of beauty that stood before him.

'Well, are you going to say something?' uttered Billy as he turned and saw the young lady.

'Can I help you?' uttered Dan.

'Hi, I am Sandy Evans. We have a room booked here for tonight,' said the lady in a strong southern American accent.

'Oh, yes, Mr. and Mrs. Evans. I will get your key now,' said Dan.

'No sir, you are mistaken. It's just Sandy and Jo Evans,' said the lady.

'Jo is not your husband?' uttered Dan.

'No, he is a she, and she is my sister,' she replied with a snicker.

'Oh I see, I am sorry, would you like to complete the register?'

Dan handed the lady a large red book and pen and asked her to complete her name and address.

'So, you're an American,' enquired Billy, which should have been a question in place of a statement.

'Yes sir, pleased to meet you. I am Sandy Evans from Dallas Texas.'

'Dallas! You killed the Irish President Kennedy!' uttered Billy.

'Excuse him for his poor manners, interrupted Dan. I am Dan Flynn, owner of this establishment.'

'Pleased to meet you, Dan.'

'We had you in room 3 as we assumed… Joe was your husband, so I have moved you to room 1, which is two single beds.'

'Oh, that is funny, but thank you.'

Dan handed her the key to the bedroom, holding onto the key for longer then was needed. His eyes glazed and stared at Sandy, who was wearing cowboy boots, tight blue jeans, and a white blouse. Her long blond hair ran down her spine and glistened from the watery morning mist that clung to her hair. Sandy's eyes caught Dan's eyes gazing at her for a slightly uncomfortable amount of time.

Sandy turned, walked outside, and stood talking to another lady, who appeared a little older but was also rather attractive. Both ladies took carry bags from the boot of a car that looked like a rental. They then walked back into the hotel and to the bedroom area.

'Have you ever seen anything as beautiful as that?' asked Billy.

Dan stayed quiet, his mouth slightly open. He was transfixed by the young Texan girl; it was simply love at first sight.

'Earth to Dan… are you hearing me. Dan?' asked Billy.

'Sorry, Billy, just something on my mind.'

'It wouldn't be that little blond lass from Texas, O Danny Boy. The pipes… the pipes are calling you, boy, but I think Cupid has hit you right bulls eye… in the heart.'

'She is something else, Billy, that's for sure,' responded Dan.

Just as Dan was getting back to the reality of preparing the coffee for the Protestants, the two young Texan ladies walked into the bar.

'Gentlemen, may I introduce you to my sister, Jo.'

Billy jumped from the stool and took off his cap as, yet again, Dan's jaw fell towards the floor.

'It's certainly a great pleasure to welcome not one… but two beautiful Texas roses to Termon Donegal… Dan, Dan, boy, where are your manners?' said Billy.

'Oh… em… sorry. I am Dan Flynn. My parents own this establishment. You're very welcome to Donegal, Cead Mile Failte!'

'Is that Gaelic?' asked Sandy

'Yes, it basically means, one hundred thousand welcomes.'

'Oh, thank you, that is kind. Say, is there anywhere we can get some coffee around here?' asked Sandy.

'Yes, yes, please, have a seat. I just put on a fresh pot of coffee.'

'Lucky it's a Sunday and the Protestants are coming, otherwise it would be from a jar,' said Billy with a smirk.

'Shut up, you, ya eejit, Billy.'

Sandy and her sister sat at a small table beside the window, with the bright sun shining and a hint of floral scent in the warm morning summer air from the fresh flowers within the window box. Dan made the coffee, glancing at every opportunity in Sandy's direction. Dan nearly dropped the coffee pot when he caught Sandy looking back at him and then quickly turn away with a blush of redness appearing in her pure white cheek.

'Two coffee's, ladies. Can I ask what has you in these parts?' asked Dan as he put the coffee on the table and tried not to look at Sandy or, at least, not make his glance an obvious stare.

'My sister Jo is doing a Masters in political history, and she is...'

'I can talk for myself, Sandy,' said Jo.

'I am doing some research on Irish political history. I decided to stay in Donegal, as I hear it's a beautiful part of Ireland and it has easy access to Londonderry... or should I say, Derry,'

'Either is fine with me, but best err on the side of caution and stick with Derry when on this side of the border,' said Dan.

'Are you talking about those British bastards?' shouted Billy.

'Behave, Billy, or I will throw you out.'

'Can I talk now, Sis?' asked Sandy. 'I came along for the ride. I have always wanted to visit Ireland, so I decided to give my sis some company.'

'Well, you came to the right place if your lookin' for a ride,' shouted Billy.

'Shut up, I am warning you, Billy,' said Dan. He turned back to the ladies. 'How long are you staying for?'

'We leave on Thursday, heading over to Belfast, then back home to Dallas via London,' said Sandy.

'I am leaving on Friday, heading to America myself,' responded Dan.

'Oh, that's swell, but why leave this beautiful country?' asked Sandy.

'I have always wanted to live in America, ever since I was a child. I got relatives in Philadelphia.'

'So, you got a job in America?' asked Jo.

'Yea, as part of getting my green card, I have to do some national service in your army, so I will do that and then maybe go see my relatives in Philadelphia.'

'Sounds fun,' said Sandy

'Sounds crazy and stupid to me. You know you will most likely end up in Iraq,' responded Jo.

'Yes, I know, but it's not forever. Nothing… lasts forever,' said Dan.

'Love lasts forever!' responded Sandy in a soft tone.

There was an uncomfortable silence for a moment or two. Finally, it was broken by the sound of the front door to the pub opening. In walked Sgt. O'Brien, who tipped his hat to the two ladies and greeted Billy.

'Dan, a word please… in private,' said the Sgt.

Dan walked over to the corner of the bar away from Billy and the two American ladies.

'Dan, when you left Fran's chip shop last night, where did you go?'

'Mickey drove me home, straight home Sgt., and I went to bed, especially after the kicking I got last night… why?'

'Somebody smashed up Joe McGuirk's BMW last night, while it was parked outside the parish hall.'

Dan smiled and laughed out loud. 'Did you talk to Mickey?'

'You smart bastard, Dan Flynn, I know where Mickey was and you do too. If I find out you or Mickey Flynn had anything to do with Joe's BMW, I will be back. The law must be enforced, and I, Sgt. O'Brien, am the enforcer in this here parish.'

Sgt. O'Brien walked out of the pub and drove away in his Garda Ford Mondeo with the siren switched on for no apparent reason.

'Is he like a sheriff?' asked Sandy.

'Well, now you could kind of call him a sheriff, ladies, but I think the word asshole would be better suited to our Sgt. O'Brien,' said Billy.

'Billy watch your words in front of these ladies.'

'Oh, that's OK, I have heard worse,' said Jo.

'Will you have some more coffee?' asked Dan.

'Yes, please,' responded Jo.

'So, are you going into Derry later on?' asked Dan.

'No, it's been a long drive, so I think we will just take it easy, stay around the area before I start my work tomorrow. Is there anything to see locally today? Any activity?' asked Jo.

'Not much happens around here. It's rather quiet, only a GAA match today.'

'A GAA match, is that like a football game for… gay men?' asked Jo.

'No… it's the Gaelic Football Association. Our local team is playing St. Colmcilles,' responded Dan.

'Oh, it sounds wonderful. We must go see it, Jo,' said Sandy.

'What time is it at, Dan?'

Dan had about as much interest in Gaelic football as he did in cricket. He quickly checked the notice board before answering, 'It's at 2:30 today in the local pitch at Termon, which is only a couple of minutes' walk from here.'

'Oh, how wonderful. We will get changed and go see the football game, Jo. Come on, it will be great fun.'

Jo and Sandy stood up. 'Charge the coffee to our room,' said Jo, and the two walked out of the bar. Dan remained transfixed on Sandy as she walked away. His eyes focused clearly on her ass, which was neatly tucked into her tight jeans. He was smitten in every way with this young Texan lady.

'I'd say you will be at the match today!' said Billy.

'Shut up and drink up.'

Dan ran out to the kitchen to phone Mickey on the house phone. No answer. He quickly dialled Mickey's mobile number. Again, there was no answer, it just rang out.

'Ah, Mickey, where the hell are ye?' Finally, Mickey's phone was answered with a deep 'Hello...'

'Mickey, its Dan. Jeepers, have I got news for you. Two American angels just walked into the bar and are staying here. You gotta come over here.'

'Well, he can't!' responded the voice on the other end of the phone.

'Who is this?' asked Dan.

'This is Sgt. O'Brien of An Garda Siochana, Termon. Who is this?'

'Sgt., its Dan. Where is Mickey?'

'Dan, I knew it was you. Mickey can't come over and won't be coming over as he is in jail, my jail, and that's where he will be a staying.'

The phone went dead. 'What the hell? Oh shit, what has Mickey gone and done. Don't tell me he thrashed Joe's BMW,' said Dan.

CHAPTER 4

ℐℛ

D an's parents had returned to the pub. Before his parents could say anything, he quickly ran out the door of the pub and got a lift from a local to the Termon Police Station. As he approached the station, he could see the Sgt.'s patrol car parked outside along with Joe's red BMW, which had been vandalized. Dan paused for a few moments to look at the BMW. Its front and rear windows were smashed and there was a large dent in the bonnet that looked as if it had been caused by somebody throwing a concrete brick at the car. The front bumper was also badly dented. The car looked a real mess but would be repairable.

Dan entered the police station. Nobody was in the small station except for the Sgt., who was sitting behind the counter, leaning back on his executive-styled leather swivel chair with his feet on the desk. The desk contained nothing more than an old Garda issued computer, a notebook, telephone, his Garda hat, a box of Marlboro cigarettes, and an ashtray that contained several cigarette butts and one lighted cigarette that belched smoke into the atmosphere like a chimney. The Sgt. had not seen Dan entering the station, as he was asleep, snoring his head off, with his hands resting on his rather rotund, very well-nourished belly. Dan approached the counter.

'Excuse me, Sgt.,' he said, but there was no response from the Sgt., who was in a sound sleep. This time, Dan raised his voice with a loud 'Hello, Sgt.' The Sgt. grunted and jumped in a startled manner as he returned to consciousness. He jumped up and looked directly at Dan.

'Ah, well, would you look at who it is, Rocky Balboa himself, or should I say Mickey Flynn's partner in crime, the… Dan Flynn himself.'

'Thanks for the compliment, Sgt., on Rocky,' responded Dan.

'It wasn't a compliment, Flynn. Don't get smart with me, or I will lock you up with the other Flynn. Now, what do you want?'

'Sgt., Mickey was with me last night. He couldn't have done that to Joe McGuirk's car!' exclaimed Dan.

The Sgt. sat on the edge of his table and took a fresh cigarette from the packet. He tried to light the cigarette with a match, but it would not light.

'Have you got a light?' asked the Sgt.

'Is it not against the law to smoke in the workplace?'

'Smart ass, I am the law in Termon.'

'No, Sgt., I don't smoke.'

The Sergeant opened his desk drawer, took a lighter from the desk, and lit a fresh cigarette. He inhaled deeply on the cigarette, and his face displayed the enjoyment of satisfying his nicotine addiction.

'So, you think Mickey Flynn did that to McGuirk's vehicle?' asked the Sgt.

'Is that not why you have him in jail?'

'Hmmm… Bollox McGuirk crashed his car last night on the way home from the dance. He must have been pissed drunk. Our patrol found the car crashed this morning.'

'But you said the car had been vandalized,' said Dan.

'That's what we thought until our Garda forensic man took a look at it. No, Mickey Flynn is locked up for a worse offense.'

'Sgt., what did he do?' asked Mickey.

'There are laws of the land, lad, like data protection, which stops me from telling you things, and then there are other laws like a father's duty to protect his daughter.'

'Sgt., what did he do? Please, tell me.'

The Sgt. stood up. He took another deep inhale of his cigarette and blew, or should I say, tried to blow, smoke clouds. He then opened his trousers and poured his large belly into his Garda uniform as he tucked his shirt back into his trousers. Once finished, he scratched his balding head and said, 'I suppose he has learned his lesson. Come on then, Dan the man, and I will release him to you, so now he will be in your sole custody and responsibility.'

Dan followed the Sgt. into the rear of the police station, which had two jail cells similar to what you would see in an American old west sheriff's office. The two cells were more like cages than the traditional solid brick cells. Upon seeing Dan and the Sgt., Mickey jumped to his feet and stood waiting for the cell door to open. The Sgt. opened the cell door, saying, 'Mickey Flynn you have served your sentence and you are free to go… but I will keep this cell for you open and ready just in case we need it again… do we have an understanding?'

'Yes, thank you, Sgt.,' responded Mickey.

'What did you do, Mickey?' asked Dan.

'Shush now, I will tell you when were outside.'

The Sgt. opened the back door of the station, saying, 'Goodbye gentlemen, I am sure I will be not seeing you again, Mickey Flynn, you useless boyo.'

Dan and Mickey started the walk back towards Mickey's house, which was about two miles from the police station. Dan was still curious as to why his friend had been arrested.

'Mickey, what happened? What did you do? Why did the Sgt. lock you up?'

'Oh, that bastard caught me in the act, red handed, it was so embarrassing.'

'What happened, Mickey.'

'Remember last night when we left Fran's and we saw Naomi in her Da's car?'

'Yes, come on, what happened, Mickey?'

'Well, after I dropped you off, I realized I had left my wallet in Fran's, so I went back and met Naomi, who had met her friends and stayed in Fran's. We got chatting, one thing led to another, and we ended up going for a spin in my car, and sure, didn't we end up at Lovers Point.'

'Mickey, that's great news,' said Dan. He knew that Mickey had had a crush on Naomi O'Brien for years, since they were in kindergarten, and at last he had made a move on her.

'So give us all the details, Mickey!'

'Things were going great. We were just talking and a bit of kissing, nothing else, but another car pulled into the car park.'

'Oh no! Not the Sgt. in the patrol car?' asked Dan.

'Not exactly, you're kind of right. It was the Sgt. in Mrs O'Flaherty's car with Mrs O'Flaherty, and they were doing more than talking'

'Ah, no way! She is rotten looking... but then the Sgt. is no oil painting... O! The Sgt. is separated, but Mrs O'Flaherty has five kids married and... gives out mass on a Sunday.'

'I didn't know it was the Sgt. until we got out of the car... and then the Sgt. seen Naomi. Oh, Dan it was so funny. He jumped out of the passenger seat of Mrs O'Flaherty's car with his trousers around his ankles.'

Dan burst into laughter at the thought of the Sgt. standing in Lovers Point with his trousers down. 'So what happened then?'

'We got back into the car, and I drove Naomi home. I went back to my place, but as I was getting out of my car, the Sgt. was waiting for me. He arrested me and brought me to the station.'

'He arrested you... for what... have you been charged?'

'I don't know why I was arrested, but he told me if I go near his daughter again, he will batter me!'

Danny laughed and patted his friend on the back as they walked along the narrow country road. His mind was firmly fixed on the young Texan girl Sandy, who was staying at his family-run hotel. All that Dan could think about was Sandy and her beauty, just perfect in every way. His heart was yearning for her. The need to be in her company was burning with a constant pain, but how could this be as he did not know her. Mickey was talking away, but Dan was not listening to him. Two young men consumed with the ambition of establishing a foundation with two ladies, each from very different backgrounds and countries, but little did Sandy Evans know how much Dan Flynn had fallen under her spell. The two young bucks continued walking.

'Beep Beep,' came the sound of a car horn, breaking the silence of the day, along with the soft purring of the new Ford Focus car engine which approached from behind.

'Hi, Daniel,' shouted Sandy as she leaned out the passenger window of the car, which slowed and stopped beside the two young men.

'Hello, Sandy, Jo,' said Dan, as he bent down and leaned against the car. 'This is my friend Michael Flynn.' Dan only ever referred to Mickey as Michael when he was being serious or trying to impress somebody.

'Hi, Michael, I am Sandy, and this is my sister Jo. We are looking for St. Colmcille's football stadium!'

'Stadium,' said Mickey. 'No stadiums in Donegal… you're going the wrong way anyway.'

'Oh, gee, would you guys mind giving us some directions, as we want to see the football game,' said Sandy.

'Well, as it happens, we are going that way ourselves, so would you like us to come along with you,' said Mickey in a friendly but overpowering manner as, by the time he had the words out, he had the rear door open in the car and had pushed Dan in behind Jo.

'You know, in America, it would be dangerous to pick up a hitcher. How do I know you're not a serial killer?' hissed Jo.

'Sis! Sorry, guys. We know Daniel, and I am sure he ain't no serial killer,' Sandy responded.

'That's a first for Dan to be called a serial killer. Now turn this car around and we will take you to the game.'

Dan sat in the rear of the car saying nothing; shyness had got the better of him. However, nobody really noticed with Mickey blabbering away. Within the short five-minute drive to the football grounds,

Mickey had obtained all the information he needed from the two girls. Jo had a long term boyfriend, and Sandy was single, which was the most important information Dan needed. However, Mickey also established that they lived in Dallas and were both university students, with Sandy being a freshman studying medicine.

They pulled into the grounds of St. Colmcille's GAA club in Termon, which did not have any stands, dressing rooms, or toilets. The rear of a truck was at the side of the pitch for the lads to get togged out, and the mobile chip van, which had Fran selling his usual chips and hot drinks, served as the refreshments for the supporters. To be fair to the girls, the stadium, as they had previously called it, was the furthest possible thing from what they would be accustomed to when viewing the Dallas Cowboys play football back home in Texas. Jo parked the car, and they all stood at the side of the pitch, with Dan trying to explain the rules of the game. Sandy had changed and was now wearing a navy tracksuit and boots, which Dan later realized were called UGG boots and not bear boots.

'Will you have a drink, girls?' asked Mickey.

'Yes, please, can I get a Coke?' asked Sandy.

'Black coffee for me, please,' said Jo.

Mickey walked over to Fran's mobile chip shop, leaving Dan on his own to talk to the ladies. The shyness had started to pass, and Dan tried to explain the rules of the GAA match. Both girls were lost but said nothing out of politeness.

'Give us two cans of Coke and a black coffee, Fran,' said Mickey.

'Coffee? Who is drinking fuckin' coffee?' said Fran as he brushed the dust off an old jar of coffee. He hit the jar against a table in an effort to loosen up the stale coffee granules at the bottom of the jar.

'Some yankee girl Dan has his eye on.'

'The wee blondie girl in the navy. Saw her coming in. A fine looking bird. Wouldn't mind giving her a poke myself,' responded Fran.

Mickey walked back over to the side line of the football pitch and handed Jo her coffee, which was in a ceramic white mug and not a plastic coffee cup as you would expect.

'My God, you call this coffee?' shouted Jo after she'd taken a sip.

'I am so sorry for my sister's manners.'

'That's OK,' said Mickey. 'Sure, the coffee is shite anyway.'

'Oh my God,' said Jo 'that guy over there has no pants on. Look, you can see his ass.'

'Good man, Frankie,' shouted Mickey. 'That's Frankie Downes. Do you know he scored two goals and four points in the last match? A trooper of a player.'

The players ran out onto the pitch as the supporters chanted and cheered their teams. It was a good turnout. There must have be at least fifty supporters standing on the side lines. The local priest, Fr. O'Shea, stood in the middle of the field beside the referee and the two team captains.

'Is that a priest? Why is he in the middle of the football field?' asked Jo.

'Just warning the lads to play fair,' responded Mickey.

The priest walked over to the far side of the pitch. Dan kept an eye on him. He did not want to see Fr. O'Shea as no doubt the priest would want words over last night's fighting. The referee blew his whistle, and the game commenced. Dan tried his best to talk the girls through the game and the scoring of points, but again, the girls struggled with the rules and his instructions.

'It looks rather violent to me, a bit like our football, but the guys don't have any protection,' said Sandy.

'It's not that bad Sandy. Sure, it's only a bit of harmless fun,' responded Dan.

'I have seen enough, Sandy. Come on, we gotta go. I have a long day tomorrow.'

'OK, Jo, I am feeling tired myself. I guess the jetlag has the better of me. An early night is called for tonight. See ya, boys.'

'Sleep well, ladies,' said Mickey.

Dan looked saddened at Sandy's departure from the playing field and stared at her as she walked from the field.

'Please, turn around… Sandy, please,' whispered Dan.

'She is way out of your league, boy,' laughed Mickey.

'Shut up, you fool.'

Sandy turned around, looking directly at Dan while walking slowly backwards. 'I maybe in the bar later, Dan,' she called. 'Will I see you there?'

'Sure, Sandy, see you later,' shouted Dan.

The two girls got into their car and started to drive away. Dan jumped into the air with delight and excitement.

Mickey quietly said, 'Well I'll be dammed. Good man, Dan, good man!'

CHAPTER 5

ol/o

Dan walked into his dad's pub with a smile beaming from his face. He checked the car park and noted that Jo's rented silver Ford Focus was parked there. Billy was still sitting at the bar, well, more leaning against the bar as he had now been there since the early morning.

'Good man, Dan. Did you catch up with the wee Texas lass?' asked Billy.

'All is good, Billy, all is good.'

'All is not good, Dan. You need to go talk to your mam out the back,' said Dan's Dad, who was working in the bar.

'Did you tell her, Da?' enquired Dan.

'I did, son. I broke the news to her.'

'What news is that now, lads? Tell Billy what's happening?' asked Billy.

Dan took a deep breath and gathered his thoughts before walking behind the bar and into the kitchen. Dan loved his Mother and did not want to upset her, but he knew he had to go to America and at least get it out of his system. He observed his Mother through the kitchen window. She was standing in the back garden, hanging some bed sheets on the washing line. Once again, Dan took a deep breath and paused for a few moments to gather his thoughts before walking out to the back garden. His mother instinctively knew he was standing behind her, just like your mother always knows when you're not telling the truth. A Mother and son relationship is one of the closest, if not the closest, relationships on the planet.

'Do you have to go on Friday, Daniel?' asked his Mother without turning around to face him.

'I have my tickets booked, Mam. I will need to leave on Friday as I fly from Dublin on Saturday morning.'

'I see. So why did you not tell me till now?'

'I told Da about a month ago, and he said he would tell you himself.'

Dan's mother turned around, leaving the washing on the line, and directly eyeballed her son. Dan could see that her eyes were red and watery from crying. She held out both her arms, and Dan ran towards his mother, embracing her as if he was only a five-year-old little boy once again.

'Oh, Mam, I am sorry. I never meant to hurt you or make you cry.' uttered Dan.

'It's OK, son. Sure, all children have to leave the nest at some stage in their lives. I just didn't think of you heading off to America at such a young age.'

'Well, Aunt Nora and Ann are in Philadelphia, and they will look out for me when I am over there Mum.'

'Yes, that's true, but who will look out for you, son, when you're in the American Army?'

Dan had been uncertain if his dad hold told her of his plans to join the army, but now his Mother was fully aware of her son's intentions. She cradled her son's head in her arms against her warm body, uttering the words, 'Holy father protect my only child, my son, as he leaves Ireland to pursue his destiny.'

'Mum, I will be fine.' Dan broke the embracement of his Mum's arms and sat down beside her as she composed herself and went on hanging out the washing.

'It's just so soon, you leaving on Friday, Dan. It's only four days away.'

'I know, Mum, but I have to go.'

'I know, son, I know. Just remember we are here for you if you need anything.'

'Thanks, Mam.'

The two of them embraced again, and Dan gave his mum a kiss on the cheek and a big hug before turning and walking back into the kitchen. He peered out the kitchen window and could see his mum wiping away a tear from her eye. This was the worst part of going away for Dan, but he just knew that he had to experience life on his own away from his parents. He sat in the kitchen at the table drinking a cup of tea. His mother walked back into the kitchen holding the empty laundry basket.

'We will have to arrange for Fr. O'Shea to say a mass for you, Daniel.'

'Ah, Mam, come on. I will be fine.'

'I also want you to get some of the Gartan clay and take it with you wherever you go. Will you promise me you will take some clay, Daniel?'

'I will, Mam,'

Dan's Mum put her hand on his shoulder, saying, 'What happened to my wee boy? He has grown up all too fast.'

'I am still your son, Mam, but I am a man now and have to experience the world.'

'I know, son, but it doesn't make it any easier on me.'

Dan stood up and wrapped both his large arms around his Mother like a giant holding a child in his arms. If Dan squeezed his mother, he would surely squeeze her to death like a giant python. But there was no chance of this as Daniel loved his mum dearly, yet he yearned to go and explore the world, knowing that his destiny was in America.

'Will you give me a hand in the bar, son,' shouted Dan's dad, which returned him to a sense of normality. He released the tight hold on his mother and walked back into the bar, leaving his mother to continue her motherly chores.

Back in the bar it had gotten busy, as the visiting club had beaten the local team with a hammering result. Dan quickly pulled pints of Guinness and opened bottles of beer for the defeated team and supporters. Frankie Downes, the key player of the team, had already downed several shots of whiskey and was now onto his third pint of Cider. It was doing to be a long, messy evening, yet Dan was still consumed with brash ideas of his young Texan girl and hoped that she would walk into the bar. While working in the bar he kept one eye firmly fixed on the small door which led to the hotel bedrooms.

'What was the score, Frankie?' asked Dan as he placed pints of beer on a table beside Frankie and a couple of other players.

'Don't ask, Dan. We were hammered out there. It ended 4 goals and 16 points to 1 goal and 5 points.'

'Yea, well, at least Frankie got our goal,' said young Pat, who was one of the other players.

'And, sure, you got a goal as well, Pat. Pity it was in our own net.' Laughter filled the small bar area as the players and supporters got happier with the ever-increasing alcohol consumption.

'Who was the wee blonde girl I saw you talking to at the match?' asked Frankie.

'One of our guests who is staying in the hotel. Wanted to see a traditional GAA football game.'

'I wouldn't mind having a go on her myself. A fine wee girl!'

Dan could feel rage and jealousy building within him at Frankie's comments, a strange feeling that he had never felt before, especially over a girl. He walked back to the bar, annoyed with himself for feeling this way but also somewhat confused as to how could he have such feelings for a girl he had only met. Now, Daniel was not the romantic type, and neither was he experienced in the ways of courting women. As for sexual activity, well, that would also score a zero, as having a kiss and a fondle with the local slapper Shelly Kelly was the limit of his experience. You could not include the spin the bottle games they used to play as younger teenagers, as the only girl kissing was Shelly. Women were in short supply in Dan's townland. The best looking woman in the area was in a long-term relationship with rich boy Joe McGuirk. Well, at least she thought it was a serious relationship, but McGuirk was off screwing girls all over the country.

Most of the locals exited the bar, leaving a well-oiled Frankie and a couple of cohorts drinking heavily at a table. It was now almost 8:30 pm, and Billy was still downing pints at the bar. Billy was a bit of a local celebrity as he was known to drink from early morning till closing time in the pub before staggering home, but without fail, he would show up for work at 6 am the following morning as fresh as a daisy. He used to boast that the whiskey and alcohol in his system would fight off any infection or potential germ, permitting him to never miss a day off work in his life. When Billy was finished with life and called to God, he would simply drop with a massive heart attack, but that was for another day and certainly not tonight.

The door that led to the bedrooms creaked open, and in walked Sandy, who looked fresh, radiant with life, and glowed as she walked into the dimly lit bar. It was as if there was an aura around her body, like a spirit glowing, as her beauty surpassed anything Dan had previously witnessed. Wearing a pink Ralph Lauren blouse and a black pair of skin-tight Levi jeans, with her long blond hair bouncing with her every step, she walked up to the bar and sat down beside Billy. There was a silence in the bar as if somebody had just died. Of course, Dan's jaw had dropped again as he tried to fight off his re-aroused shyness once more. Frankie looked over at Dan and grabbed his groin, shaking it as if trying to show Dan what he would like to do to his young Sandy. Once again, Dan tried hard to control his temper, but then Sandy was not his young Sandy, and any of the young bucks in the bar had the right to try out their chances with her.

'Hello, Billy, do you mind if I sit beside you?' asked Sandy.

'Look who it is, the beautiful Texas rose, and she wants to sit beside owl Billy. Will you have a wee drink?'

'A glass of white wine would be nice, thanks, Billy.'

Dan took a bottle of unopened, chilled Chardonnay from the fridge, even though there were several opened bottles within the fridge. *Only the best for Sandy*, he thought to himself, pouring the crisp wine into a large wine glass, which he also personally ensured was in pristine condition.

'Thank you, Daniel,' said Sandy as Dan poured the glass in front of her.

'Call me Dan, Sandy,' Dan stuttered.

'I'd rather call you Daniel, if that is OK.'

'Sure, call him what you want. Most people call him gob shite around here.'

'Thanks, Billy. Daniel is fine with me, Sandy.'

Sandy made small talk with Billy, who had not received this much attention from a female in the whole of his life. Dan was trying to look busy restocking the small shelves with bottles of beer and wiping down the bar area. Any onlooker could see that Dan could not take his eyes off Sandy and was constantly glancing in her direction, feeling awkward and uneasy about himself.

Frankie and two of the lads from the football team remained sitting at a small table when Frankie shouted over to Dan, 'Another two pints of cider and a Guinness, Dan.'

Dan poured the drinks and brought them over to Frankie, who had a bird's eye view of the rear of Sandy, who was sitting on a stool beside Billy at the bar. As Dan placed the drinks on the table, Frankie nudged Dan on the shoulder and said, 'Look at that ass. The things I could do to that. You can see her silk knickers sticking out of the top of her jeans. Oh yea, I think I will have to have a go on that.'

Once again, Dan could feel the rage and jealously build within him. He glanced over at Sandy, and Frankie was correct, her white silk lingerie was protruding from the top of her trousers. It was a vision of beauty and sexiness built into one. Dan walked back to the bar, slightly embarrassed at not being able to control his manly urges.

'So, Daniel, what is there to see around here? Can you recommend anything?' said Sandy as she fluttered her beautiful bright blue eyes at Dan while playing with the tips of her long blonde hair with her fingers.

'Em, well now, Letterkenny has a shopping centre. You might like that,' responded Dan.

Frankie had overheard Sandy's question and decided to muscle in on the conversation. He stood up and took a gulp of his cider, which dripped down his chin onto his shirt, leaving a horrid yellow stain. He put his shoulders back and walked over to the bar area, standing beside Sandy. There was a distinct smell of sweat off Frankie, as he had obviously not taken a shower after the match. A day or two of stubble growth was on his face. He looked like a bum and smelled like one too.

'So, you need a guide to show you around wee Donegal,' said Frankie as he leaned on the bar, looking in Sandy's direction, displaying his filthy, unwashed yellow teeth and breathing his cider-fumed breath in her direction.

'No, I am just fine, thank you,' Sandy replied with a shiver down her spine as she looked disgusted and somewhat distressed at being chatted up by such an unwashed creature as Frankie.

'Am I not good enough for you, Ms. Yankee?' asked Frankie in a drunk and aggressive tone.

'No, not at all, I just have plans.'

'Plans to be with me, you wee sexy thing, ya.' Frankie put his arm around Sandy, displaying a rather large, wet sweat stain under his arm.

'No, I am fine, thanks,' responded Sandy as she tried to shrug him away.

Frankie got more aggressive, dropping his hand from her shoulder to her ass and putting his other hand on her long blond hair.

'I'll show you a good time, you sexy wee thing, ya.'

Sandy pushed Frankie away. 'Please stop. Leave me alone.'

On hearing those words, Dan sprang into action and leaped over the bar like a knight coming to the aid of a damsel in distress.

'Back off, Frankie,' sounded Dan in an aggressive, authoritarian tone.

'Are you looking to start something?' responded Frankie as he stuck out his chest in an apelike manner. Sandy jumped behind Dan, placing her hand on his shoulder and peering out from behind his back like a defenseless chicken trying to avoid the onslaught of a vicious wolf. Dan towered over Frankie, who retreated to the table where his two friends remained seated.

'Come on, Frankie, it's time to go home,' suggested one of his friends.

Frankie, took a gulp from his remaining pint of cider while looking at Dan with an aggressive, angry expression on his face. He simply stood up and walked out the door. Just before leaving, he turned and said, 'I'll see you later, Dan Flynn,' and then he exited into the night.

Billy also stood up and staggered towards the door. Having being drinking all day, he was locked drunk once again. 'Goodnight to you both. I am away home.' As Billy exited the hotel, he whistled and called for Alfred, who came trotting from behind the hotel.

Dan turned and faced Sandy, who was still standing behind him, frozen at the aggression shown by Frankie. Dan could see that she was visibly shaken by the events.

'It's OK, Sandy, he is gone now. You're safe. Relax,' he said as he encouraged her to sit on the high stool once again. Sandy sat down, and as the bar was empty, Dan quickly locked the front door and sat on a high stool beside Sandy. He was delighted as at last he now had Texas Sandy to himself.

'Would you like another drink?' asked Dan.

'No, thanks, I am fine. I guess I had better go to bed.'

'Are you sure you won't have a drink, Sandy?'

Sandy stood and gave Dan a kiss on the cheek, saying, 'You're a good man Dan Flynn. You saved me tonight... Could you help me out tomorrow?'

Dan was feeling saddened at Sandy deciding to go to bed, but he was curious to know what she needed for tomorrow.

'Sure, Sandy, anything,' he said, sounding desperate. Sandy had hooked Dan, and her wish was his command.

'Jo is going into Derry tomorrow morning. I was wondering, if you were free, maybe you could show me some of the local sights.'

Without thinking he quickly responded, 'Sure, Sandy. What time suits you?'

'Say about 9:30. Would that be OK?'

'That's just perfect for me, Sandy. I will see you here in the bar at 9:30.'

'OK, see you then.' Sandy walked towards the door to the bedrooms. Dan's eyes were fixed firmly on her body, his eyes ravishing and devouring her every move. Sandy stopped at the door, turned around, and looked at Dan. 'Well, good night... Daniel Flynn,' she said in a flirtatious tone.

'See ya... Sandy,' he replied as the door closed behind her.

Dan's dad walked into the bar from the kitchen. He could see that his son was smitten with the young American girl.

'Oh, Danny me boy, have you eyes for that wee Texas lass?'

'No... Da... I... em... can I borrow your car tomorrow?'

'Just make sure you bring it back with fuel in the tank.'

'I will, Da, I will. Thanks.'

CHAPTER 6

✌

That night Danny could hardly sleep with the anticipation of having Sandy to himself, not to mention his first real date with a woman. There would be no rude interruptions from Frankie, Mickey, or any of the guys. He had meticulously planned the day in his head. He would take Sandy to Killybegs to see the fishermen and onto Slieve League to see the highest mountain cliffs in Europe. The cliffs of Moher in Clare, which are also beautiful in their own right, claim to be the highest cliffs, but Slieve League would be higher, only they are cliffs from the side of a mountain. Either way, both points are spectacular viewing areas. On a clear day the vision out over the Atlantic from both vantage points simply takes your breath away. Yes, Daniel was planning on showing Sandy the best of Donegal, West Ireland.

Dan awoke from his sleep just after 6:30 am. The only guests in the hotel that night where the Texas girls, so Dan's Mum was also up at this time and had prepared a cooked Irish breakfast for the two girls. Dan shaved and, not being happy with the first, went and had another shave.

Then he had a long shower, washing and gelling his hair back. He put on his new Levi's jeans and leather jacket. Looking in the mirror he resembled Danny Zuko, the character portrayed by John Travolta in the movie *Grease*, without the T Birds logo on the jacket. Dan was happy with his look and went downstairs, took his Dad's car keys, and drove his car to the local petrol station. His Da's car received a complete valet and car wash. The six-year-old Toyota Avensis looked in pristine condition. The car was also full of fuel, which must have been filled by his Dad the previous evening. Our Danny was ready for his big date – although he liked to think of it as a date, he did not consider it such as it was his duty as an Irishman to show the Americans the beauty of Ireland. But then it was something solid to try and build on for the future, and he would be alone with Sandy.

Danny drove back to his parents' hotel and sat in the kitchen. His Mother was busy doing her motherly chores while his Dad sat reading the newspaper. His Dad looked up at Danny and said, 'Would you look at that, a dashing young man, our young Danny!'

'Thanks, Dad.'

'One thing, Daniel, what's the smell?'

'Smell… what smell?'

'Do you not think you have overdone it a bit on the after shave?'

'Do you think so, Dad?' asked Danny as he tried to smell his face in his hands.

'Ah, will you leave him alone,' said his Mum as she loaded the washing machine.

'Where are you going to take her?' asked his Dad.

'Killybegs and the Slieve League cliffs.'

'Well, you have a nice day for it. Supposed to hit eighty degrees today.'

Dan smiled as he sat at the table, thinking of the day ahead and the warm temperature of his blood as he escorted Sandy, or more paraded her, around Donegal.

Just then there was a knock on the kitchen door that led into the bar dining area, and in walked Jo. Dan's dad jumped up. 'Good morning. Are you OK?'

'Yes, I am fine, slept like a log in this fresh Irish air.'

Jo looked at Dan. 'Wow, you sure do clean up well!'

Dan blushed with embarrassment and whispered a soft 'Thanks.'

'Would you have an adapter for an American plug?' asked Jo.

'It just so happens, that I do,' said Dan's Mum as she took the adapter from a shelf and handed it to Jo.

'Thank you... Daniel, Sandy will be down shortly... just doing her hair,' sounded Jo in a flirtatious manner, giggling as she walked out of the kitchen.

'Looks like you in for a nice day, Daniel!' said his Dad.

'Now you listen to me, Daniel. You treat that wee American girl with respect. None of your showing her lovers point!'

'Mam...' Daniel blushed.

'No hanky panky, Daniel,' said his Dad.

'I can't believe you two. I am twenty years of age. Bloody hell.'

'Just remember she is somebody's daughter.'

'Thanks, guys, for the vote of confidence. You two are truly inspirational,' Dan said as he stood up and walked back towards the bar dining area.

There was another knock on the kitchen door.

'Come in, come in,' shouted Dan's Dad.

Sandy's head peered around the door of the kitchen. 'Is it Ok to come in?'

'Of course, come in and sit down. You're most welcome.'

'Thank you. You Irish are just so friendly.'

Dan felt a serious bout of shyness come over him. He was embarrassed by the beauty of Sandy as she stood before him. Sandy was wearing her blue jeans, a tight white Ralph Loren Polo top, and a pink cardigan. Her long blonde hair was hanging perfectly straight down her back.

'Has the cat caught your tongue... Daniel?' asked Dan's dad.

'Leave him alone, will ya,' sounded his mam as she flicked the T cloth at her husband.

'You look amazing,' uttered Dan.

'Why... thank you. You look pretty good yourself.'

Dan could feel the excitement building within him and just about managed the words, 'Shall we hit the road so?'

'Hit the road... what?' enquired Sandy.

'Sorry, its Irish slang. I mean, shall we go now?'

'OK, can't wait.'

'Enjoy your day,' said Dan's Mam and Dad as Dan held the door open for Sandy. Outside, when he opened the passenger car door for her, he could see his parents peering curiously out the window.

'Do you... want me to drive?' asked Dan.

'No, of course not.'

'Silly me, I forget this is the passenger side, still stuck in America,' sighed Sandy.

Dan's Dad gave him a wave as he got into the car, placing his arm around his wife. 'This is the first time our wee boy has gone on a date. Doesn't seem that long ago he was playing with his soldiers and lego,' said Dan's dad.

'Yes... how time flies. I just can't bear saying goodbye to him on Friday. This is going to be hard, really hard.'

'I know Rose, I know.'

CHAPTER 7

D an drove from the car park, accelerating hard in an effort to be cool, which was hopeless as he was driving a family sedan. Sandy, being from Texas, was used to large, powerful engine sports vehicles such as Buicks and Ford Mustangs. Dan quickly realized that he was thinking in the right direction when Sandy asked the question, 'Why are all the cars so small in Ireland?'

'I guess it's because we have small roads,' responded Dan.

'That figures.'

'So, what do you think of Ireland?'

'It's really nice and so green, small, and quaint. Have you ever been in Texas?'

'I have never been in America, let alone Texas.' It dawned on Dan that he was heading to America on Friday and this time with Sandy could be his only time with her. The thought made him anxious and scared, but equally, he wanted Sandy to enjoy her time in Ireland and their precious time together that he was hoping might develop into something more lasting. But how would a long distance relationship work? His mind raced as he tried to relax and enjoy the moment.

'So you're heading to the states on Friday, to join our army?'

'Yes… No, I head to Dublin on Friday and fly to Atlanta, Georgia, on Saturday.'

'You're flying Delta? Good airline.'

'You fly home on Friday via Belfast.'

'No, we fly on Thursday from Belfast to London, then pick up the flight to Dallas.'

'Would you like some music?' Dan switched on the radio, 2FM. Ryan Tubrity was chatting on the radio.

'What's on the CD.'

Before Dan could stop Sandy, she pushed in the CD, which was Clannad.

'Sorry, that's my Dad's CD.'

'This music is awesome. Is it Irish?'

'Yes, in fact they are from Donegal… well, originally anyway. Think they live abroad now, maybe even America.'

'Great music,' said Sandy.

Dan drove along the main road heading towards Killybegs, which is a fishing village and harbor located in West Donegal. The sun was now shining, and it was getting warm.

'Phew, getting hot out. Should be a nice day.'

Sandy looked at the temperature in the car, which read 70 degrees. 'Back home in Dallas at midday, the temperature is about 100, so this is really nice for me… in Atlanta it will be a similar heat, so make sure to drink plenty of water.'

'Water... I just love your Texan accent.'

'I love your accent too, Daniel.' Sandy reached over and rubbed Dan's hand, which was on the gear stick, not in a sexy manner but flirtatious enough for our inexperienced Dan. The very gentle touch of her hand on the back of his made Dan feel relaxed and hopeful that the relationship might develop somewhat throughout the duration of day. That being said, Dan had certainly fancied women before. After all, he was a red-blooded male, but with Sandy he wanted to take things slow and was satisfied just being in her company.

Soon they arrived in Killybegs, a few fishermen were mending nets and getting their boats ready for the afternoon fishing trips into the Atlantic. Dan and Sandy walked onto the pier, which was littered with fishermen's nets and crab pots. Sandy peered out at the vast Atlantic Ocean.

'It's so beautiful. The nearest beach to Dallas is a six-hour drive.'

'Six hours. Texas must a big place. To drive from the east coast of Ireland to the west coast would take no more than three hours.'

'Golly gee, Ireland is small. You can drive all day and still be in the state of Texas.'

The two walked to the end of the pier. Dan felt a real sense of joy in spending time alone with Sandy. The day was passing fast, and he did not want it to end. The two of them stared out into the blue yonder with Dan taking more than the occasional look at Sandy as he admired her radiant beauty.

'It's a big ocean, Sandy.'

'Yes, it's so blue and beautiful.' The reflection of the sun in the water created a beautiful turquoise color within the sea.

'Next stop, Boston,' sounded Dan.

'Excuse me?'

'If you crossed that there ocean, you would hit land at Boston.'

'Yes, I guess you would. That is awesome.'

Dan laughed at Sandy's use of the word awesome, as she hung on the 'aw' with her strong Texan accent.

'Are you laughing at me?' asked Sandy as she hit out at Dan, slapping him on his chest in a giddy and childish manner.

'No, only kidding with you.'

Dan caught Sandy's blue eyes as she looked into his, and the two stared into each other's eyes. It was clear that the feelings Dan had so quickly developed for Sandy were growing and, just maybe, she was having the same feelings for him. Dan could feel the shyness growing within him once again. He broke off the stare. 'Come on, I have something else to show you.'

The two walked back the short distance to the car and drove on to the mountains of Slieve League. There was an uncomfortable silence in the car as they drove, so Sandy switched on the Clonnad CD and turned up the volume.

It was not long before they arrived at their destination. Dan parked the car in a car park, which was deserted. Although it was a beautiful day, people were working, so making a trip to Slieve League for the locals would be unusual unless it was the weekend.

'It's a bit of a walk, Sandy, but I think you will like the view.'

'That's OK. You mean it gets better?'

'Yes, Sandy, you're in for a real treat.'

The two walked up the narrow pathway along the mountains until they reached the cliff view edge some 1,200 feet above sea level. Nothing but a sheer drop to the Atlantic Ocean below. The sun was now high in the sky, without a single cloud to be seen. A perfect sunny day, which is a rare sight in Ireland.

'Oh my lord, I have never seen anything like this before. This is amazing.'

'Yes, I think it's one of the nicest views in Ireland.'

'We are up so high. Look at those boats down there. They look like tiny specks in the sea.'

Dan ushered Sandy towards the edge for a better panoramic view.

'I am close enough,' shouted Sandy as she put her hand around Dan's waist. Dan instinctively put his arm around Sandy's shoulder, rather clumsily. Sandy tripped over a rock. As she was falling, Dan flexed his arm, grabbed her, and pulled her close, saving her from injury. Sandy pulled herself to the left and found herself face to face with Dan. Once again, their eyes met and stared at each other.

'Saved me again. I think you might be my hero, Daniel.'

'Yea,' whispered Dan as their faces moved closer.

'I like you too,' whispered Sandy, their faces now only a couple of millimetres apart.

'I like you more,' whispered Dan.

'Kiss me and prove it,' whispered Sandy.

Dan moved his inexperienced lips and kissed Sandy, who responded to the kiss, placing both her arms around his neck in a loving, passionate manner. Dan responded by putting his arms around her waist and lower back, pulling her closer to him, almost squeezing her to the point of causing pain. The two kissed passionately as if they had known each other for years. It was hard to believe that this was a first kiss, as it seemed to go on and on.

Eventually, Sandy broke the passionate kiss, and the two lovers touched foreheads while still looking into each other's eyes.

'Wow, that was some kiss,' whispered Sandy.

Dan remained speechless for a moment. 'Would you like another kiss?'

There was no response from Sandy of the verbal kind. How could there be? Her mouth was once again busy passionately kissing Dan.

This time Dan broke the kiss as he hugged and held onto Sandy. If anybody had seen them, they would have assumed that the couple had been lovers for years, and not that this was the first and second kiss and that the two were not officially in a relationship.

'This could get serious,' said Dan as he held Sandy in his arms, looking out towards the sea, perched high on the Donegal cliffs.

'It sure does feel that way,' responded Sandy as she maneuvered back in front of Dan, kissing him passionately once again.

Eventually, the two broke the embrace, ending the kissing, and walked along the cliff face, arms around each other's waist.

'I wish this moment would last forever,' said Sandy.

'Me too, but we best make a move towards heading back to the hotel,' said Danny.

'Yes, I know. Jo will be back from Northern Ireland, and I will need to see her.

The two lovers walked back to the car, which took double the time it took to walk from the car to the cliffs. You see, they kept stopping, embracing, and kissing passionately. The drive back to Termon also took three times as long, as again there were intermittent stops for refreshments of the kissing and the hugging kind. Both of them where so happy in each other's company. It was going to be the start of a long and beautiful relationship; at least, that is what Dan had in mind.

'I was starting to worry about you,' said Jo as Sandy got out of the car and walked over to her sister, who was standing at the entrance to the hotel talking to a local man.

'I had the best day ever, sis. You have got to see the photos I took.' Sandy grabbed at her sister's hand and pulled her into the hotel, turning to Dan who was walking from the car. 'I will see you later, Daniel,' Sandy said as she turned back, looking at Daniel, winking and making a kiss shape with her lips. Daniel winked back and gave a slight wave as he walked into the bar.

The bar was empty except for Dan's mum and dad, who were stocking the shelves with bottles of beer and soft drinks, and cleaning the large mirror located behind the bar.

'Did you have a good day, son?'

'I did, Mam, a great day. Sandy really enjoyed herself, and before you say anything, Ma, I was the perfect gentleman.'

'Good boy. She is nice girl, Daniel, but remember she goes home on Thursday, and I just don't want to see you get hurt.'

'I know, Mam, I will be fine.'

'Will you help me in the bar tonight, Daniel? We're having a traditional music night, and it may get busy. Why don't you invite the Texan girls to come along? Nice for them to see some real Irish music.'

'That's a great idea.' Dan ran to the internal phone to call Sandy and extend the invitation, which was joyfully accepted. 'Be down at 8.' said Sandy.

CHAPTER 8

✑

D aniel took another shower and put on a fresh black shirt. He
washed his hair again and combed it back, applying hair gel. He
looked pretty cool as he stood in the mirror checking his look, with his
navy jeans and black cowboy boots. All he was missing was the cowboy
hat. His Dad joked at him as he walked into the bar.

'Did you leave your horse outside, Dan?'

'Oh, well, would you look at him. Must be trying to make the wee
Texas lass feel like she is at home in Texas,' said Billy, who was back sitting at the bar, peering into a whiskey and a half-drunk pint of Guinness.

Dan sat at the bar, talking to Billy and bringing him up to date on the
events of the day, without going into the intimate details of the kissing
as this would be kissing and telling and not right for a gentleman like
Daniel. The traditional band 'The Attic Boys' were warming up in the
corner: Barney on the bodhran, Jimmy on vocals and guitar, and Seamus
on the fiddle.

'Hello, Dan… heard you had a nice day. Sure, we may even have a song or two for the girls tonight,' shouted Seamus.

Dan nodded at Seamus and the band as he placed a reserved sign on a small table with two seats right beside their corner. 'Good man, Daniel. We will keep an eye on the Texan girls for you whilst you're behind the bar,' laughed Jimmy.

The bar was starting to fill up with the locals, including Fr. O'Shea, who loved a bit of traditional music. Thankfully, he must have forgotten about the fighting the previous Saturday as he said nothing to Daniel other than 'Two pints of Guinness.'

The door to the bedrooms opened, and in walked Sandy and Jo. Sandy had a big smile on her face, showing off her perfect pure white teeth.

'Sandy, you look amazing.'

'You look mighty fine yourself, Daniel,' she said as she gave him a kiss on the cheek.

Dan showed the two girls to the best seat in the house, located right in front of the band, and provided them with two glasses of wine, leaving a bottle of Chardonnay on the table.

'The drink is on the house,' sounded Dan as he walked back towards the bar.

'Oh, sweet Lord, that's great. Free drink,' said Billy.

'For the Texan girls. Not you, Billy.'

'Well, isn't that just fine. You give the free drink to the girls and nothing to your regular man. Well, you're only a hungry bastard.'

'Have a whiskey on me, you owl fool.' Dan poured a glass of whiskey for Billy without using a sprit measure.

'You're a fair man, Dan!'

Frankie the footballer and two of his heavy friends had entered the pub, and they sat at the bar drinking. Frankie eyed up Sandy, who had turned him down the previous evening, resulting in the standoff with Dan.

Mickey also walked into the bar with his arm around Naomi O'Brien and sat at a small table to the rear of the pub. He walked over to the bar and ordered a pint of Guinness and a glass of Coke for Naomi.

'Well, I see you have been busy, Mickey,' said Dan.

'You're one to talk, Dan the man. She is a fine looking woman, that wee Texas lass.'

'Are you taking your life in your hands? If Sgt. O'Brien finds out, he will put you back in jail.'

'Feck him. Look at her sitting over there, Dan. Isn't she just gorgeous? It's amazing to think that that fat bastard could produce such a beautiful daughter.'

'I... it is, Mickey. Just don't let him catch you.'

'I won't. I will see you later, Dan.' Mickey winked at Dan as he walked back to Naomi.

The music started up with a few slow ballads of traditional music. The girls tapped their feet to the music and nodded their heads. Jimmy sang a beautiful version of Danny Boy.

'It's a bit slow, the music. I thought it would be faster,' said Sandy as she stood at the bar talking to Dan.

'Right, so I am off. God bless all in this house,' said Fr. O'Shea. On seeing Fr. O'Shea standing up, the band stopped playing, and Jimmy the singer said, 'Good night Fr. O'Shea.' The band stayed silent for a few moments.

'Right so, let's get this party going. Barney beat that Bodhran with all your might,' said Jimmy.

Barney beat the bodhran, with a strong beat, and the music became much faster and louder. Many a great was played, including 'Whiskey in the Jar,' 'The Siege of Ennis,' and 'Black Velvet Band.' Sandy, Joe, Billy, Dan, his parents, and all the occupants of the pub became high on the music and traditional Irish dancing, and the Guinness was drunk like there would be a drought tomorrow. Even Sandy and Jo downed a few sips of Guinness. The music, atmosphere, and fun was electric and palpable. The hours passed like minutes, and the fun, or Irish craic, was mighty. Sandy was so happy and excited to be with her Daniel that she did not want the night to end. Jo could not take anymore and had decided to go to bed, but sleeping would have been impossible with the noise in the bar as the bedroom was directly linked to the bar.

'Would you like to go and get some air?' asked Daniel.

'Sure, Daniel,' replied Sandy, and the two lovers walked outside into the clear night sky. No sooner were they outside than a now very merry Sandy put her arms around Dan's shoulders and kissed him passionately. Dan was in heaven and could feel himself falling deeper and deeper under Sandy's magic spell.

'Look at how bright the moon is, Daniel, and I have never seen so many stars.'

'Yea, we don't normally have this clear a sky.' Dan paused a moment before continuing. 'Sandy, Jimmy is taking his boat out tomorrow. He has to do some work on Inismore and has asked if you and Jo would like to come along.'

'What is Inishmore?'

'It's an island off the coast, part of the Aran Islands, really popular with you yanks.'

'I ain't a yank, I am a Southerner.'

'Sorry.'

'I am only kidding with you, Daniel. I am Daniel's yankee southern girl,' said Sandy as she slightly slurred her words from the alcohol consumption.

Once again, the two passionately kissed under the clear night sky.

'Daniel, this is so romantic. Hold me in your arms. I don't want this night to end.'

'Me neither.'

'What time would we be leaving at for the boat trip?'

'Jimmy said he would collect us here at 10 am. It will be a long day. Won't get back till about 10 tomorrow night.'

'Well, Jo is gone again all day tomorrow, so I guess it sounds pretty good to me.'

'Great, that sounds...' Dan could not finish the sentence as Sandy began to devour him with passionate kisses.

'Dan, Dan,' shouted Seamus the fiddle player from the steps of the pub. Dan, who was wrapped around Sandy a short distance from the pub, shouted back, 'What's wrong, Seamus?'

'Fight! Hurry! Frankie and Mickey are going at it.'

Dan, broke the embrace and ran into the pub. When he entered, his friend Mickey was on the floor, being punched and kicked by Frankie and two of his friends. This was an unfair fight. Dan left Sandy at the door. 'Stay here. I will get this sorted.'

Dan pulled Frankie's two friends off of Mickey, who jumped up and punched Frankie square in the face with a powerful punch. Frankie's two friends, who were more like henchmen, grabbed at Dan but were no match for the mighty Dan. One of them punched Dan in the stomach, which had hardly any effect. Dan lifted up the two lads and bounced them out the door. He then grabbled at Frankie and, with the assistance of his dad, threw Frankie out of the bar.

'Consider yourself barred from this establishment,' said Dan.

'Fuck you and your American whore,' shouted Frankie, which Sandy heard as she was standing at the door to the pub. On hearing the words 'American whore,' Dan turned and walked into the car park with Sandy pulling at him. 'Leave it, Daniel.'

Dan grabbed Frankie and punched him again in the face, which had already been bloodied by Mickey's punch. Dan's Dad jumped in the middle of the two of them and said, 'Leave it boys. Come on, or I will call Sgt. O'Brien.'

Dan walked back towards the door, but Sandy was gone, nowhere to be seen. 'Mickey, did you see Sandy?'

'No, I didn't.'

Dan frantically searched for Sandy as the locals were leaving the pub and the band was packing up.

'See you at 10:30 in the morning, Dan,' said Jimmy.

Dan did not respond as he could not find Sandy. He walked up to her bedroom but did not want to knock on her door as he knew that Jo would be sleeping.

'Did you find her?' asked Dan's Dad.

'She must have gone to bed.'

'I wonder if she is gone on her own, Dan,' said Billy.

'Shut up, Billy, ya fool,' responded Dan as he felt lonely without Sandy. He walked outside and looked up at her bedroom window just as her bedroom light switched off, leaving a darkness in the room and a darkness within Dan's heart. He wondered and hoped that she would go on the boat trip with him tomorrow. The chance of spending more time with her was possibly dashed by Frankie and his cohorts.

CHAPTER 9

ℐℐℐ

The following morning Dan was up early. When I say up early, he was out of bed after only sleeping for about three hours. His mind was racing, wondering if Sandy would go on the boat trip. He knew that Jo would be leaving for Derry at about 8 am, so he shaved and showered, as he wanted to look good and always give a good impression to Sandy's big sister.

Dan walked downstairs into the bar, which was now clean and tidy again. His Dad would never go to bed leaving the bar dirty. The bar was so clean you could not believe that a few hours earlier there had been a hooley night in full swing with the small bar packed to capacity with customers.

Jo sat at a small table drinking coffee and reading a book. Dan walked over to her and sat down. 'Morning, Jo. Is Sandy OK?'

'Hi, Dan. Think so. She was fast asleep when I left the room. Why? What happened?'

'Nothing, just a problem with one of the guys in the bar. It got a bit physical.'

'Sandy does not like fighting.'

'Me neither. Just couldn't stop myself after what Frankie said about her.'

'Defending her honor again, Dan. You don't know my sister. She would have preferred it if you simply walked away!'

'But Jo, he a called her a fuc... well, not a very nice thing.' Dan did not want to curse in front of Jo.

'Dan, he called her a fucking American whore. So what? Is that worth getting in a fight over, maybe getting yourself killed?'

'I won't have anybody insult her like that. 'Tis not right!'

'You really don't know my sister, Dan, but I can see you like her.'

'Like her? Jo, she is the best thing that ever happened to me. She is great, magic, and I... well, you know what I mean.' Dan could feel a bout of shyness coming on again.

'You what, Dan? Please continue.'

'Yes, please continue, Daniel,' said Sandy, who reached over and picked up a croissant from the table.

'Sandy... how long have you been standing there?'

'Long enough. So, I guess you like me, Daniel, but please, continue!'

'Yes, Dan, I am enjoying this,' said Jo.

'You're making me embarrassed,' said Dan as he stood up and went to get Sandy the coffee pot. The two girls giggled.

'So, are we going on the boat trip today, Daniel?'

'Yes... of course... would you like to...' Dan stumbled over his words with the excitement of Sandy confirming the trip.

'Sure, I want to spend another day with my Daniel, my big strong Irishman.'

Dan went red with the embarrassment at Sandy's comments in front of her sister. It was tough keeping his hand steady as he tried to poor Sandy's coffee.

'Ah, coffee, that's just what I need. My head is sore from all the drink last night.'

'Sandy, I am sorry about the trouble last night, but I won't have anybody talking about you like that.'

'Sticks and stones, Daniel, sticks and stones,' said Sandy.

Dan looked somewhat confused at Sandy's comments. Jo, seeing Dan's confusion, intervened.

'Dan, what Sandy is saying is that she does not mind. She is not hurt. That Frankie guy is an asshole... it's just as well we are not in Texas, as bar room fights can get people killed. Remember, we have guns in Texas.'

'Just as well we're not in Texas, as there would be a lot of dead people in Donegal.'

'Sandy, I gotta go. Enjoy your trip... Dan, take good care of my Sis, or you will have me to answer to.'

'She is in good hands, Jo.'

'It's not the hands I worry about... Dan!'

Sandy sat at table drinking her coffee and eating a croissant. Dan sat down beside her, feeling a little more confident and managing to control the shyness, he held her hand.

'I am sorry about last night.'

'Well, that's the third time, Daniel!'

'Third time for what?'

'Saving me. I guess you really are my knight in shining armour.'

'You look beautiful, Sandy.'

'You need glasses, Daniel. I have not put on any makeup, have not had a shower, and my hair is a mess.'

'Well, I think you look great.'

Sandy looked at the clock, it was just after 9 am.

'I need to go take a shower and get ready,' said Sandy as she stood up and gave Dan a kiss on the cheek.

'I can see your ready already, Daniel,' she said as she walked from the bar, back towards her room.

Dan quickly cleared up the table and then went back to his room to double check his look and make sure his hair looked good.

Dan sat in the bar, drinking coffee and talking to his Dad, who was once again cleaning glasses and making sure the bar was in perfect condition.

'Tuesday today, Daniel, and you heading off to America on Friday. Ma's going to organize a little Mass for you tomorrow afternoon.'

With falling for Sandy and being consumed by his passion, Dan had lost all thoughts of going to America and joining the Army. His Dad's words brought him back to reality with a shocking blow. Not only was he going to America, but the day after tomorrow, Sandy would be leaving. Reality was biting him on the ass. He could feel a real sense of loss within the pit of his stomach, and it hurt like hell. How was he going to say goodbye to Sandy? The idea was just all powerful and consuming his though process. There was nothing he could do; the reality was that Sandy and Daniel would have to part company.

'Morning, lads,' said Jimmy as he entered the bar.

'Swell night last night.'

'It was great session, Martin. Did the wee Texan girls enjoy the night?'

'Yea,' sounded Dan as he felt deflated in facing reality.

'So, are we ready to go? I need to catch the tide, so let's hurry,' said Jimmy as Sandy walked into the bar. Dan's eyes feasted on Sandy, who had taken some time to make herself look amazing.

'Morning, Ms. Texas, you look amazing,' said Jimmy.

'Why, thank you, kind sir.'

Dan just stared at the vision of beauty before him. Words could not describe Sandy's beauty as they walked to Jimmy's car. Dan, being a gentleman, insisted that Sandy sit in the front of the car with Jimmy, who filled her head with Irish tales of woe along the journey to the harbor. Once again, it was a beautiful day with the sun rising up high in the clear blue sky.

At the harbor, Jimmy parked the car while Dan walked Sandy to the boat. The boat was nothing fantastic, not like the boats you would see in Miami or even Dublin. It was a small fishing boat with a deck cabin and steering house, with enough room for no more than three people. It was a safe and sturdy boat, but not the sort of vessel you would want to be caught out in an Atlantic sea storm in. That being said, Jimmy was himself from the Arran islands and was an expert traditional skipper. He could read the weather, and today was a perfect calm day for sailing to the isle of Arran.

'I like the name of the boat. *Dolphin's friend*. Just hope it's safe,' said Sandy as she climbed aboard.

Dan had never noticed the name of the boat even thought he had been on the boat several times.

'Sandy, the boat is fine. Jimmy is one of the finest sailors in the whole of Ireland.'

'I hope so.'

Dan could see that Sandy was a little nervous and apprehensive about the trip. He put his big arm around her and said, 'Don't worry. Sure, isn't your knight here to save you.'

'I can't swim, Daniel.'

'You can't swim? What sort of a person can't swim?' said Jimmy as he boarded.

'I know, I just never got around to learning, I guess.'

'Here, put on this lifejacket. You too, Dan. Don't want any accidents around here.'

Dan assisted Sandy in putting on the lifejacket and ensuring it was secure. It was also a good reason to be close to her body.

'I hope we will be OK!' said Sandy.

'You have nothing to worry about. I am known as Jimmy the pirate around here. Sure, the water between here and Aran is my home and my father's home and his father's, so just relax now and enjoy the trip.'

Jimmy started the engine and cast away as the boat tugged out of the safety of the harbor. The water was unusually calm, with no swell, almost like a pond.

'It's a beautiful day. I hope you will enjoy the view. I will bring her down the south coast around Mayo, Achill island, down by Galway, and sure, you may even get a glimpse of the cliffs of Moher before we cross to Aran.'

'Jimmy, that's taking you a good bit out of your way,' said Dan.

'Sure, it's no trouble at all. Let's show the girl the real beauty of Ireland, and sure, we can come back direct.'

'How long will the boat trip take, Daniel?' asked Sandy.

'I'm not sure. Once we get out of the harbor area, Jimmy will increase the speed and take us south down the coast. The scenery will be really nice. Maybe three or four hours,' which was a guess on Dan's part, in reality he had no idea.

Sandy sat down on the deck of the boat and loosened the top button on her blouse, starting to relax in the warm sun. Dan went into the steering cabin and thanked Jimmy.

'Sure, it's no bother at all, Dan. I tell you should try and hold onto that girl. She is gorgeous and very nice too… I wonder, can she cook?'

Danny laughed and went back outside to Sandy. He held onto her hand as Jimmy accelerated to a fast but comfortable speed and exited the harbor into the Atlantic Ocean.

'Next stop Boston or New York,' said Danny.

'I hope not. It's hard to imagine how big the Atlantic is… Next stop, home!'

'Are you missing home?'

'No, I am having the time of my life, Daniel, here with you,' she said, and she reached up to Daniel and pulled him towards her, giving him a kiss. 'But I do miss my Dad.'

'Not half as much as I will miss you when you're gone,' said Danny.

'I know, but let's enjoy our time together, Daniel, as I go home the day after tomorrow… I wish I could stay with you forever.'

Dan put his arm around Sandy and held her tight, realizing that he was powerless and that time stops for no man. Indeed, with the passing of time, Sandy would be back on the far side of the ocean, and he would be there also, in the army, seconded for two years and most likely deployed to Afghanistan or Iraq.

'Nobody can see the future,' said Daniel.

'Dolphins beyond the forward bow,' shouted Jimmy.

The two lovers jumped up and ran to the front of the boat. Two dolphins raced along beside the front of the boat as if playing or toying with it.

'How pretty. I have seen dolphins in Sea World in Florida, but they are in a fish tank. To see them in the sea, their natural environment is just so amazing.'

The boat trip continued with all three of them basking in the sun and Jimmy full of song and laughter. None of them had a care in the world; all worries and concerns had been washed away by the sea.

'That's Croughain, the largest Mountain on Achill island, County Mayo, over to the left.' The huge mountain towered over the sea like a giant. With a large cliff face bellowing down to the ocean and seagulls and peregrines playing in the uplift of air, it was a spectacular view. They continued on south before Jimmy said, 'I am turning her out now to cross the Atlantic to Aran. Those cliffs to the yonder are the cliffs of Moher in Co. Clare. You yanks love that place. Real popular with the tourists.'

'It will get a little bumpy as we cross the Atlantic, a bit of swell which is normal as the currents between the mainland and Aran are strong,' said Jimmy.

Once again, Dan put his arm around Sandy as she checked her bright orange lifejacket to make sure it was secure. 'You will be fine,' said Dan with a confident grin displayed on his face. Sandy rested her head on his shoulder. 'I know I will.'

The crossing was not as bad as expected, and before long they were in the harbor of Kilronan on Inismore Island, which was busy with tourists and boats docking. Jimmy reduced the speed of the boat as they approached the pier and prepared to dock. Dan threw a line of rope to a young lad who was standing on the pier, which secured the boat.

'Thanks, young Terry,' said Jimmy as he handed the young boy a two euro coin. Jimmy then helped Sandy and Dan onto the pier. 'It's ten past four. Let's meet back here for the five thirty sail, which will have us back on dry land by eight-ish and home to Termon by nine. That OK with yee?' asked Jimmy.

'Sounds good to me,' responded Sandy as she put her arm around Dan, and the two lovers walked off down the pier.

'You must be starving with the hunger?' asked Dan

'I have all I need right here with you, Daniel. There is time for eating when we get back to the hotel.'

The two young lovers hired a jaunting car, which, according to the driver, was powered by Speedy the fastest horse on the island. 'Where would you like to go?' asked the driver.

'Would we make it to Dun Angus fort and back in an hour?'

'Yes, but you will only have about 10 minutes at the fort.'

'That's perfect, let's go for it.'

'Giddy up Speedy, away with ya!' And with that, the horse took off at a fast speed. Dan had his arm wrapped around Sandy's shoulder, and her head was on his chest.

'Oh, Daniel, this is so romantic.'

The horse sped along the road, which was littered with tourists on bikes and a few other horses.

'Daniel, there are so few cars on the road. Is this a back road?'

'This is the main road or, you might say, highway. Actually, I think it's the only road. Remember, we are on a small island.'

'It's like going back in time, to Ireland of many years ago.'

'Life is nice and slow out here, so I guess you are correct.'

'Have you ever been in a jaunting car before?' asked Daniel.

'Just once when I was a small child with my dad in New York City. We went around Central Park. It was great.'

Soon the jarvey pulled up in front of the entrance to Dun Angus fort, which was busy with tourists. Dan helped Sandy from the jaunting car and asked the driver to wait, which he agreed to do as long as they were fast.

Dan quickly ushered Sandy over to the side of the fort, which had a drop, not as steep as the previous cliffs she had already witnessed, but still a significant drop. The Atlantic waves crashed against the bottom of the cliff, with the spray reaching the two, who were holding hands.

'Now, Sandy, you are officially on the edge of Europe, the western-most point in Ireland, so next stop across that ocean is America.'

Sandy peered out into the ocean. Danny stood behind her with his arms around her upper body. He could smell the sweet perfumed smell from her long blonde hair, which was just below his chin. Her hair was shining once again from the slight wetness of the moisture in the air from the sea below. Daniel had not been this happy in his life before. He was truly at one with nature and the beauty of Sandy. I guess you could say he was experiencing love for the first time in his life.

'I want this moment to last forever, Daniel.'

'Nothing lasts forever, Sandy.'

'Love... true love will last forever, Daniel.'

Sandy turned around so that she was facing Dan, her face only a few centimetres from his, and she rubbed her hand over his cheek.

'Daniel, I need to tell you something.' Dan felt a sense of apprehension and fear come over him. As he was about to speak, Sandy put her index finger over his lips, shushing him.

'Daniel Flynn, I think I am in love with you.'

The sweetest softest and nicest words Dan had ever heard. Was he dreaming? He wanted to pinch himself, to check for reality. His eyes stared directly into Sandy's, and he responded without thinking, just a pure spontaneous reaction.

'I love you too Sandy.'

The two kissed passionately and embraced each other, and onlookers moved away from them with a sense of embarrassment or awkwardness as this was the most passionate kiss to date and not the sort of thing you do in a public arena. After a couple of minutes and gasps for air, Dan said, 'Quick, Sandy, we gotta go, we have a boat to catch.'

The two ran back to the jarvey, who had waited for them at the gate.

'Did you see all you wanted?' asked the jarvey.

'Sure did, but we have twenty minutes to get back to our boat,' said Dan.

'That's cutting it tight. Come on then, Speedy, let's see what your made of.'

The jaunting car made it back to the harbor, and Dan paid the driver while Sandy thanked him. The two then ran down the pier and met with Jimmy, who was standing on the pier beside his boat.

'Hold your horses, guys, we have a problem,' said Jimmy.

'What's wrong?' asked Dan.

'A piston in my boat engine has blown, and I can't get the part till 10 pm tonight on the last sailing from Galway. Barney is bringing the part to Galway and will put it on the last sailing.'

'So, we are here for a few more hours then,' said Sandy.

'I can't make the crossing in the dark. It's just too dangerous. We will book into the local guesthouse and leave at first light, say 6 am in the morning.'

'I will need to phone Jo,' said Sandy.

'I have already phoned your dad, Daniel, and made him aware of the problem. He will tell your sister, Sandy. Oh, and Dan, we are all booked into Mrs. Murphy's guesthouse... sorry pal, your dad made me book separate rooms.'

'Sandy, I am sorry about this, but it's out of my control.'

'What are you sorry for, Daniel? We get more time together, so that's cool. Now, I am starting to get hungry, so let's go find a place to eat.'

'We best go check into Mrs. Murphy's guesthouse first.'

CHAPTER 10

ₒⱼₚ

Mrs. Murphy's guesthouse was similar in many ways to Dan's parents' hotel and bar in Donegal. The only difference was that there were twelve bedrooms, all equipped with two double beds and an en-suite bathroom. Mrs. Murphy was originally from Buncrana in Donegal and had gone to school with Dan's mother before marrying Patrick Murphy and moving to the Aran islands. Dan and Sandy walked into the reception area of the guesthouse and were greeted by Mrs. Murphy.

'Hello, Daniel Flynn, it's lovely to meet you after all these years. The last time I met you was at your Communion when you were only seven years of age. Oh, how you have grown into a fine young man, and is that the Texas lass? Well, you're very welcome. Now, do you need anything as I heard all about the boat engine, isn't it terrible, but I want you to know that you're welcome here and this place is your home from home.'

Sandy was amazed and impressed at Mrs. Murphy, who rattled off the words without stopping to take a single breath of air. However, it was well known that Mrs Murphy was a local gossip and knew everybody's business even though she lived on an Island.

'Thank you, I may need some pajamas,' said Sandy.'

And Mrs. Murphy was off again. 'Well, that's certainly not a problem, you may be a little small for borrowing one of my night dresses, sure, you're only about a size 8, maybe even smaller. Now Sindy Byrne's shop would be closed at this time, but maybe my daughter Linda may have a pair to fit you. Now, she is only sixteen years of age, but I am sure she can help you. Now, will you have a cup of tea?'

'No, we are fine. If we could just get the key to the room.'

'Its rooms....two rooms I have for you. Dan, you are in room 8, and you are in room 10. Now, they are side by side, but I told your Mam, Daniel, that I will make sure that you would have separate rooms and that everything would be OK. Now, am I right in saying that?'

Dan nodded in agreement, and Sandy laughed. 'You would think you were only 14 years of age, Daniel.'

The two were shown to their bedrooms by Mrs. Murphy, who left after announcing that she would return with the pajamas for Sandy. The rooms were well decorated with views of the ocean, and Sandy also had a small balcony. Within seconds of Mrs. Murphy leaving them, Dan was knocking on Sandy's bedroom door. Sandy opened the door and pulled Dan into her room, giving him a kiss.

'Isn't this wonderful, Daniel?'

'Yes, wonderful,' said Dan as he fell on top of Sandy, who pulled him onto the bed on top of her. However, Dan quickly jumped up off the bed and apologized.

'Daniel, relax, just relax, will you. I am so happy. You know, this room and view is amazing. It reminds me of the Hilton hotel in Key

Largo with the balcony view of the sea, only I am sure it costs a lot less and the people are much friendlier here.'

'Well, if you are happy, then so am I.'

There was a knock on the bedroom door, which was followed by it being opened by Mrs. Murphy. 'Daniel Flynn, what are doing in this room?'

Dan looked scared as if he were a school boy caught smoking behind the school shed. Before Dan could say a word, Sandy answered. 'I invited him in to talk to me.'

'Well, that's OK with me as long as she invited you in to talk, that's fine, fine with me, and it is only talking after all. Now, here are the pajamas belong to my daughter, I will leave them on the chair for you. I have a nice stew on the stove, so if you want some just drop down, and if there is anything else, just call me.' Mrs. Murphy was known as motor mouth and continued to race away with herself as if her very life depended on getting the words out of her mouth.

'Thank you so much, Mrs. Murphy, I am just fine,' said Sandy.

Mrs. Murphy nodded and rubbed her hands together as she exited the bedroom.

Sandy walked over to the pajamas and picked them up. A grey pair of woollen pajamas, horrid and unattractive with absolutely zero sex appeal. A sack for holding potatoes would have had more sex appeal. Holding them in her hand she burst into laughter along with Dan, who, feeling more relaxed, jumped on her and gave her a kiss and big hug.

'Come on, let's go and get some food,' suggested Dan.

'As long as it's not Mrs. Murphy's stew.'

The two sneaked out of the guesthouse as they did not want to offend Mrs. Murphy's hospitality in not taking up the offer of her stew.

They had passed a small Rocket's-styled 1960s diner earlier in the day. It was only a mile down the road, which was now deserted as most of the tourists were either gone back to mainland Ireland or were in the bars with the locals.

After the short walk, the two sat in the diner, placing an order for burgers, chips, and milkshakes. Dan placed a 50 cent coin in the old music jukebox at the door that played golden oldies from the 1960s and 70s. He sat across from Sandy in the booth, with his hands on Sandy's hands, which were on the table in front on them.

'Oh, Daniel, what a choice. How did you know that '*Unchained Melody*' is one of my favourite songs? It's such a special song to me.'

'I didn't. I just really like the song since seeing it in the movie *Ghost*.'

'That movie gets me every time. It's so sad and yet happy. Makes you think… Do you believe in the afterlife, Daniel?'

'Yes, sure I do, but I don't think that Christians, Jews, or Muslims have it right. What I mean is, we are all one and believe in God.'

'Wow, boy, that's a bit heavy. I just believe in God.'

The food was placed in front of them, and they both devoured it with the intensity of starving animals feasting on a dead carcass. They were both starving and needed to satisfy their hunger for food.

'Daniel, would you mind playing that song again?'

'Sure.' Daniel once again placed another 50 cents in the jukebox and selected *The Righteous Brothers*' famous song.

'Dance with me, Daniel.'

'Here in the diner?' he asked, feeling a little embarrassed.

However, once in Sandy's arms, swaying slow to the song, the shyness passed, and comfort and enjoyment took over.

'It's lovely to see young love,' said the elderly waitress who walked past them. When the song was over, the few occupants of the diner clapped in appreciation.

Sandy said to everyone, 'Thank you, folks.' Daniel just went bright red.

The two sat back down in the booth, and the waitress said, 'It's nice to see some life in here again. Dessert is on the house.' She handed them two knickerbocker glories.

'That's very kind of you, thank you,' said Sandy.

They finished their ice cream, and Dan said, 'We better head back to Mrs. Murphy's, as there is lightning in the sky. Looks like it's gonna rain.'

The two thanked the waitress, settled the bill, and walked into the night air, with Dan putting his arm around Sandy's shoulder. As they walked, there was a loud clap of thunder and a flash of lightning.

'I hate thunder and lightning. It really scares me,' said Sandy as she rested her head on Dan's chest while walking. It was still a rather warm and pleasant evening as long as the rain held off, as neither of them had coats.

About half way into the walk, the rain started, really heavy rain, big raindrops, the kind that explode when they impact on your head and dribble down your neck, leaving that wet, uncomfortable, soggy feeling. Within minutes of the rain starting, the road was badly flooded with large puddles that splashed water onto their shoes and trousers. By the time they walked into Mrs Murphy's, they were soaking wet.

'Well, would you look at you two, you're like drowned rats. Go upstairs and get out of those wet clothes, and I will put them in the dryer for you. There are bathrobes in the main bathroom, so take them and get changed.'

'Thanks, Mrs. Murphy,' said Dan.

As they walked up the stairs to the bedroom, Dan said to Sandy, 'Can you imagine what the bathrobes are like?' However, when they entered the main bathroom, they were pleasantly surprised, as the bathrobes were good quality, if a little on the big side for Sandy, but a good fit for Dan.

'I need to take a shower. Meet me in my room in 30 minutes,' said Sandy.

'Ok... sure.'

Sandy kissed Dan and went into her room. Dan quickly got out of his wet clothes, having to peel his jeans off as they were stuck to his legs. The shower was fantastic, making lovely hot beads of water on his rain-soaked body. Leaving the shower, he checked his watch, and there was still another 10 minutes to wait. Each minute, as it passed, felt like an hour. He pleaded with the minute hand of his watch to move faster. After exactly 30 minutes, he put on the bathrobe and quickly ran to Sandy's room, knocking on the door.

'Just a minute,' sounded from inside the room. Then the door opened and Sandy was standing in her large robe, which completely covered her body. However, she looked amazing. Without any makeup and just out of the shower, she was raw in Dan's mind, and he liked what he saw.

Just as Dan was about to kiss Sandy, he heard Mrs. Murphy's voice from behind him, 'I will have these clothes ready and dry for you before I go to bed. Sure, I will bring them back up to you when they are ready.'

'Thank you Mrs. Murphy, but we would like some privacy so maybe just leave them outside the door,' said Sandy in a forthright and forceful manner.

'Privacy.'

'Yes, privacy. Thank you, Mrs. Murphy, I am sure you understand,' said Sandy.

Mrs. Murphy exited the bedroom, and Sandy closed the door. She put her arms around Dan and said, 'Now I have my man all to myself.'

Dan was impressed with the way Sandy had spoken to Mrs. Murphy. She was respectful but direct, and Dan liked that about her. The two sat on the side of the bed, with Sandy jumping with fear with each clap of thunder.

'Do you not get thunder and lightning in Texas?'

'Yes, we do, and I hate it. It's the noise of the thunder that gets me.'

'Well, there is nothing to be scared of anyway. You're safe with me.'

'Daniel, you're so romantic. I want you to sleep with me tonight.'

Dan had very little experience with sexuality. He was also confused, as a woman asking him to sleep with her was, in Dan's mind, exactly that: get into bed and sleep with her. But maybe sleeping with someone in American terms was full-on sex.

Sandy climbed into the small double bed and held the sheets back for Dan as he somewhat clumsily climbed over Sandy to the other side of the bed. Sandy kissed Dan, who responded to the kiss. Sandy then removed her robe and pulled it from the bed. Dan was in heaven; he had only ever seen this happen before in James Bond films with such an action being followed up with *Oh James!'*

'Take off your robe, Daniel.'

'But I have nothing underneath.'

'Daniel... don't be shy, come on.'

Dan somewhat reluctantly removed the bathrobe as Sandy once again snuggled up close to him while kissing him and rubbing her hand through his hairy chest. Dan was somewhat non-responsive.

'Daniel, is there something wrong?'

Dan responded, 'Em… no… just… I am not that experienced.'

'Are you a virgin, Daniel?'

'Em… well… yes.'

'Daniel, we don't have to do anything you don't want to do, so relax.'

'What do you mean, don't want to do? I am in bed naked with the woman of my dreams, who is also naked. There is nothing more to be said.'

'Well then, kiss me quick and make love to me Daniel Flynn.'

Sandy climbed on top of Daniel and reached over, switching off the main light and leaving on a side lamp. The feeling was intense for Dan. He looked up at Sandy and put his hands on her firm and pert breasts as she straddled him. Dan was terrified of making Sandy pregnant as his mother would kill him, but there was no way of buying any contraceptives, so it was just take your chance and hope all would be OK. Anyway, Dan was not going to let the moment pass. In his mind this was fate, destiny, and he wanted Sandy's beautiful, petite young body.

Sandy lowered herself onto Dan, who was now as hard as a rock. Sandy let out some moans and groans of pleasure, muttering in between, 'Oh, Daniel.' After a few moments, Dan flipped Sandy onto her back and climbed on top of her in a missionary position. Nature took over, and Dan was bucking away like an expert bronco bull rider.

'Slow down, Daniel.'

'Sorry.'

Dan slowed his pace. Sandy screamed as she released one orgasm and then another. As expected, Dan was not far behind and went to withdraw at the point of no return. However, Sandy held onto him, and they shared an intense moment with Dan's full tank flowing into her. On completion, Dan collapsed on top of Sandy, exhausted.

'Daniel, I love you so much,' whispered Sandy, and Dan responded, 'I love you too, Sandy. That was amazing.'

The two fell asleep in each other's arms, before awaking simultaneously and making love again in many varied positions. By morning, Dan would be an expert lover. Once finally and completely exhausted, the two fell asleep to the sound of the occasional clap of thunder, which sounded as if the sky were applauding their performance from outside.

The following morning, they got dressed and left Mrs. Murphy's early in order to meet Jimmy on the pier. Dan was ecstatic, bursting with energy and playing with Sandy as they walked, picking her up and carrying on her on his shoulders to the pier. They were the ideal couple, the picture of happiness. They were in love, but time was running out for them, destiny was waiting to whisk them away in different directions. But would love conquer all and bring them together?

CHAPTER 11

⨳

The trip back to Donegal was uneventful. However, the Atlantic crossing was much bouncier as there was a larger swell in the ocean following the night's rain and thunderstorm. On the way back, though, they took a more direct route, and before long, they arrived back at Flynn's guesthouse.

'Sandy, let's go and get some lunch.'

'I need to get some fresh clothes and have a shower, so give me an hour, Daniel.'

Dan kissed Sandy as they parted company for a short time. Dan knew that the time was coming when they would be parting for much longer, possibly parting never to see each other again. This was scary for Daniel. He did not want his heart broken, but how could he avoid this trauma?

Dan went into the kitchen. His Mum, as normal, was cooking at the stove, and his Dad was laying the table for lunch.

'Danny, you're back. Did you have a nice time?' asked his Dad.

'Yes, we both had a great time, Da. It was nice of Jimmy and Mrs. Murphy to let us stay.'

'Noreen Murphy. I haven't seen her in years. Is she still talking non-stop?'

'Yea, Ma, non-stop.'

'Dan, invite Sandy down for some lunch, will ya? It will be ready in 15 minutes.'

Dan phoned Sandy on the internal phone, and she advised that she would love to have lunch with his family. Before long they were all sitting at the kitchen table, eating Dan's mum's famous bacon, cabbage, and potatoes.

'So, you go home tomorrow then, Sandy, or is it Sandra?' asked Dan's Dad.

'Yes… sadly, I do… back to Dallas… Sandra is my name, but I prefer Sandy.'

Dan looked sad at the news of Sandy leaving him and heading back to America, but they both knew that this day and time would come. Sandy reached over to Dan's hand and held it openly on the kitchen table. This was a first, and most unusual for Dan's mum to see a woman, another woman holding her Daniel's hand.

'I am going to miss this place and Daniel so much.'

'What do you think of that eejit joining the American army. You know he leaves on Friday,' said Dan's dad.

'Well, he will be in America with me, and maybe I will be able to come see him.'

Dan's Mum got up and walked over to the kitchen sink. She was visibly upset at the thought of her only son heading off to America. Dan jumped up and walked over to his mam, putting his arm around her.

'It will be alright, Mam.'

'I know son, I know. Sure, don't mind me, I am fine.'

Dan walked back to the table and sat down beside Sandy, who remained silent and upset at seeing his mother crying.

'I have arranged for you to pick up some Gartan clay this afternoon, Daniel. You will need it,' said his mother.

'Sandy is going home tomorrow, Mam. I was planning on spending the day with her.'

'You can take an hour out of your day, son. This is important, and Fr. O'Shea and Jennifer are not available tomorrow.'

'Dad, I don't need this today.'

'Sure, can't you bring Sandy with you... maybe pick some up for her as well, won't do her any harm.'

'What have you to do, Daniel?' asked Sandy.

'It's a load of rubbish.'

'You have respect for your mother, Daniel... I will explain it to Sandy,' exclaimed Dan's dad.

'It's an old Gaelic Irish tradition from times past. Legend has it that, many years ago, Colmcille our saint was born in the townland of Gartan, which is not far from here. A young Flynn helped deliver the baby Colmcille. The afterbirth fell onto a stone and the ground, turning the ground to a clay, white in color. According to the legend, only the sons of the Flynn, the direct descendants of the Flynn man, can pick up the clay.'

'What's so special about the clay,' asked Sandy.

'It has mystical powers... As long as you carry it about your person whilst you travel, it will keep you safe, and no harm will come your way.'

'Did you ever hear such a load of baloney,' said Dan.

'No, it sounds so sweet and traditional. I think it's great, a little like King Arthur,' said Sandy.

'This is no myth, Sandy, it is an Irish reality and a tradition that has been passed from Flynn generation to generation. Young Daniel there is the last in the direct bloodline of Flynn sons, and only he can pick up the clay from the ground. If another person picks up the clay, it has no effect, it loses its mystical powers. Daniel has to pick it up and nobody else.'

Sandy turned to Dan's dad. 'But what about you, you're a Flynn. Can you not pick up the clay?'

'Alas girl, I am not a Flynn, its Rose who is the Flynn. We carry her name as it has such importance in these lands.'

'Oh, I see, how wonderful. Can I bring my sister Jo?'

'Of course you can. Gartan is not far from here, but you must not reveal the location of the clay to anybody as it's a secret place.'

'No sir, no I sure wont. I can promise you, the secret will be safe with me.'

'Dad... Mam... ah for feck sake.'

'Watch your language, son,' echoed Dan's Father in a strong tone.

'What time are we going at, Daniel?' asked Sandy.

Dan's Mum answered, 'I have arranged to meet at Gartan for 3pm.'

'Wonderful, Jo will be back shortly. This is wonderful,' said Sandy.

Dan looked somewhat bemused at the situation and rested his head on his hand and elbow, which was placed on the table in front of him.

'I had better go and make myself ready. See you down here at about two o'clock. Is that OK?' asked Sandy.

'That's perfect... and we have arranged a little surprise for you two tonight seeing as it's your last night in Donegal,' said Dan's mam.

'Mam, what sort of a surprise?' echoed Dan with a sense of embarrassment.

'You will have to wait and see, son.'

CHAPTER 12

ગℓ

Sandy walked back into the kitchen after freshening up and applying fresh makeup. *She looks pretty good*, Dan thought to himself.

'Is it OK if Jo takes her car and we can follow you?'

I will do one better for you, Sandy. I will travel with you and Jo, and I can show you the way,' said Dan's Mum.

'Ok, that's great.'

As they set off on the drive to Garton, Sandy asked Dan's Mum to explain the story of Gartan and the Flynn's in more detail so that her sister Jo could hear it first-hand.

'Let me tell you of the mystical tale of Gartan.' All remained quiet in the car, especially Sandy, who was totally in awe at the legendary tale.

'It is history, and it is written, that before St. Colmcille was born to his parents Eithne and Felim, that Eithne had a vision. An angel of Christ showed her a beautiful coat or maybe a cloak of magical colors. But when she reached out to touch the coat it went out of reach into the air. The coat floated over the sea and land until it rested on the side of a mountain. The vision informed her that she would have a son who would rise to become a great man and leader of people. He would travel overseas and land until resting.'

'Ah, Mam, that's enough,' sounded Dan.

'No, please continue, this is fascinating' said Sandy.

Dan's mum took a deep breath and then continued.

'On the 7th of December 521 in the land known as Gartan, Tyrconnell, Donegal, St. Colmcille was born unto this world. Some blood from the birth of the child ran onto a stone and clay, which turned white, a pure white. The stone is known as Leac na Cumba, which translates to the stone of loneliness. It is said that this stone has powers and that the clay will protect you wherever you may travel. You should keep the clay on your person at all times, and you will be protected. It is written that whoever has Gartan clay on them will never be burned, will not die at sea, and will never die without a priest. However, the Gartan clay can only be collected or picked up from the ground by a male with the surname Flynn. If a non-Flynn collects the clay from the ground, the clay loses its power, it will become worthless. Daniel is the last of the Flynn men, and only he can pick up the clay or until he has a son.'

'Why can only Flynn guys pick up the clay?' asked Sandy.

'That's a very good question, Sandy. Unfortunately, some of the legend has been watered down with the passage of time. Legend has it that when Eithne was giving birth she was assisted in the task by a kind person named O'Flynn. This area became sacred and blessed, and for the kindness show by Flynn, the clay from the place of birth was given to them as a holy relic. '

Is Flynn an Irish surname? Does it have meaning?'

'Yes, O'Floinn is the ancient Gaelic word which translates to 'gallant man."

'Well, that's for sure, as Daniel is certainly a gallant man and has been a true gentleman, taking such good care of me, especially on the island.'

Sandy finished her sentence with a wink at Dan, which caused him to blush with shyness and embarrassment, especially as he thought of the previous night's bedroom activity.

Before long they arrived in a small car park, which was more of a grassy field with enough spaces for five cars. Jo parked her car alongside of Dan's dad's car. They were in a beautiful green grassy field that had a view of Mount Errigal in the distance, which is the highest mountain in Donegal. There was a slight, warm breeze blowing from the south, and once again, the sun was shining from a clear blue sky.

'It's only a short walk now,' said Dan's mum as she ushered them to walk from the car along a hedge row into a smaller field that was away from the road. There was a silence with only the sound of the birds singing and a few whispers between Jo and Sandy, who walked behind Dan and his mother.

When they passed through the hedge, they came upon a large stone cross and the Priest Fr. O'Shea, who was dressed in his clerical church clothing, and a woman who was dressed in white priest-like clothing.

'This is the Reverend Jennifer Brooks, she is the local Protestant Reverend,' said Dan's mum.

'Why do you have a vicar,' asked Jo.

Dan's mum answered, 'When Colmcille lived, there was only one Christian religion, and we believe that both religions should be represented here at this most holy location.'

The priest asked that they all lower their heads, and he read a prayer in Gaelic, the old Hibernian language of Ireland.

Ar nAthair ata ar neamh,
go naofar d'ainm
Go dtaga do ríocht
Go ndeantar do thoil
ar an talamh mar a dheantar ar neamh.
ar n-aran laethuil tabhair dúinn inniu
Agus maith dúinn ar bhfiacha
Mar a mhaithimidne ar bhfeichiunaithe féin
Agus na lig sinn i gcathu
ach saor sinn o olc.

'Wow, that's the traditional Irish language. Is that a poem,' asked Jo.

Dan responded, 'No it's the Lord's prayer. You know, Our Father who art in heaven in the Irish language.'

'That's amazing,' responded Jo. The priest then said, 'Daniel Flynn, of the clan O'Flynn, come forward and pick up this clay of Gartan that it may protect you and all that you give it to as promised by our hold St. Colmcille of the lands of Donegal.'

Dan walked forward and picked up a handful of the white clay, which resembled baking soda, and placed it in a small clear plastic bag. The priest put his hand on Dan's bowed head and blessed him, making the sign of the cross and saying:

"Yea, ce go shiulann me trid an ghleann"

Dan's Mother turned to Sandy and Jo, 'That's the Irish version of Psalm 23:4. Yea, though I walk through the valley of the shadow of death, I will fear no evil, for thou art with me; Thy rod and thy staff, they comfort me.'

Jennifer, the Protestant Reverend, then made the sign of the cross in front of the small gathering of people, saying, 'Go in peace and follow the light of the Lord.

Amen.'

Dan returned to Sandy and Jo, who were both standing beside his mum.

Jo stated, 'That was awesome. It was a privilege to witness such a traditional ceremony.'

'May I see the clay,' asked Sandy.

Dan opened the bag and handed a small amount of the clay to Sandy, who placed it in the palm of her hand. She played with the clay, poking it with her index finger and feeling its texture, saying, 'It's so soft.'

'Come on, let's get out of here,' said Dan as he grabbed Sandy by the arm and pulled her towards the car. Jo followed, having arranged a lift back for Dan's Mam with her husband.

'I don't know why you are so embarrassed. We don't have such traditions in the United States. It's all modern history for us,' said Jo as she drove the car from the field, with Dan sitting in the back and Sandy in the front.

'What's the harm, Daniel. Sure, if the clay protects you, well, isn't it worth carrying some with you on your journey?'

'I guess so,' responded Dan.

Soon, they arrived back at the hotel car park. 'I am going to miss this place,' said Jo.

'Jo, you haven't seen the places I have, the mountains, the cliffs, the fields, the island. This has been the best vacation ever.'

'Oh, yes, the island. Strange how the boat ran into mechanical problems, leaving you stranded on the island… how convenient!'

'Jo, that's not nice,' said Sandy.

Dan intervened. 'I can assure you, Jo, I had no part to play in the boat breaking down, but it does look a little suspicious…'

'Indeed, what would Dad think, Sandy?'

'Jo, I am 20 years of age. Stop treating me like a child.'

'You need to wise up, Sandy. You're leaving tomorrow, and you will not be seeing Danny boy or this place again.'

On hearing the words 'not seeing Danny again,' Sandy jumped out of the car and stormed off into the hotel. Dan ran after her, catching up with her just before she got into her bedroom.

'Sandy, Sandy, stop running, come on, let's talk,' shouted Dan as he grabbed her arm and turned her around. Sandy was softly crying with a single tear coming from her left eye.

'It will be OK,' said Danny as he pulled her towards him, giving her a hug.

'I don't want to leave, Daniel. I want to stay. I don't want to go back to Dallas and college. I want to stay with you.'

'Me too, Sandy, me too.'

'I have an idea that will cheer you up. Get yourself ready, and I will meet you in the bar in say 30 minutes,' said Dan.

'What idea?'

'You will see. It's a surprise. Come on, we don't have much time, so go get ready. We have one night left together, so let's enjoy it.'

'Ok… now you have me excited.'

Dan walked back down to the bar, meeting Jo in the hall area.

'Jo, I had nothing to do with the boat breaking down on the island, honestly.'

'You're lucky. If Daddy was here, he would most likely have shot you!'

Dan walked after Jo, who continued to walk towards the bedroom. 'Jo, I really like Sandy and want to make this work.'

'Make what work? We are going back to Texas tomorrow. Sandy will have a broken heart, and I will be the one who has to try and get her over you. Do me a favour, Daniel, do us all a favour. Let her down gently as I have never seen her this keen on a guy before. You may well be a nice guy, and I genuinely hope, no, think that you are, but long distance relationships don't work.'

Dan went downstairs into the kitchen. His Mum was back from Gartan and working in the kitchen. 'What's wrong with you, Daniel. You look down in the dumps.'

'Sandy is leaving tomorrow.'

'She certainly is, but you knew this time would come when you would have to part your ways, so look, enjoy your last night together. Do you need money, son?'

'No, Mam, I am fine, but can I borrow Da's car tonight?'

'Sorry, no can do. I need it tonight,' said his Dad, who'd just walked into the kitchen.

'Dad, I really need the car. Come on, its Sandy's last night.'

'Sorry, son, no can do!'

Dan rang Mickey, explaining the situation. Mickey agreed to lend Dan his Ma's Ford Escort XR3i if he supplied Mickey with a few pints in the bar before he left for America.

CHAPTER 13

Dan sat on the step outside the hotel, pondering his thoughts, when he felt Sandy's warm soft hands wrap around him from behind.

'I made myself ready as soon as I could.'

Dan quickly jumped up and turned to look at Sandy. She looked simply amazing, wearing tight leather trousers, a white blouse, and cowboy boots, with her long blonde hair flowing down her back.

'Wow, Sandy, you look amazing.'

'Why, thank you, kind sir, I decided to dress like the Dallas cowgirl that I am.'

A few moments passed as Dan rubbed his hands all over Sandy's body while kissing her at the entrance to the pub. Dan did not see or hear Mickey pull up bedside him in his mother's car until he opened the window, his trade mark Bee Gees music playing loudly.

'Hello, boys and girls,' shouted Mickey.

Dan broke off kissing Sandy and opened the passenger door, assisting Sandy into the car. Dan then escorted Mickey into the bar and pulled him a pint of Guinness from the tap.

'Looks like you're in for a good night, Dan the man. She looks hot!'

'Hope so, Mickey. Catch you tomorrow. What time do you need the car back?'

'Hold on to it till the morning. Go on, Danny the lad... and don't stain my seats,' shouted Mickey as Dan walked from the bar.

Dan got into the car, quickly customized the steering controls, and drove away, turning down the Bee Gees CD as he drove. Sandy checked the CD container beside the hand brake; every CD was the Bee Gees.

'I guess he sure likes the Bee Gees.'

'Yep, he certainly does. Sorry, I think that's all we have.'

'No problem, I like them too, especially the slooooowww songs,' said Sandy as she reached over to kiss Dan's neck and ear.

'So, where are you taking me, Daniel?'

'We are going to the most beautiful beach in all of Ireland. It's called Port Salon. It has the whitest sand and large waves that come in from the North Atlantic.'

'Sounds amazing, especially for a Dallas girl who has to drive five hours to get to the sea.'

Danny drove the coastal route over Fanad head, which has spectacular scenery, and along the narrow country roads, which were deserted other than for some brave sheep who had ventured onto the road. Sandy had switched on the Bee Gees CD, which played 'Fanny be Tender,' which she sang along to as Dan drove.

'We really are a bit dated, driving this old car and listening to the Bee Gees,' said Dan.

'Great music never gets dated, Daniel. Anyway, I love *Barry Gibb*.'

They arrived in Port Salon and went walking arm in arm along the white sandy beach, with large Atlantic waves hammering the shore line. Even though there was no music, Sandy continued to sing the Bee Gees songs as they walked. The beach was deserted except for two brave kids who battled the cold water in an attempt to surf. The two walked for miles along the beach, sharing stories of their very different childhoods, which were worlds apart. Sandy's mum was from Houston, Texas, and her dad was a successful businessman from Dallas. They lived on a small ranch, as Sandy called it, which consisted of 200 acres of land and a few cattle, and her mum had seven horses. 200 acres of land may have been a small amount of land in Texas, but for Ireland that was a good size of land.

'So, do you like horse riding, Daniel?'

'Never been on a horse in my life.'

'We will have to change that. You will have to come visit my place in Dallas, and we can go horse riding.'

'I would like that very much.' Dan had a different idea of riding in his head and that did not include horses; he was thinking more of the intimate kind.

The two sat on the beach, enjoying their time together. Every minute passed like a second. The sun was setting across the sea, and Sandy clung onto Danny as if her very life depended on their relationship.

'I wish we had more time together, Daniel.'

'Me too,' said Dan as he kissed Sandy, allowing his hands to wander and explore her body, with her offering no resistance. Dan could feel the red-blooded male taking over his mind and body and the instincts of nature taking control. Sandy was also feeling the same, and after all, it was her last night in Ireland with her Daniel.

'Let's go somewhere a bit more private,' said Sandy as they walked back to the car park. Danny, getting more excited which each step he took, stopped on occasion to explore his passion with Sandy via physical expressions of emotion and love. Once back in the car, Dan drove to the infamous Lovers Point, as it was known locally. He was toying with his feelings as although he loved and respected Sandy; he also had male needs. He did not feel it appropriate to be making out with Sandy in the car park at Lovers Point, but he was struggling to control his male sexual urges. From the way Sandy was responding to his passionate kissing and heavy petting, she too was lost in the moment of passion. Dan opened her trouser button, but the leather jeans were so tight on her it was as if they had been spray-painted on. Opening a lady's bra is a feat of skill for a young man while in a passionate embrace. However, removing Sandy's leather jeans was an impossibility.

'Would you like a hand?' asked Sandy as she tried to remove her jeans. However, before she could, there was a flashing blue light from outside that lit up the dark sky. Dan and Sandy quickly tried to make themselves respectable, adjusting their clothing. They were momentarily blinded by the bright car headlights that shone in their direction. Then a voice shouted at them from the car.

'Mickey Flynn, I have you now. This is Garda Sgt. O'Brien. Get out of that car with your hands in the air. You're going to jail for a very long time.'

'Daniel, what are we going to go? Jo will kill me. We had better cooperate with the police officer. I don't want to get tased or, worse still, shot.'

'Nobody will be shooting anybody. Relax, Sandy, our boys in blue don't carry guns.'

Dan got out of the car and shouted, 'Sgt., it's me, Dan Flynn'

'Dan Flynn… but that's Mickey Flynn's car… Don't tell me Naomi is with you.'

'No, Sgt., I am here with Sandy, the visitor from America.'

'The wee Texan lass… Well, I hope you're showing her a good time… Dan the man.'

The Sgt. got back into his car and drove away.

'Come on, Sandy, let's head back to the bar. This is no place for a lady.' Dan had managed to suppress his male urges and had decided to take Sandy back to the bar.

The only person sitting in the bar was Billy, who was well oiled, and Dan's Dad, who was watching the TV. Ireland was playing a soccer match on the TV. Jo came in from the kitchen area talking to Dan's mother.

'Hi, Sandy, I have settled our bill, so we are good to go in the morning,' said Jo.

'What time are you leaving at?' asked Dan.

'We need to be out of here by 10am, as we have to drive to Belfast. Sandy, we have a long day tomorrow, so don't let lover boy keep you up late tonight.'

'It's almost 10 pm, so I am going to call it a night. Good night all and thanks for your kind hospitality,' said Jo as she walked towards the bedrooms.

Sandy and Dan sat peering into each other's eyes with a mixed bag of emotions, happy they had met, but sad as they had to part company, not sure if they would ever see each other again. Billy spun around on the bar stool, which was stationed in front of the bar and said, 'Do you know guys, you two remind me of a great film, and sure, ya have the same names of the two characters, Sandy and Danny. The movie was *Grease*.'

'Sandy laughed. Billy you're right, it's one of my favorite movies…
but there was a happy ending in that film.'

'Aye, that is true, but remember, you make your own luck in life,
and if you two want to be together, then let nothing get in the way or
stop you… Destiny is the word, but only you two can decide,' said Billy.

'Billy, you're a smart man. I have never heard something so true.
Thanks, Billy,' said Daniel, feeling a bit more upbeat.

'I had better be heading home. I have things to do myself. Sandy, it was
a pleasure and an honor to meet such a Texan beauty as yourself,' said Billy
as he struggled to stand up given Sandy a hug before walking out the door.

'Alfred, Alfred, come here to me,' shouted Billy once he was outside.

'Who's Alfred?' asked Sandy.

'It's a long story. Don't ask,' said Dan.

Dan's Dad switched off the TV and locked the front door. 'Goodnight to you two, I am off to bed. We will see you in the morning before
you go, Sandy. Night, now.'

Dan's dad walked out, leaving the two lovers sitting at a small table
in the dimly lit bar, which was now quiet and peaceful. The night was
passing by, and before long, it would be over. Sandy and Dan remained
sitting, talking to each other about the things they had done in the past
few days and, most of all, the island bedroom fun.

Dan then had a brainwave. 'Sandy, would you like to spend the night
with me again?'

'Would I! Of course I would, but we don't have a room, and let's
face it, Daniel, we would require a bed!' she replied in a flirtatious tone.

'That's not a problem,' responded Danny as he went behind the bar.
'Only one room taken tonight, and that's yours and Jo's. Let's see, yes,
this room we call the bridal suite.'

'What are we waiting for? Take me to bed and love me forever,' said Sandy.

There was no time to be wasted. Dan picked up Sandy, cradling her like a baby, and carried her up the stairs to the bedroom, which was called the bridal suite as it was the best decorated bedroom in the house. Quickly, the two of them almost swallowed each other with their tongues, wildly exploring each other's mouths. It took some effort to peel off Sandy's trousers, but the effort was very much worth the reward. What followed was a night of passionate lovemaking, with the two eventually falling asleep in each other's arms.

The following morning, the two of them snuck out of the room, with Sandy returning to Jo, where they had words. Dan simply went to his room, showered, and put on fresh clothes. He then went to the kitchen where his mother was preparing breakfast for the two guests.

'Did you have a good night, son?'

'Yea, Ma, great night, thanks.'

'Shame she is leaving today. I really started to get to like her.'

'Me too, Ma, me too.'

Sandy and Jo walked into the bar area and sat at a small table. Jo looked furious, while Sandy sat on her hands, staring at her Cornflakes.

'A word please, Dan,' said Jo as she pulled out a chair for Dan to join them at the table.

Dan sat down, wondering what he had done wrong.

'Dan, Sandy tells me that the two of you had an enjoyable night last night with plenty of bedroom fun afterwards.'

Both Dan and Sandy went pure red, with Sandy protesting that her love life was none of Jo's business.

'Sandy, it may well not be my business, but who will explain to Dad if two of us went on this trip and three of us come back!'

Dan realized that they had not used any contraceptives during the bedroom antics. On the island there may have been an excuse, but last night was inexcusable. There are condom machines in the hotel toilets.

'You had better pray, Dan, that she is not pregnant, or my Daddy will be back with two of his friends... Mr. Smith and Mr. Wesson, you get my drift?'

'Come on, Daniel, let's go outside,' said Sandy as she took Dan by the hand and walked outside the bar. Dan put his arm around Sandy and hugged her in the car park.

'Jo, is right, We should have taken precautions.'

'My big sister is always right... I know, but I love you so much... Would it be that bad if I was pregnant with our child?'

Dan thought for a moment. The idea of being a Dad this young was scary, but he did love Sandy. 'I guess not. If she was a girl with your looks, then she would have every man chasing her!'

The two hugged and kissed, which was interrupted by Jo saying, 'Sandy, get your stuff. Time to go now.'

Sandy reluctantly broke the loving embrace and went upstairs to pack her bag.

While Jo was packing the car, Dan took the opportunity of trying to talk to her.

'Jo, please don't be angry with Sandy. I am the one to blame.'

'Dan, you don't understand, if she is pregnant, my Dad would come to Ireland, hunt you down, and have you killed... I am serious.'

'What is he, some sort of Special Agent?'

'Yes, he is U.S. Secret Service and ex Special Forces.'

Dan felt the pit of his stomach ache as he pictured Sandy's dad like the Sylvester Stallone *Rambo* character.

'Sandy said he was a business man.'

'He is now as he is retired from the service... Sleep well tonight, Dan... lover boy.'

Sandy walked out to the car, and Dan assisted her by putting her bag into the boot. The two hugged and kissed, and Sandy said, 'I guess this is it, Daniel, time to say goodbye.' She wiped a tear from her face.

'It may be goodbye, but it's not the end. Sandy, nothing lasts for-ever... except love.'

'Hey, that's my line,' said Sandy.

'Come on, Sandy, we gotta go,' shouted Jo as she revved the car engine.

Finally, Dan let go of Sandy, who handed him half of a US$10 bill and a small box, which was wrapped.

'What's this for?' asked Danny.

'When we meet again, it will be in the United States, so let's put the money together and buy some condoms to keep Jo happy,' laughed Sandy.

'Open the box tonight when you go to bed... Goodbye, Daniel Flynn... I love you.'

'I love you too, Sandy,' said Dan as the car drove from the hotel car park and out of his line of sight...

CHAPTER 14

⨳

D an walked back into the bar and into the kitchen where his Mam was preparing the lunches for a few customers in the bar.

'Sit down, son, till I make you a cup of tea,' said his Mam, who put her arm around his shoulder. It's a well-known fact in Ireland that an Irish mother and son have a special relationship, a form of a bond. The same can be said for an Irish Father and his Daughter. Dan was sad but realized that this time would come. In essence, Dan also could feel that he would meet with Sandy again. It might take the passing of time, but he just knew that Sandy was the one for him. He was never more certain of that fact, and he was prepared to walk on fire if needed to get back to his Sandy.

'I had better go upstairs and start packing myself, Mam.'

'Daniel, do you have to go yet? Let's spend some time together.'

'We will, Mam. I just need a little time on my own right now.'

Dan walked upstairs and was passing by Jo and Sandy's bedroom. He opened the door and walked into their room. As he entered the room he could still smell Sandy's perfume. The beds were made, and the room would require little in the way of cleaning. He sat on the bed and pondered his thoughts, memories filled with fun and enjoyment of his time spent with Sandy. It felt like they had spent months together as if he had known her all his life. He knew that he had met his soulmate and that, just possibly, they had been together in a previous life, not that Dan believed in reincarnation. He looked down at the small, wrapped box, which looked like a bracelet or watch box, annoyed with himself at not having thought of giving her a going away present. He quickly opened the box, which contained a small ring that just about fit on his little finger and a small love heart note, which read: *Dan, this ring belonged to my Grandmother. Please hold on to it and remember me when you look at the ring. Always remember, I love you. Your Sandy xx.*

Dan immediately put the small ring on his finger. He picked up the pillow on Sandy's bed and put it against his face. He could get the smell of Sandy from the pillow. Dan was pining for Sandy, and that was obvious for all to see.

On hearing his Mother's voice calling him, he went back downstairs and sat moping around the kitchen, sitting on a chair, and basically getting in his Mother's way. His Mother did not complain as she knew that her son would be leaving in the morning on his voyage to the other side of the world. Dan's mother sat down beside him.

'Would you like some lunch, son?'

'No thanks, Mam, I am not hungry for food.'

'You really like young Sandy.'

'Yes, Mam, I do. She means the world to me. I really do...' He stopped before saying the love word in front of his mother as this would be embarrassing. Most men who are close to their mothers will never admit loving another woman until getting married.

'You have grown into a fine young man, Daniel. I just want you to be happy.'

'I am happy, Mam, I just really miss Sandy.'

Dan's mum gave him a hug just as Mickey walked in to the bar, calling for Dan.

'Hello, Mickey, how are things?' said Dan as he walked into the bar.

'All is cool with me, Danny boy. Bet you're missing wee Sandy.'

'You better believe it, Mickey.'

'Sweet little ass on her in those jeans. What a butt. Oh, sorry, Danny. I didn't mean that… but she was kind of hot all the same!'

'Yea, she sure is hot, Mickey.'

'How are things with Naomi? The Sgt. thought I was you the other night when I had your car. It was kind of funny, me in the car with Sandy at Lovers Point and the Sgt. with his blue lights and siren going.'

'You weren't doing it, were you Dan, when the Sgt. showed up?'

'No, sure, I couldn't get those spray-painted leather trousers off her.'

'Oh, Danny, when I think of her now… she sure was a hot babe.'

'She sure is, not was, and Mickey my friend, I promise you this, I will marry that girl someday… What are you laughing at Mickey?'

'Ha ha, when the Sgt. was following you around in my Ma's car, wasn't I getting the leg over with Naomi… in his bed.'

'Mickey, you're playing with fire. He will fuckin kill ya.'

'Come on, Dan, will we head out for a few hours?'

'I need some sleep. I was up all night with Sandy.'

'Oh, go on, you dirt bag Danny boy. Well, I will be back at seven tonight, and we will have a few beers.'

Danny went to bed and tried to sleep. Thankfully, he had downloaded the photos from Sandy's camera to his laptop. He reminisced over the photos, thinking of all they had done over the past few days. Sandy must have taken over a hundred photographs. Dan scanned through the photos, thinking in particular of his time with Sandy when no camera had captured the bedroom antics. Dan fell asleep looking at the photos, which included a few printed photos of his favorites.

Dan woke up to the sound of Mickey's voice, who was standing over at him as he had slept.

'You're a dirt bird Danny boy. Fell asleep playing with yourself, looking at the photos. You're a dirty lad.'

'Fuck off, Mickey! What time is it?'

'It's seven o'clock. I told you I'd be here at seven.

'Go on downstairs. I will be down in twenty minutes.'

Dan got into the shower, pausing for a few moments before switching on the power, as he did not want to wash away the sweet smell of Sandy from his body. After the shower he went into the bar, where there was a crowd of about fifteen people, who all welcomed him. His mother and Mickey had arranged a surprise send-off party for him. All the locals were there, even Frankie, who apologised for his drunk action the previous evening. It was a great party, if you were in the mood. Dan did his best to enjoy the party for his Mother's sake, but deep down all he wanted was Sandy, who was now well on her way back to Texas.

The following morning Dan awoke early. He had a long day ahead of him. He needed to catch the midday McKinley's bus to Dublin as he was staying in a Dublin Airport hotel overnight before catching the Delta flight to Atlanta. He knew that saying goodbye to his mam and dad was going to be difficult, in particular to his mother as this was going to be tough on her. He had all of his belongings and needs packed into a single suitcase. He drew back his window curtains and looked out at the sky, which was dull. It certainly looked as if it was about to start raining. Dan heard the Skype on his laptop ringing. Quickly, he answered it…

'Sandy, hello,' shouted Daniel.

'Hello to you from sunny Texas.'

'How was your flight home?'

'Fine, British Airways is great. Got back, flew direct from London into Dallas, and we only live a few miles from the airport, so it was all good. Danny, I miss you so much. It feels like we have been apart for years. I want to see you!'

'I miss you, too. It feels like we have been apart for a year, and yet it's only been hours.'

The computer screen flashed intermittently, as Danny's broadband was not so good in remote Donegal.

'It's morning time here in Donegal. It must be the middle of the night in Dallas.'

'1:15 am, Danny, and I am about to go to bed. I am still stuck on Irish time. I wish you were in the bed beside me, then I would sleep much better.'

'Me too.'

'You flying to Atlanta today?'

'Heading to Dublin today, flying to Atlanta tomorrow, and then on to Fort Benning. I am all packed and ready to go, not looking forward to saying goodbye to my Mam.'

'Oh, no, she will really miss you, Daniel, but not as much as I miss you now. I got to go and get some sleep, so skype me from Dublin and, remember, I love you Daniel Flynn.'

'Love you too, Sandy.'

Dan was delighted at Sandy contacting him. He jumped out of the bed with much excitement and energy. Quickly, he dressed and then slowly walked downstairs with his packed bag. Saying goodbye to his mum and dad was going to be difficult. Dan walked into the kitchen. His dad was sitting at the table, and his mother was, as usual, standing at the kitchen sink.

'Sit down and have some breakfast, Dan,' said his dad.

'I don't have time, Dad, I have to go and get the bus to Dublin.'

Dan's dad stood up and took Dan's bag. 'I will be in the car, son, when you're ready.'

'Mom, it's time for me to go now.'

'I know, son, I know. Give your Mum a hug.'

Dan and his mam embraced at the kitchen sink, Dan's mum fighting to keep back the tears. The morning sun was shining brightly through the kitchen window, and it radiated through Dan's Mam's greying silver hair.

'I remember we watched Superman on the TV, and do you remember the young Superman had to say goodbye to his Mother. Well, I know how he felt right now,' said Dan.

'Have you got your Gartan clay with you Daniel?'

'I do, Mam. I have it in a small locket around my neck, and I also have some in my bag. I will be fine, Mam.'

'When will you be back, Daniel?'

'I am not sure, Mam. Training lasts four months. After that, who knows?'

'Will you keep in contact over the internet and phone?'

'I will, Mam. I have set up Skype on the computer. Use it in the bar as that's the best reception for the broadband signal.'

Dan and his Mam walked out to his dad, who had the car running. He hugged and kissed his Mam.

'I will miss you, son, and never forget your home and the land of Donegal. It's in your flesh and blood.'

'I won't. Goodbye, Mam.'

Dan's Dad drove into Letterkenny and stopped at the bus station. His Dad was also now a bit teary eyed, which was unusual as Martin was never one to let his guard down and show his feelings.

'Look after yourself, Daniel, and say hello to America for me.'

'I will, Dad.'

The two shook hands, and Dan got on the bus for Dublin.

As the bus pulled out of his hometown, he glanced over at the Donegal mountains and pictured his own mother and the many generations of Flynn's who had left the mystic land of Donegal in search of the American dream. His head was full of mixed emotions, happy at hearing from Sandy, sad at leaving Donegal, and most of all sad at leaving his Mother. However, his head was also full of excitement at the road that lay ahead. Young Daniel Flynn was embarking on a voyage of discovery and could only dream of the many roads and journeys that lay ahead.

CHAPTER 15
THE UNITED STATES OF AMERICA

స్ప

T he following morning Danny awoke in one of the hotels located in
the grounds of Dublin Airport. After breakfast he tried to log onto
the internet but was unable to get a connection as the hotel internet was
out of order. He had a long telephone conversation with his Mother, who
now appeared a little more adjusted and to have come to terms with him
emigrating to America.

After checking in for the Delta airlines flight, he once again tried to
log onto the internet, this time without any difficulty. However, when
he Skyped Sandy there was no answer, which initially made him feel sad,
but then he realised with the time difference it would only be about 4
am in Dallas.

The flight to Atlanta was uneventful with the flight running on time
and the crossing of the Atlantic lasting no more than eight hours. The pilot
had informed them of a strong tailwind, so this reduced the flight time

by at least an hour. Dan thought once again of his Flynn relations who'd crossed the Atlantic Ocean many years previously. When his Mother and Aunts Nora and Ann had moved to America or travelled back to Ireland, there was little or no way of keeping in contact other than the posting of a traditional letter or the occasional phone call, which was expensive. Yes, the modern day travel to America in the comfort of a Delta airlines aircraft and having the ability to call home on Skype, email photographs, or use Facebook was fantastic. Danny had planned on keeping his parents and Mickey well informed of his activities while in America.

The aircraft landed in Atlanta, with Danny spending the last hour of the flight peering out the window at the vast United States of America down below. It was a beautiful sunny day in Atlanta, so the descent into Atlanta gave the passengers a birds-eye view of the state of Georgia and Atlanta. As the wheels of the aircraft touched on the runway of Atlanta, Danny felt proud of his achievement in at last reaching his long dream of becoming an American. The flight attendant called out on the intercom, 'Ladies and Gentlemen, welcome to Atlanta. The local time is 3:15 pm, and it's a hot 95 degrees.' Danny thought to himself, *95 degrees, even in the best Irish summers we don't get that heat in Donegal!*

After clearing customs and collecting his bag, Danny made his way to the bus stop for Fort Benning, which was located outside the main terminal. There was a line of about ten guys standing at the bus stop. Dan recognized one of the men in the line from the Delta flight from Dublin.

'Excuse me, were you on the flight from Ireland?' asked Dan.

'A fellow paddy! I'm Patrick O'Kelly, but just call me Jelly?'

'Nice to meet you. I am Dan Flynn. So, why are you called Jelly?'

'Ah, sure, I will tell you again. You heading to Fort Benning?'

'Yea, joining up the U.S. Army.'

'Me too, should be fun!'

'Fun? Are you crazy?' said one of the guys standing in the line.

'Why not fun? Dan Flynn, nice to meet you.'

'James Roberts, but you can call me Coffee.'

'Why Coffee?'

'The part of Boston I am from there are only a few blacks. Hence, I am called Coffee.'

'But why Coffee? Sure, isn't coffee white, especially if you put a drop of milk in it?' innocently said Dan.

'Hey, man, not sure if you're a bit stupid or just innocent, but I like you,' said Coffee.

A fourth guy stood reading the newspaper. Dan reached out his hand and said, 'Nice to meet you, I am Dan Flynn.'

The man turned his back on Dan and muttered something.

'Sorry, didn't get that,' said Dan.

'I said I don't have no time for micks or blacks, so you leave me alone, and I will leave you alone, and we will all get on just fine.'

Dan was a bit shocked at the way the man spoke to him, especially in modern day America. He thought that racism in particular against black Americans was now a thing of the past. He had also only ever heard of the Irish being discriminated against and had never witnessed it first hand, so Dan decided to just ignore the man and continue talking to his new friends.

A few minutes later a coach arrived with the words Fort Benning printed on a paper sign stuck to the bus window. A man in army clothing got off the bus and asked the guys for their names before permitting them to board the bus. The guys boarded the bus, which only had a handful of other guys sitting on the bus. Dan sat beside Patrick, who he knew as Jelly, and James, known as Coffee, sat opposite. The ignorant man sat at the rear of the bus.

'So what part of Ireland are you from?' asked Coffee.

'I am from a small town called Termon in Donegal.'

'Mallow, also a small town in Cork.'

'Mallow. I have never been to Cork,' responded Dan.

'Termon. Well, I have never been in Donegal,' responded Jelly.

'And I have never been to Ireland,' said Coffee as they laughed.

'So what part of Boston you from?' asked Dan

'I was born in the Bronx in New York but moved to Boston when I got married.'

'Married? You seem a little young' said Dan.

'Married, yes, and divorced.'

'What happened?' asked Jelly.

'I got caught screwing her mother. Very sexy lady,' responded Coffee.

'Welcome aboard the Benning Express. It's 114 miles to Fort Benning, which is about a two-hour drive from here, so sit back, relax, and enjoy the ride,' said the driver across the bus microphone. Dan fell into a sleep with the motion of the bus as they maneuvered along the Georgia interstate roads. Before long they arrived in Fort Benning and were ushered from the coach.

The three young men stood in a line of twenty or so misfits of every nationality, creed, and color. The only form of commonality amongst them was that they were all young men with untidy hair, dishevelled looking, and all somewhat lost. A tall man in an army uniform approached the group of misfits.

'I want you men to stand in five lines of 10 and 10… now.'

The group of men quickly muddled around each other, flapping and holding their bags, coats, and other belongings. Eventually, the group managed to find themselves standing in two lines.

'My name is Sgt. David Bell. Whenever you address me, it's, yes, Sgt. Bell, do you understand?'

'Yes sir, Sgt. Bell,' the group responded.

'Excellent. I think we are going to get along just fine. Welcome to Fort Benning. Over the next four months, we will train you to become members of the greatest fighting army the world over. You boys will become soldiers of the United States Army.'

Danny put his shoulders back and looked up at the beauty of the American flag, which appeared to wave at him as it flapped in the gentle breeze of the warm sunny Georgia day. His new friends Jelly and Coffee stood beside him, also trying to stand at attention, with their non-muscular chests pushed outwards.

'You will be fitted out with your training uniform and necessary equipment.'

'When do we get our army uniform?' asked one of the group.

'You will get your United States Army uniform when you become a United States Army soldier. None of you people are ready to wear the uniform. You disgust me with your filthy, long hair, fat bellies, and scruffy look. You guys are what I would call Fat Fucks, in particular you. What is your name and where are you from?' bellowed the Sgt. The Sgt. pointed at one of the group who was standing in the front row. He appeared to be well overweight and looked very unfit.

'Sgt., Jeremy Clarke, sir, from San Diego, California.'

'Well, Mr. Jeremy Clarke, as you are the fattest member of the team, you will be known as Fat Fuck, that is, until you lose some weight and get fit.'

'You at the back, tall boy, who are you?'

The Sgt. pointed at Daniel, who felt somewhat intimidated by the Sgt. who shouted his questions. It reminded Daniel of his school days in the Christian Brothers School in Donegal.

'Sgt. I am Daniel Flynn, from Donegal Ireland, sir.'

'Well, I'll be dammed, an Irish boy, the fighting Irish. You micks make damn good fighters.'

'Thank you, sir.'

'I didn't say you would make a good soldier. What sort of a name is Flynn? Tell you what, let's call you Daniel Free, the free Irishman!'

'Thank you, sir, but I am not the only Irish man here.'

'You mean there's more than one mick in my platoon? Show yourself, mick,' shouted the Sgt.

'Sgt., sir, Private Patrick O'Kelly, known as Jelly here.'

'Who said you could call yourself a Private. That is a rank in my army, and you're not yet a soldier. You're nothing, son. Do you hear me? Nothing!'

'Yes sir.'

'I don't want to know why they call you Jelly, but I like jelly and ice cream, so Jelly you are. I wonder if I will get to like you?'

'Yes sir.'

'Now, you boys are going into intensive training. From 08:00 tomorrow morning your ass is mine, so go call your Ma's and Pa's and say goodbye, as there will be zero telephone calls while I own your ass. Good training makes good soldiers. Get your asses into barracks four… now!'

The untidy group of men quickly grabbed their bags and belongings and walked into Barracks 4. On entering it was very much open plan, with little privacy, just rows of single bunk beds with showers and toilets to the rear of the room.

'Home sweet home. This is it for the next four months, boys,' said Coffee.

'Just as I imagined,' responded Dan.

'Ain't going to be much opportunity of getting ladies in here,' continued Jelly.

Sgt. Bell walked into the room, shouting, 'Attention men, stand to attention in front of your sleep pit… now.'

Dan stood beside Jelly and Coffee, who had placed their bags on selected beds.

'This your home, boys. When you leave here in 16 weeks, you will be soldiers of the United States Army, or you will have died trying to become a soldier. You are about to start a program of OSUT. That's One Station Unit Training. Remember what I said, use the phones to call your girls or Mommas now as from 08:00 tomorrow it's all gone. No girlies in my army. Goodnight, gentlemen.'

'Good night, Sgt.,' responded the group at the same time.

'That Sgt. thinks he is in the marines. He thinks he is like the Sgt. in *Full Metal Jacket*,' said Jelly.

'He is a Marine,' responded one of the guys. 'Nice to meet you micks. I'm Paul Tallouzi from Albuquerque, New Mexico, but you can call me Tango, and this is my brother Dave, known as Chico.'

'Hi guys,' responded Dan, Coffee, and Jelly.

'He looks like a mean son of a bitch,' stated Jelly.

'Yep, he is. He served in Iraq and got a Purple Heart. Seen heavy combat, but he is what we need for the best training,' said Tango.

'I agree,' responded Dan.

Dan took out his laptop and walked towards the reception area, as he had been informed there was Wi-Fi. He was anxious to talk to Sandy and was pretty cut up about not being able to talk to her for the next 16 weeks. Dan entered a small reception area, which had a slender, attractive female with blonde hair tied up under her cap. The color of her hair reminded Dan of Sandy. She was wearing a full Officer uniform and standing behind the desk.

'Excuse me, can I use the Wi-Fi?'

'It's excuse me, ma'am,' responded the officer.

'Sorry, I am new around here.'

'Where are you from?' asked the officer.

'I am Dan Flynn from Donegal, Ireland... Ma'am.'

'Ireland, nice place. Yes, use the Wi-Fi. It's free, and there is no password.'

'Thanks... ma'am.'

Dan quickly logged onto his laptop and called Sandy on Skype.

Up popped Sandy in excellent high-definition quality. She looked great.

'Hi, Sandy.'

'Hello, Daniel, are you in America?'

'Yes, I made it. I just arrived in Fort Benning.'

'Oh, it's great to see you, Daniel,' said Sandy as she kissed the camera, and Dan responded by kissing his laptop camera.

The officer at the reception sniggered at seeing Dan kissing his laptop.

'I miss you so much, Daniel. I really would like to see you.'

'Oh, Sandy, I miss you too, but when can I see you? How?'

'Daniel, love conquers all. We will find a way.'

'Yes, but I won't be able to Skype you for 16 weeks,' as my sgt. will not let us contact the outside world whilst we are in training.'

'16 weeks, that's so long.'

'I know, but what can I do?'

There was an eerie silence on the skype call, and Dan could see that Sandy was distressed at not being able to talk to him for 16 weeks.

'Maybe I could write to you,' sounded Dan.

'Yes, yes, you see, there is always a way. Write to me, Daniel. I have to go. Will you call me in the morning?'

'I will, but it will be early, maybe 07:30, as training and my curfew from the outside world starts at 08:00.'

'I will be waiting. Love you, Daniel.'

'Love you too, Sandy,' he replied, and they both once again kissed their laptop cameras.

Dan sat back with his hands around his head, delighted that he had made contact with Sandy, similar to a junky getting his drug fix.

He then decided to try and Skype home to his Mam and Dad in Donegal. To his surprise, his dad answered within a couple of seconds. His dad had a big smile on his face, which crackled as the poor internet quality of Donegal did not permit a solid connection. Before Dan could even say hello, he could hear his Dad shouting for his mother to come to the computer.

'Daniel, my son, it's so good to see you. Are you OK? Did you make it? Don't forget Aunts Nora and Ann are in Philadelphia,' said his Mom, without permitting Dan to answer her never-ending questions.

'Mom, Mom, relax, I am fine. Yes, I made it, and I am in Fort Benning, so all is fine, no problems.'

'That's great, Daniel,' responded his mum.

Billy was sitting in the background on the kitchen armchair and was locked drunk, shouting abuse at nobody.

'Will ya shut up, ya fecking ejit Billy, Daniel's on the computer.'

Billy stood up. 'Hello, Daniel me boy. How did you get into the computer?' said Billy

'I told you to sit down, Billy,' said Dan's dad.

'Mam, I will have to go now, and I won't be able to call you for 16 weeks. There is a curfew whilst we are in training.'

'16 weeks, Daniel, that's so long.'

'I know, Mam, but it's the rules. Mam, I have to go now. I love you and will call you when I can, and don't worry, I am fine'.

The signal for the broadband was poor and cut out before Dan's Mother could respond. Dan stood up, closed his laptop, and started to walk towards the door.

'Nice to see young lovers,' stated the officer as she looked towards Dan.

'Yes… ma'am,' said Dan as he paused to address the officer, then continued walking.

'Hey,' shouted the officer as Dan opened the door and turned back towards her.

'Don't mind Sgt. Bell. You're allowed to call at weekends. Just don't tell him I said that,' said the officer as she winked in a flirtatious manner at Dan.

'Thank you, no, ma'am,' said Dan as he joyfully fumbled out the office door and skipped back towards the barracks.

'Well, would you look at the smile on him. Did the cat get the milk?' asked Jelly.

'Feck off, ya Cork rebel, Kelly,' responded Dan.

'Get the fuck out of my… Nigger boy!' shouted the ignorant member of the group from the bus stop as he lashed out, pushing Coffee to the ground as he tried to put his stuff in a locker. Dan quickly jumped to Coffee's defence and pushed the ignorant man, who fell to the ground just as Sgt. Bell walked into the barracks.

'Fucking Irish micks fighting already. Get your ass over here now!!'

Dan quickly ran over to the Sgt. and stood to attention in front of him.

'Yes sir, Sgt., sir,' shouted Dan.

'What the fuck is going on in here? You boys will be brothers at the end of my training. You want to fight? We will soon enough be fighting the scummy chicken shit terrorists.'

'Yes sir,' responded Dan.

'You get over here now,' shouted the Sgt. at the ignorant man, who quickly also stood in front of the Sgt.

'What is your name, boy?' asked the Sgt.

'Sgt., Chris Adams from Mississippi, sir.'

'What are you fighting over?'

'Nothing, sir, just a misunderstanding.'

'Just a misunderstanding. Good, well, you are both on head duty, boys, for two weeks. Let's see if you can get along now.'

'But…' responded Adams.

'But nothing, boy. The words you're looking for are yes, Sgt., do I make myself clear?'

Sgt. Bell moved closer to Adams and directly eyeballed him with an evil stern look no more than one inch from his face.

'Yes…Yes sir, Sgt., sir,' responded Adams.

'Good. Now you boys get your calls made, get to bed, change your socks, wank your cocks, and be ready for 08:00. Goodnight, gentlemen.'

'Good night, Sgt.'

As the Sgt. walked from the barracks, Adams turned to Dan. 'Watch yourself, you Irish scum, nigger-loving shit, or I will fuck you up.'

Dan felt rage and could feel the blood running into his now bright red face, but he simply said, 'Go for it, ya redneck fuck.'

Jelly, pulled Dan from the confrontation, pushing towards his bunk. 'Let's keep our heads, Dan, fighting for another day.'

'Yea, he is not worth it, but thanks, man,' said Coffee.

That night most of the guys slept with one eye open, a restless night, thinking of what was to come: the training, Sgt. Bell, shipping out and potentially entering the killing fields of Afghanistan or Iraq. The only exception was Dan and Jelly, who were suffering from jetlag, and they both slept like babies that night.

CHAPTER 16

ℐℛ

'Get your asses out of beds and fall in now!'

'Huu, what, it's only 05:30, what,' the platoon sounded.

'Yes, it's a fucking beautiful day. No time to waste, gentlemen, the clippers are waiting. Get your asses dressed and over to the barbers in barracks one, then pick up your training gear and get back here asap.'

A half-awake Dan and Jelly made their way over to barracks one, along with the rest of the group. Upon arrival the anticipated ritual of head shaving began. Rows of barbers stood lined up next to their chairs with anxious clippers in hand, waiting to shave the hair like hungry wolves waiting to feed on the flesh of an antelope. One by the one, the guys had their heads shaved, leaving the bald scull and protruding ears. This was not a styling contest, more of a sheep-shearing operation. Less than two minutes would pass, and all the years of styling, gelling, and brushing hair were gone. Dan was no different, other than the fact that his ears protruded more from the side of his head. 'Ha Ha, Dan, new name for your boy… Radar with those ears,' shouted Jelly, and the group laughed out loud.

After getting their hair cut, the men were quickly ushered into a small room and issued three pairs of combat army trousers, five army green T shirts, socks, and a pair of new dock martin style boots, which when tied almost touched the knee. The guys quickly got dressed and once again were ushered into the main square outside barracks four. Standing holding his spare gear, Dan looked at the guys. They still looked a dishevelled group of young men, yet they were starting to look more like infantry soldiers, at least if only from wearing the same uniform.

Sgt. Bell, walked out in front of the group and shouted 'Attention.' Quickly, the group stood to attention with their arms down by their sides and the spare uniform on the ground in front of them.

'Nice haircuts, men, nice,' shouted the Sgt.

'But you still look like a group of fat fucks, especially you, fat boy Clarke from San Diego.'

'Yes sir, Sgt., sir,' responded Clarke.

'Now, let's see, I think we should start the day with a little run, maybe five miles for warm up,' shouted the Sgt.

'Sgt., sir, are we not supposed to start at 08:00 this morning,' asked Tango.

'You Mexican Spanish fuck, lazy good for nothing! So, if the enemy are going to attack, they won't attack before 08:00. You will learn the element of surprise in my troop. You will be ready at all times. Now leave your shit on the ground and let's start running… Now, move it!'

The group of men began running at a slow jogging pace behind the sergeant. Dan was not so good at running long distance and struggled from the start. Jelly and Coffee had no issues with the running. Poor fat boy Clarke struggled with walking, so jogging, let alone running, was going to be a challenge for him. Dan started to fall back a little after the first mile but still maintained a steady enough pace to keep him within the main group. He looked up at the Sgt., who was out leading the troop, running without any obvious signs of difficulty, his fit toned body bouncing with every step. He was no more than forty-five years of age and was super athletic, with a fit muscular body. He was a most aggressive character and always wore a cowboy hat.

The other guys struggled with the running, and after the two-mile mark, everybody except the Sgt. was starting to slow down. It was now just after 08:00 am, and the sun was starting to rise, which can get hot in the state of Georgia, especially for two Irish boys who would be used to seeing the sun in Ireland no more than a couple of times a year. Dan, although trying to concentrate on the running, realized that Sandy expected a call from him this morning. He was now faced with the potential of 16 weeks and not being able to talk to her. This was upsetting him, but he needed to keep his emotions in track as surely, if the Sgt. saw a weakness, he would exploit him. The red sand of Georgia seemed to be magnetic as it pulled their feet like glue onto the ground, making lifting their boots with every single step more difficult.

The Sgt. suddenly stopped in the middle of a field and gathered the group of men around him. The men struggled to catch their breath, and most fell to the ground.

'Get you asses up and stand to attention. I don't recall telling any-body to sit down. You men are a disgrace. I will turn you from a group of men into a troop of professional American soldiers if it's the last thing I do. Now get up.'

The men tried to stand to attention, most of them exhausted from the running and some of them hungry from not having had any breakfast.

'You men, see that small hill over there,' bellowed the Sgt.

Dan looked and saw a hill, which was more of a small mountain. It was steep but could be climbed without using ropes. However, after a run, climbing the mountain was the last thing that the guys wanted to do. The guys groaned, which infuriated the Sergeant.

'You will do what I say. Now move your lard asses.'

Once again the Sgt. ran without any difficulty and picked up the pace. All of the guys had slowed to almost a fast walk. Poor fat boy Clarke was really struggling and looked as if his heart was about to give out. The Sgt. ran up the mountain, leaving the guys struggling at the base with a couple of them now stretched out flat on their backs. It wasn't long before all of them lay on the ground. The Sgt. returned with his shirt completely covered in sweat and shouted at the men.

'Get your asses up and follow me back to the Fort, you group of useless lard asses.'

The Sgt. started to jog with the group of men all pulling themselves up from the ground, with some jogging or, at best, fast walking. Others walked at a snail's pace, and Jelly and Coffee carried Clarke, who was now struggling to breathe. The group of men walked into the yard area outside their barracks and collapsed in a heap on the ground. It was a sorry sight of perspiring, exhausted bodies all lying on the ground, similar to a group of unfit people having just completed a city marathon. The Sgt. stood in front of the group, shouting abuse at the men.

'A useless shower of lard assess, a disgrace to the United States Army. Collect your shit and get into the barracks. Shower off and be in the mess hall in an hour for chow. Dismissed!'

The men helped each other into the barracks, most of them completely exhausted and struggling to walk. Dan was aware he was unfit but had no idea how gruelling the training would be on his body. He was exhausted. After showering and putting on a fresh uniform, the men somehow managed to make their way into the mess hall and all stood in line waiting to be served food. Dan, Jelly, and Coffee sat at a table, the three having developed a good friendship. However, none of them spoke as they were too busy eating, or should I say devouring, the food. Dan was starving, and to be fair, the standard issue army food was of a good quality. However, the guys were so hungry that the food tasted as if it had been served in a five-star restaurant. On completion of eating the food, the Sgt. appeared, shouting, 'On your feet, men. Attention!'

The men quickly stood up to attention.

'I hope you all enjoyed your food, boys. I know you did, fat boy,' said the Sergeant as he looked at Clarke. 'Now, time for another run, men. Quickly, outside now!'

The men looked shocked and could not believe that they would have to run again, especially having just had food. Once again, the Sgt. set off running, with the group of men fast walking at best. However, this time another Sgt. was at the rear of the group shouting abuse at them, which made them walk a little faster; some even broke into a slow jogging.

Coffee was the first of the group to stop and violently empty his lunch and the contents of his stomach onto the field. He was quickly followed by Adams, Chiko, and most of the other guys, who all puked their food onto the grass while continuing to attempt to run. As poor Chiko was empting his lunch from his guts onto the grass, the new Sgt. shouted abuse at him, 'You Mexican Spanish shit, getting sick on my field, you will run, boy, you will run!'

Dan continued to try and run, but his legs felt as if they had anchor weights attached to them. By now the Georgia sun was high in the sky, and the temperature was getting hot, especially for the Irish boys. Jelly kept on falling over but managed to continue a fast walk. Sgt. Bell stopped, gathering the men together, telling them to sit down in a circle. It was a sorry sight of exhausted men, with puke on their sweat-soaked shirts. Some of them had even shit themselves. The smell was repulsive, reminding Dan of a blocked toilet drain in his dad's pub, but it didn't appear to bother the two Sergeants.

'Well it may be time to introduce you boys to Staff Sgt. Chris Vickers. Sgt. Vickers is from Tucson, Arizona, and he specializes in being a mean son of a bitch. He hates white folk who don't like blacks. So I guess, Adams, that kind of singles you out, so you best watch yourself.'

Adams was flat on his back with exhaustion, looking over at Sgt. Vickers, who grinded his perfect white teeth, which seemed extra white from his dark black skin.

'Now, Sgt. Vickers is from the desert, and yes, you can see he is a black American, but his grandfather was an Apache Indian, and when he is not being a mean bastard, he likes nothing more than desert warfare. Now, that kind of makes him an asset for you boys, especially where you boys will be going. Stick with Sgt. Vickers, learn from him, and you may just survive your first deployment. Now, on your feet, men, and back to the Fort.

The men pulled themselves up once again and limped back to the base. Fat Clarke was in a heap, lying flat on his back some distance back from the group. Jelly and Tango picked him up and helped him back to the fort. When back at the fort once again, the guys showered and put on fresh clothes. This time there was little or no chatter from the men.

Their bodies ached, and some of them were embarrassed at having gotten sick and shitting themselves. After getting dressed they sat on their beds, some of them already asleep. This was the end of the first day. What terror was the Sgt. going to bring them the following day? The men's anticipation, however, was overpowered by aching tired bodies that cried out for sleep and rest.

CHAPTER 17

T he following morning, the boys were awoken by Sgt. Bell and Sgt. Vickers walking into the barracks and blowing two bugles loudly. It was just about possible to hear the men's groans as they pulled their aching bodies out of bed. Dan quickly checked his watch: it was 04:15 am.

'Get out of bed, get dressed, and be ready for parade in fifteen minutes. That includes you, fat boy Clarke.'

Sgt. Bell had taken a particular dislike to Clarke, who was wondering how he was still alive. His large body ached and even sweated during the night, which was strange considering that the barracks were air-conditioned.

Once again, the men stood to attention in front of the two sergeants, who quickly did a role call to make sure that the men were all present and ready for action.

'Good morning, men, hope you all slept well. Are you ready for a nice leisurely, let's see, three mile run and then a sprint to the top of my mountain?'

All the guys groaned with the anticipation of the hard running, along with the aching limbs and blisters on their feet.

'Move out, gentlemen,' bellowed Sgt. Bell.

Once again, the merry bunch of men jogged from the fort and out into the Georgia training fields. As they ran or attempted to run, another group of twenty or so men ran past them. They looked fit, trim, and like a real fighting machine. The men soon arrived at the bottom of the hill and once again collapsed in a heap of sweaty and tired bodies. Sgt. Bell and Vickers stood in front of them, also dripping with sweat.

Sgt. Bell shouted, 'The group of soldiers who ran past you on the way here graduate tomorrow as soldiers of the United States Army. Looking at those fine boys it's hard to believe that they were like you bunch of ass wipes a little under 16 weeks ago. Yes sir, Sgt. Frank Brickley sure did a fine job on those boys.'

The guys remained flat on their backs on the ground attempting to catch their breath, some coughing and others breathing heavily. Even the hard ground against the men's backs felt comfortable. Fatso Clarke was walking towards the group, having been left behind a couple of miles previous.

'Tell you, boys,' shouted Sgt. Bell. 'Let's have a little wager. If any of you boys can beat me to the top of this hill, I will give you a day off tomorrow. Yes sir, a full rest day for all of you.'

Adams jumped up. Even though he was an ignorant racist American who had no time for Irish or black Americans, Dan hoped that he would beat the Sergeant. Adams was by far the fittest member of the group, and just for a moment, Dan thought that he had a chance at beating Sgt. Bell.

'Adams, isn't it? Well, let's just see now. Say, I tell you what. If you win, not only will I give all the guys tomorrow off, but hey, I might just arrange for a crate or two of Budweiser for you boys,' said Sgt. Bell.

Even though exhausted, all of the men climbed to their feet and urged Adams to win. Even Coffee was cheering him on. The hill, as it was known, was better described as a small mountain. Running at a steady pace, you would reach the top in no more than twenty minutes, that is, assuming you were fit and had not just jogged three miles. Sgt. Bell handed his radio to Sgt. Vickers, who also had a set of binoculars.

Quickly, the two of them set off, Sgt. Bell running at a steady pace and Adams sprinting. Adams was already a good twenty metres in front of Sgt. Bell, who was running at a steady and solid pace. The men quickly ran after them; attempting to keep up would be a major problem, but they did their best, as they could taste the Budweiser beer and dreamed of a day of leisure. After about ten minutes of running Adams had started to slow, but he tried to keep up the pace with the motivation of the men who shouted from behind. Sgt. Bell closed in on him to a distance of about ten metres, but once again remained at a steady pace. All of the men now struggled but still kept on moving, which was a significant improvement over the previous day.

As the summit of the mountain approached, Adams had reduced to a fast walk and was breathing heavily as he pulled himself up the mountain. Sgt. Bell continued at his steady pace, but had slightly slowed, and the distance between them had dropped to only two metres. With the summit in sight, Adams collapsed in a heap on the ground, completely exhausted. The men all huddled around each other in despair. Sgt. Bell stopped at Adams, bent down, and picked him up in a fireman's lift over his shoulder and continued on running. The men looked on and also continued jogging as Sgt. Vickers shouted at them from behind. Sgt. Bell reached the top of the summit with Adams on his back. He then dropped Adams to the ground and waited a few moments for the group to arrive at the top of the hill. All of the men once again collapsed on the ground. Sgt. Bell, perspiring with sweat, looked at the group and shouted...

'In the United States Army, we leave nobody behind.'

Although Adams was beat, he gave a brave attempt, and I salute him. The rest of you have improved on yesterday and will improve again tomorrow and the day after until you are soldiers. Today we reached the top of my hill, and that is more than you did yesterday. Like the group of men that passed, you too, in time, will become like them. I will make you soldiers, and that is a promise.'

Dan, although extremely tired felt a sense of pride in the Sgt.'s words. He could see that the Sgt. was using psychology to get the best from the men. Although tired, they all made it back to the barracks by somehow managing to fast walk. Even Fatso Clarke managed to make it today without being carried. The men stood in their lines outside the barracks, exhausted and dirty with sweat, but all inspired by the words and leadership of Sgt. Bell.

Sgt. Bell stood in front of the group. 'Men, I want you showered, changed, and in the mess hall in 40 minutes. Chow is good today. I also want you to eat well at lunch as there will be no more running today.'

On hearing no more running, the men were delighted. However, they were still a little unsure as it could have been a trick like yesterday's unexpected running. Even though their bellies ached with hunger pains, they would eat cautiously just in case they had to run again. Having been dismissed, the men showered, changed, and quickly made their way to the mess hall. Dan ate like a pig, as did some of the other guys. They gulped down their food and drank cups of coffee like it was going to be rationed. Once again, Sgt. Bell and Vickers arrived in the mess hall.

'Oh no,' sounded Coffee.

'Relax, men. Us Sergeants have got to eat too,' said Sgt. Bell.

On hearing these words, Dan relaxed and went up for a second helping of food, which tasted almost as good as his mother's home cooking back in Donegal. To the surprise of Coffee, Jelly, and Dan, Sgt. Vickers and Bell sat at their table.

'You boys don't mind if we join you.'

'No sir, please do,' responded Coffee.

'So. you two boys are from Ireland.'

'Yes sir.'

'I was in Ireland, Dublin, with my wife and landed in Shannon in transit to Iraq.'

'Did you like Dublin?' asked Dan.

'Yes I did, and I liked your Guinness. Great beer.'

'Technically speaking, it's not beer, it's a stout,' responded Jelly. Dan kicked him under the table.

'All I know is it got me drunk, and that was fine with me. Eat up, boys, we have got a busy day ahead of us.'

'But Sgt., you said no more running,' responded Coffee.

'Yes, I did, son, and I am a man of my word. This afternoon's training is in the classroom, so get your thinking hats on boys.

After lunch, the group were assembled in a large classroom near the main reception building. Dan wondered if he would be close enough to try and get a Wi-Fi connection on his laptop, as he longed to call Sandy.

Although they had all been warned by the Sgt. about using their laptops and phones, there was to be no contact with the outside world. Dan could only imagine the wrath of the Sgt. if he broke his rule. He decided not to take the chance.

Dan found the classwork interesting, as it covered the ranking system of the United States Army from Private through to Sergeant Major in the enlisted men and Second Lieutenant through to General in the Officer class. Dan remembered that Sandy's Dad had been in the army and then the United States Secret Service, he wondered what rank he was when he'd left the army. According to Sgt. Vickers, their training would consist of three phases. The first was Patriot phase, consisting of the Drill Sergeants taking full control of their lives. This sounded like the hardest part to Dan. The second phase was the Gunfighter phase, consisting of combat training, both armed and unarmed. Finally, the third phase consisted of examinations, fitness tests, and advanced armed training. Most of the guys in the group had previously owned firearms of some type, which gave them a distinct advantage over Dan and Patrick O'Kelly, also known as Jelly. It is illegal to own a firearm in Ireland other than a target shooting .22 caliber rifle or a shotgun for a farmer. This worried Dan as he had never shot a gun in his life, and he also had a fear of guns. A strange fear considering he was now a soldier in the United Sates Army.

CHAPTER 18

❦

T he following morning it was out of bed again at 04:00, quickly dressed, and out onto the parade ground. Dan and the guys expected the usual three to five mile run and then the climb up Red Belly Mountain, as it had been affectionately christened, which was due to the red sand and the pain in the guys' guts from running up the hill. They would not be disappointed; only today it would be a five mile run before climbing the mountain. Once again, the guys collapsed in a heap at the bottom of the mountain. However, as the days passed, the guys began to get stronger and fitter. Before long the first week was completed, and the men were given the news that they would have a Sunday off to rest and recuperate. Now, a day off in army training does not mean a day of staying in bed or watching TV. No, a day off in army training is a day to get up early an hour or two later than the normal 04:00 and to catch up on your personal hygiene and chores. The guys needed to wash their clothes, change their bedding, and polish their boots along with the two Sergeants, as this was the custom for new recruits, at least it was Sgt. Bell's custom.

Adams and Dan had the job or punishment of cleaning the toilets and shower area. It was not just a quick squirt of bleach like back home in Donegal. No, these toilets had to be sparkling clean just in case the Captain decided to use them. Dan had hoped to call Sandy on the day of rest, but once again, it was risky as, if the Sgt. caught him, well he knew the punishment would be severe.

However, that Sunday evening he could wait no more, and with a fully charged laptop, he decided to try and Skype her from outside the reception area. All mobile phones had been removed. A couple of the guys including Dan had persuaded the Sgt. to permit them to retain their laptops. In Dan's case he told the Sgt. that his spelling was poor and that he needed to use Microsoft Word to type his Mother letters. The Sgt. permitted him, but Dan new that the Sgt. was not soft and that the only soft word associated with Sgt. Bell was in the word Microsoft.

At 01:00 am Dan picked up his fully charged laptop and tiptoed out of the barracks, away from the guys, who lay in bed snoring. Dan walked across the open parade ground, which was silent in the dead of the night. The only light flickered from the bright full moon and the small lights within the compound area. Dan was scared of being caught by Sgt. Bell but just knew that he had to try and get a message to Sandy, possibly a quick email. Skyping a call would be fantastic but would be too risky.

Dan arrived outside the reception area and checked the door, which was locked. He quickly switched on his laptop, which was in hibernation mode. He crept in behind the garbage cans to the side of the reception, hoping that the internet Wi-Fi would be switched on in the reception area. 'Yes,' he silently said as he got a good Wi-Fi signal and logged onto Google. Dan opened his Gmail account and was shocked in disbelief as there were some twenty messages from Sandy. Quickly, he read through the messages, trying to download them as fast as possible so he could read and enjoy them later. He quickly pasted a note from Microsoft Word into his Gmail account, which was effectively a long love letter, and hit the send button.

'Well, well, what have we got here?' asked a military police officer who stood over Dan with his flashlight shining on Dan's eyes. Dan stood up and walked out, closing his laptop, hoping that his email had been sent. 'What is your name?' asked the MP.

'Dan Flynn, of Sgt. Bell's trainee platoon, sir.' Dan stood to attention with his chest pushed out, grasping his laptop in his hand.

'What are you doing outside Captain Larmon's quarters? Are you spying on her?'

'No sir, no.'

The MP grabbed the laptop from Dan and held it in his hand, which angered Dan, but he realised he was powerless to do anything.

Before the MP could ask another question, the door to the reception area swung open, and the MP quickly stood to attention.

'What's going on?' asked the lady, who was standing in her pajamas.

Dan looked at the lady and realized that it was the same female officer he had seen standing at the reception a few days previous.

'I found this man, trying to look in your window, ma'am.'

'I wasn't looking in the window. I was—' sounded Dan.

'Silence,' shouted the MP.

'He had this computer, ma'am. Is it yours? Did he steal it from you?' asked the MP.

'Steal! That's mine, I don't steal.'

'Shush now, I will take the laptop. Now escort him back to his quarters. I want to go back to sleep.'

'You heard the Captain, now move it,' sounded the MP as he walked Dan back to his quarters.

'Captain?' asked Dan.

'Yes, Captain Larmon to you,' sounded the MP.

Dan returned to his bed, extremely disappointed that his planned operation had failed and scared of the consequences he would be face the following morning from Sgt. Bell.

The following morning had the usual 04:00am start, with Sgt. Bell running the troop hard for five miles, followed with Red Belly mountain, and then on to the obstacle course, which consisted of rope climbing, balancing bars, net climbing to rather extreme heights, which Dan was not overly happy about, and crawling through muck and dirt while carrying fellow trainees on their backs. However, he did it and did not complain.

As usual, it was back to the parade ground, a warm shower, fresh clothes, and a hot breakfast. Dan wondered why Sgt. Bell had not called him out to account for his actions the previous night and had decided not to tell any of the guys. That afternoon it was into the classroom for more training and drilling on combat situations.

While Sgt. Vickers was lecturing on the art of warfare and tactics in the field of combat, there was a knock on the classroom door. Sgt. Vickers stood and talked to a young soldier at the door before ordering Dan Flynn over. Dan stood up and walked towards the door. He knew that he was in trouble and shivered at the thought of the dressing down he would get from Sgt. Bell and Vickers.

'Flynn, you are to go with this Officer to the reception area for an important message,' stated Sgt. Vickers.

'Yes sir,' responded Dan, who walked from the classroom somewhat nervous about what he was about to face. Dan expected Sgt. Bell to be waiting for him, ready to sound off with verbal abuse. Dan's mind drifted back to his school days and walking to the Br. O'Connor's office, the Christian Brothers principal, for being bold in school or doing something stupid. Although it resonated in his mind that he was normally in trouble at school for chasing girls during school time, and here he was again in trouble under similar circumstances, except this time it was more serious: he was in the army now.

'What's this all about?' asked Dan as he walked beside the Officer.

'No questions,' responded the junior Officer.

Within a few minutes they arrived at the reception area. The young Officer and Dan walked into the reception, which was empty.

'Wait here,' stated the young Officer as he knocked on an internal door. 'You can go in now,' sounded the young Officer.

Dan walked into an office area behind the reception, which was furnished with a large oak desk and a leather executive chair. There were several books and certificates on the wall and a computer on the desk. Captain Larmon was sitting on the executive chair behind the oak desk, typing on her keyboard.

'Please, have a seat,' stated the Captain.

Dan took a seat in front of the captain's desk and felt somewhat nervous, expecting Sgt. Bell to come shouting into the room at any minute.

'I am intrigued. What were you doing last night?' asked the Captain.

'It's a little embarrassing, ma'am. I was trying to send an email to my girlfriend Sandy.'

'Oh, I see, breaking Sgt. Bell's rules is a serious matter.'

'Yes ma'am.'

The captain stood up and walked over to a large four drawer filing cabinet.

'What part of Ireland are you from?'

'Donegal… ma'am.'

'My grandfather was from Galway. Immigrated over here in the 1950s, settled in New York City.'

'Galway, nice city,' responded Dan, who was now a little more relaxed.

'So, why did you join the U.S. Army?' asked the Captain as she took his laptop from the filing cabinet.

'Well, that's a good question. I guess I believe in what America stands for, Liberty and Freedom for all its people. After 9/11 I wanted to do my bit.'

'Interesting,' responded the Captain.

'Well, Daniel Flynn, today is your lucky day. I believe in karma and romance, so tell you what, I will sort it with the MP.'

'Thank you, ma'am,' sounded Dan in high tone as if a large weight had been lifted off him.

'And tell you what, you have a few bars of power left on your laptop. Why not give your girl Sandy a call?'

'Sandy… how do you know her name?'

'I had to check your laptop. Wouldn't want you taking photos of me and putting them on the internet,' sounded the Captain in a flirtatious and yet funny tone.

Dan hadn't thought of the Captain in that way, but the more he looked at her, he realized that she was rather attractive in her uniform and had curves in all the right places. He quickly logged onto his computer, which had two bars left on the power meter.

'I will be back in five minutes. Make your call, lover boy!' said the Captain as she walked from her private office.

Dan quickly logged onto his Skype account and called Sandy. 'Please answer,' Dan said softly. To his amazement Sandy answered on her iPhone.

'Daniel,' sounded Sandy.

'Oh, Sandy, I have missed you,' said Dan.

'It's so great to see you, Daniel. I got your long letter. Did you get my mail?'

'Yes, I got the emails. I have them saved and will read them later.'

'No, I posted you a regular snail mail letter.'

'Not yet. I haven't got long. I will have to go shortly,' sounded Dan.

'I am back in college. It's really hard going. I miss you so much.'

'I miss you too, Sandy. Training is really hard.'

'Just thinking of your big army muscles, Daniel, you're making me so horny and hot.'

'Ah, will ya stop now!'

Bleep, the low battery warning displayed on Dan's computer.

'I am low on power. I will have to go, Sandy. I love you.'

'I love you too, Daniel.'

'I am not sure when I can call you again, but will try soon.'

'Write me, Daniel… I love you.'

Bleep, and his computer shut down just as Captain Larmon walked back into her office.

'Well, look at that for a smile, lover boy,' said the captain.

'Yes ma'am, thank you very much, ma'am.'

'You're welcome, but let's keep it our little secret.'

'Yes ma'am.'

Dan quickly walked and skipped back towards the classroom, re-joining his colleagues. That afternoon he was happy and content in making contact with his Sandy and the friend he had made in Captain Larmon. He was only two weeks into training, but as he looked at his ever-developing muscles and relationships he was making with his army buddies, especially Jelly and Coffee, Dan knew he was going to make it through the army training.

CHAPTER 19

⋰⋰

The hours grew into days and the days into weeks. It was not long before Dan and the guys were getting used to the daily routine and activity. The uniformity of the early morning starts, running, then climbing Red Belly Mountain, marching, and classroom training. One thing that the guys were surprised at was the quality of the food and the amount of it. The American army is very well fed. I guess it is true what they say: an empty sack will not stand.

The guys had now moved on to weapons training. The standard U.S. infantryman is equipped with a Colt M4 rifle and a knife. Normally, they don't get a sidearm, but if they do, it's a 9mm Beretta. Special Forces carry a larger selection of weapons. The equipment is well maintained and effective when used correctly. However, the most important part of the equipment is the man behind the weapon. Target practice using the M4 rifle was something that Dan was good at, more than good. Without any training and on his first attempt, he hit six of the eight targets. Jelly and Coffee hit nothing, and to be fair, most of the guys missed all of the targets.

'Well, would you look at the Flynn. You're damn good with that rifle, son,' said Sgt. Bell as he stood over Dan, who was lying in the red dirt shooting at the targets.

'Thank you, Sgt., sir.'

The Sgt. knelt down beside Dan and looked down at the targets. He then said in a soft voice, 'Your good at this, son. You think you're aiming at British soldiers in Northern Ireland?'

'No, Sgt., sir,' responded Dan.

'Good. Remember, those Brits are on our side, son, and they may just save your ass in combat.'

'Yes sir, British are my friends, sir,' responded Dan.

'Good, good, I think you will be our sniper, son. Flynn the Irish sniper.'

'Sniper, yes sir.'

The Sgt. stood up and walked over to Jelly, who was missing all of the targets, not even getting close.

'Are you two boys from the same country?'

'Sir, yes, Ireland, sir.'

'Flynn has the aim of a true professional and will only get better. Why are you so bad? Why are you here in my army?'

'Sir, never fired a gun, sir. I want to be a U.S. soldier, sir.'

'Never fired a shot. Flynn, your fellow mick never fired a shot. Is that the same with you, Flynn?'

'Yes, Sgt., sir. I also never fired a gun, other than my Dad's shotgun.'

'Your Pa's shot gun? Work with your fellow mick and get me a shooting Irish team, you hear me Flynn?'

'Yes, Sgt., sir.'

The Sgt. continued on, walking down the line, shouting abuse at the guys who were missing their individual targets. Dan was an excellent shot and was clearly well above the class average. Little did he know how much this was going to be tested in the future; his sniper skills might just save his life.

That afternoon the guys had some time off to relax and have a few hours to themselves. Training was coming to an end, and the men were fit beyond their wildest dreams, like a group of athletes waiting for the Olympics to commence. Dan Flynn remained on the shooting range with his M4 rifle. Apart from having the natural aim of a true professional, he really enjoyed the shooting. Sgt. Bell looked on from his office and was impressed with the young soldier. Dan was ambitious, physically fit, a great shot, and above all was committed to becoming a United States soldier. Sgt. Vickers approached Sgt. Bell, holding a paper clipboard.

'The Irish boy, Daniel Flynn, is a good shot,' said Vickers.

'He is the best I have seen in years. He is a natural shot.'

'You considering him for sniper school, Dave?'

'Maybe… but I think he needs some combat experience first. He would benefit from a tour of duty before we consider him for a specialist role.'

'Yea, your right. Still, with the right training, we can improve his natural skill,' said Vickers.

'He is not a killer. We need to make him into a killing machine first. He will get that in Afghanistan.'

'Afghanistan. Are these boys heading to Afghanistan? When?' asked Sgt. Vickers.

'I got word this morning. They will be shipping out in four weeks.'

Four weeks, fuck, that's only one week after they complete their basic training,' responded Vickers.

'Just like Vietnam and Iraqi freedom all over again, Chris.'

'Fuck, man, we need to get these boys fit and ready fast.'

'Yea, Chris, but before we break the news to them, I am going to give them a three-day break. They need some time off.'

'Time off, Sgt. Bell? These boys need all the training we can give them.'

'I agree, but they're heading to war, Chris. Let's give them some time to spend with their families before they ship out.'

'You're all heart, Bell, all heart, man.'

'Yea, fuck you, Vickers.'

Dan couldn't explain why he was so good with the rifle. He was a natural and really enjoyed taking out the targets. Even in his spare time he was on the range shooting at bottles and other targets. He was not so hot with a sidearm, but put a rifle in this soldier's hands, and he would be a deadly weapon. At this stage it had not dawned on Dan that in time he would be aiming his rifle at humans, living individuals possibly with wives and children, but this is something that all soldiers must face on their own and be comfortable with their choices to take lives. A soldier's conscience is the same as all human's. However, from training and battle experiences, they become hardened and less vulnerable to their thoughts.

Sgt. Bell, walked back from his office over to Dan, who was still lying down flat on his chest, shooting the rifle. Sgt. Bell stood behind Dan, who was unaware of his presence. Dan was muttering to himself while taking aim and firing at the targets. Every one of his shots hit its target perfectly. If it was a dart board every shot would have been a bull's eye.

'You're one of the best shots I have seen in training, Flynn,' said Sgt. Bell, startling Dan, who was unaware that Sgt. Bell was standing behind him.

'M… Ah, thank you, Sgt.'

'I think you're a natural, son. I was talking to Sgt. Vickers, and we think you could be a candidate for sniper training school. You interested Flynn?'

Dan, put his rifle on safety and stood, dusting the red dirt from his clothes.

'Sniper school. What would that involve, Sgt.?'

'Well, let's see now, I was talking it over with Sgt. Vickers, and we both feel that you would be a good candidate for the training. Its difficult training, not all make it, but you would need some combat action first, maybe a tour in Afghanistan or Iraq before the training.'

'Yes, Sgt., thank you, Sgt.'

'What are you thanking me for, Flynn? Iraq is a killing ground. You ever kill a man before, Flynn?'

'No, Sgt., never.'

'Sure you never picked off a couple of British troops in Northern Ireland… You can tell me, Dan,' said Sgt. Bell as he put his arm around Dan's shoulder, making Dan feel somewhat uncomfortable.

'No, Sgt., I told you before I never had any interest in the troubles in Northern Ireland, Sgt. I have nothing against the British.'

'Good, Flynn. As I said, the British are on our side, and they may just save your ass someday, but just think about what I said. Are you a killer, Daniel Flynn?'

Sgt. Bell, walked off into the distance while Dan packed up his rifle and thought about Sgt. Bell's question. The word 'killer' echoed in Dan's mind, making him feel uneasy. Dan was aware that soldiers are required to take life, but he had never given it much thought. He had a blinkered view of being a soldier, the splendour of the uniform, the marching bands and honor, but then it had finally dawned on him that he was being trained to kill.

Dan had had enough of the shooting range and quickly packed up his gun, walking back to towards his shared room. As he entered the room, Jelly was stretched out on his bed, snoring his head off, even though it was only early in the evening. The sergeants had been working the troop hard. The men were fit but equally exhausted from all the training. A little bit contradictory maybe, but the troop needed rest and a few beers.

'Atten Huh!,' Sgt. Vickers shouted as he walked into the room accompanied by Sgt. Bell. The men quickly jumped up and stood to attention in front of their beds. Well, all except Jelly, who was still snoring his head off in bed.

'Get your ass out of bed… now, boy,' shouted Vickers.

Jelly jumped out of the bed and stood to attention in his boxer shorts.

'Men, you are three weeks away from graduating from your training. You have come a long way and are starting to look like American soldiers, the finest soldiers in the world. Now, as you know, we are at war with terrorists in the Middle East, and as I speak, we have several operations in place in Afghanistan and Iraq. You men will be shipping out to Iraq just after Christmas to support our efforts in combating Al Qaeda. Now, as this is your first tour of duty, you will be mainly involved in supporting the troops out in the field. This will mainly involve providing security duties at base camp along with some less risky patrols. Men, you have three weeks training left. Ask questions from us, keep up your fitness, remember your buddy and your firearm, which is your best friend, and you will be fine. For the next week, or possibly more, I want you to continue to spend time on the shooting range. You need to be able to hit the target before they hit you. Remember, men, you are heading to war, the killing zone. It will be kill or be killed. Any questions?'

The full troop responded, 'No, Sgt., sir!'

'Excellent, men, as you were. Oh, and Flynn, report to my office at 18:30 hrs.'

'Yes sir,' responded Dan.

As the sergeants exited the room, the men quickly began talking amongst themselves, which resembled a group of old women chatting. The atmosphere instantly became tense with the eventuality and realization that they would be shipping out to fight in a war.

'So, Danny boy, wonder what the Sgt. wants you for,' enquired Jelly.

'I don't know, but what I do know is that none of us are ready for combat.'

'Yea, that's true, Dan, but there's nothing like on the job training.'

'Patrick, it's not a job in the local supermarket. This is serious.'

'You always call me Patrick when you're being serious, don't you, Daniel Flynn?'

'Well, it is serious. This is for real, Patrick,' responded Dan in a loud voice.

'Hey, guys, knock it off. Come on, let's relax, man,' sounded Coffee.

Some of the guys went out of the room while Danny opened up his gun case and once again began polishing his rifle. Jelly sat back on his bed talking to Coffee, who was trying to sell him a porn magazine.

Before long it was 18:30 hrs. Dan knocked on Sgt. Bell's office door.

'Enter,' sounded a voice from inside the room.

Dan walked into the room, which was filled with the aroma of cigar smoke. The smell reminded him of his Dad's bar back home in Donegal. Sgt. Bell sat behind a desk with an open bottle of Scotch whiskey. Two whiskey shot glasses sat on the desk, each half filled with golden single malt whiskey.

'Flynn, this is Major Robert Redmond from the U.S. Ranger Sniper School,' said Sgt. Bell.

'Sir,' sounded Flynn as he saluted the major, who returned a short salute while staring at Dan and chewing on a cigar. Dan glanced at the Major, who remained sitting, noting his rank clearly displayed on his shirt. There was an eerie silence in the room as the Major continued to eyeball Dan. Major Redmond looked to be about sixty years of age and had a nasty scar down the left side of his face. He looked tough, real tough, an emptiness and coldness in his grey eyes. After a few moments, Major Redmond stood up and put out his right hand and shook Dan's hand.

'I hear you got an eye for target shooting, son.'

'Yes sir, I like to shoot.'

'The question is, are you a killer, or are you shooting blanks?'

Dan didn't answer the Major, who bent down and picked up a rifle bag with his left hand and the whiskey glass with his other. He continued to eyeball Dan as he quickly gulped down the whiskey.

'Well, son, let's see how good a shot you are. Go and get your rifle.'

'Now sir...? It's getting dark for target shooting.'

'So what, you think the enemy will only attack during the day, son?'

Sgt. Vickers and the major sniggered.

'No... I guess not, sir.'

'Then go get your gun, boy, and meet me on the range.'

Dan stood still for a moment until Sgt. Bell jumped up from behind his desk.

'Flynn, you heard the Major, move your ass!'

Dan rather clumsily fell over the bin as he quickly ran from the Sgt.'s office and back towards his buddies, who were now mostly getting showered and gearing up for tomorrow's training. Dan quickly grabbed his rifle bag, with Jelly shouting after him, 'What's the rush, Danny.'

'Having some target practice with Major Redmond. Need my gear.'

'Ya here that, boys, a shoot off with Dan Flynn and a Major. Come on, boys.'

A group of about fifteen of the guys quickly ran after Dan, who made his way to the shooting range. By the time he arrived, the Major, still smoking his cigar, had his large rifle in his hands and was adjusting the scope. He looked over at Danny, who was fumbling, trying to get his rifle from the case. It was now almost dark, with just a low light simmering over the shooting range. The major glanced at Dan's weapon, which was now out of its case.

'This is the M107 50 caliber rifle, one of the finest weapons for the United States forces. One of these in a trained and skilled soldier's hands can hold up a whole army. A good sniper can both defend and attack.'

'Yes, Major, sir.'

The major got down on the dirt and adjusted his sights on his rifle. Within a few moments he let off five rounds from the rifle and hit each of the five targets straight in the center. All targets fell to the ground, five kills with ease. The major then stood up and looked at Dan, who was stood behind him.

'Well, son, you want to try her out?'

'Your rifle, sir.'

'Yea, why not give it your best shot.'

Dan quickly got down in the dirt and adjusted the sight, which was a night heat seeking scope. The targets were almost as clear as daylight. Dan let off a shot, which pushed him slightly back with the recoil and missed the target.

'Pull the gun into your shoulder, son, and hold her tight. When you squeeze the trigger, she packs a powerful punch.'

Dan did what the major advised and pulled the gun into his shoulder, gently squeezing the trigger. He let off four shots and hit each of the targets as the major had done previously. He then adjusted his stance for the final shot, which was the furthest target, squeezed gently on the trigger, and hit the target straight between the eyes.

'That's good, damn good shot, son,' said the major, who was standing behind Dan, using a set of night binoculars.

'Thank you, sir.'

Dan stood up and brushed the dust off his trousers while the men behind him clapped with appreciation of Dan's shooting skills.

'Alright, that's enough fun for tonight. Return to your quarters, men,' shouted Sgt. Vickers.

'I like your aim, Daniel Flynn, it's a good aim. I think with my training you will do good, son. Would you like to join my team?'

'Sir, yes sir, thank you, sir.'

'Excellent. Sgt. Bell, do the paperwork. Get this man reassigned.'

'Sir, I will need the Captain's sign off first.'

'Cut the crap, Sgt., get it done and change his weapon to a 107.'

'Yes sir.'

CHAPTER 20

 ✑

The training was complete, the men ready for combat and itching to get experience in the warzone. Although training was over, they still needed to stay fit and sharp; maintaining body fitness and keeping their minds within the combat zone is crucial for any professional soldier. All of the men knew that, come the 27th of December, they would be shipping out to Iraq to face an enemy like no other previously faced by the United States.

Danny would spend a few hours a day polishing his weapon. It was as if his new M107 50 caliber rifle was an extension of his body. The rifle was in perfect condition, as was Danny, whose body resembled that of an Olympic athletic champion. The U.S. Army had trained him to be a fighting killing machine, either with or without a weapon. Although Danny was still part of his original team, Major Redmond had started training him as a sniper, and in time, Danny would join one of the elite fighting units of the U.S. Army.

Danny was on the shooting range with his sniper rifle, taking out targets with ease. Sgt. Bell approached Daniel from behind.

'Never let a man sneak up on you from the rear. He may just slit your throat.'

'No, never, sir,' responded Danny.

'You're going good, Danny. You got one hell of a shot, son. It will be Rangers and possibly Delta when you return.'

'Delta squad, sir?'

'No, ya thick mick, Delta Force. Major Redmond wants you for the Rangers, but if you play your cards right, you may get a shot at Delta.'

Danny stood up beside Sgt. Bell and looked somewhat confused.

'Sir, I don't want to leave my unit. We are a team, sir.'

'Yes, Dan we are a team, but let's talk about it when we get back from the tour of duty. You might do me a favor and keep our little conversation to ourselves, wouldn't want to spook the troop.'

'Yes sir,' responded Dan in a somewhat appreciative but still confused tone.

'Now Dan, pack up your things. You've got some leave for Christmas. Not long enough to get you back to Ireland, but a couple of days, maybe, to go see your Texas Rose.'

Dan's heart melted at the thought of seeing Sandy. It had been such a long time since they'd parted in Donegal.

'Sgt. Bell, we ship out on the 27th, and we are confined to the fort.'

'Not you, Danny. Captain Larmon has arranged a three-day pass for you. Think she likes you, son.'

'A three-day pass, from when... Sgt.?'

'From 06:00 tomorrow, son.'

Danny jumped into the air with the excitement of getting some time off away from the fort and training, but he was aware that he would not have enough time to make a trip to Dallas. Even still, some time away from the army to do what he wanted and have a few beers would be nice. Dan quickly packed up his rifle and returned to his quarters. Some of his colleagues were sitting watching TV, writing letters, and playing on the Xbox. It was possible to feel the tension as the countdown continued before their deployment. Dan quickly polished his rifle and placed it back carefully in its holder.

'Hey Danny, a couple of us guys are heading for a few beers tonight. You coming?' asked Tango.

'Yea, maybe, why not save our money for tomorrow when we can leave the fort,' responded Danny.

'Leave the Fort? Nobody said anything about leaving the fort. Sure, we ship out in a couple of days.'

'Oh, OK, sorry man, my head is a bit of a mess.'

'Leave the fort, I wish, Dan. Its standard Bud in the mess hall. That's all the beer and pussy we will be having before we ship out, and I sure don't fancy any of those Iraqi women.'

'Me neither, Tango, me neither,' responded Dan.

'At least when the guys were in Vietnam, they got free time in Thailand. Some nice ladies there. What will we get, Dan? Dubai, and they still cover up their babes' faces.'

'That's to keep their women away from horny yanks like you, Tango,' shouted Jelly as he threw a pair of socks, which bounced off Tango's head.

'I would rather an Arab woman than your ugly Irish girls.'

'Hey, Tango, have you ever seen an Irish or Arab girl?' asked Jelly.

'No, man,' responded Tango.

'So what ya saying is that something you have never seen is uglier than something you have never seen!'

'Ah fuck you man.'

Tango walked away, leaving Danny sitting on his bed with Jelly standing beside him.

'So, what's happening, Danny me boy?' asked Jelly.

'Not sure. Sgt. Bell told me I was getting a three-day pass from 06:00 tomorrow.'

'What... nobody told me... unless it's just for you, boy!'

'I don't know what's going on...'

'Attention,' shouted Sgt. Bell, who walked into the room with Captain Larmon.

All of the men quickly jumped up and stood to attention. Captain Larmon walked over to Danny, who was standing up straight to attention, and gave him a secretive but sexy little wink.

'Stand at ease, men,' sounded the Captain as the men all relaxed their muscles.

'Daniel Flynn has earned a free pass for the next three days for himself, to take himself out of here for some R&R. Now, we are a team, and you men are shipping out on the 27th, so if Dan Flynn can get a pass, I have decided to give you all a pass, but stay near the fort.'

All the men had large, banana-shaped smiles on their faces as Captain Larmon handed Dan a small envelope.

'Enjoy your trip, Daniel...'

The Captain exited the room along with Sgt. Bell. All of Dan's colleagues came over and patted him on the back, with fair play well done.

Dan quickly ripped open the envelope, which contained one single piece of white folded paper. Unfolding the paper, he read the words typed in black ink:

24TH DECEMBER

DELTA AIRLINES DL1772 10:00AM TO VAIL COLO-RADO

26TH DECEMBER

DELTA AIRLINES DL1172 12:35PM VAIL TO ATLANTA DANIEL YOUR FLIGHTS ARE BOOKED AND PAID FOR ALONG WITH TWO NIGHTS IN A HOTEL. I WILL MEET YOU IN VAIL APPORT. NOT A WORD TO ANY-BODY THIS IS A **CONFIDENTIAL OPERATION**

Dan was bemused and sat back on his bed, staring at the note. He wondered who was behind the note, what was he required to do, and what would the mission entail. He quickly walked over to the captain's office reception area and logged onto his laptop. He had an email from Sandy, which simply stated, I am going to Barbados with my family for Christmas. How I wish you were coming with me. Love you, Daniel. Sandy xx.

Daniel skyped Sandy but got a signal that she was not online. Sgt. Vickers entered the office with an angry growing look on his face. He walked over to Dan, who was busy typing on his laptop.

'Well, Dan, you happy now, getting the squad some R&R before shipping out?'

'Yes, Sgt., very pleased, sir.'

'Those men need all the training they can get, not sipping beer and chasing skirt... I hope your actions do not cause any of my men their lives!'

'Sir... no... sir.'

'Sgt. Vickers, that's enough,' said Captain Larmon as she walked from her office.

'Yes ma'am,' responded the Sgt. as he walked away, directly eyeballing Dan.

'You enjoy your time off, Daniel, you have earned it,' said the Captain before giving Dan another wink of her eye.

'Yes ma'am.' responded Dan as the captain walked back towards her office, with Dan eyeing up her sexy, womanly curves displayed from under her tight pencil skirt. Although mature compared to Sandy, the Captain took care of herself and was ageing well, like a good bottle of expensive wine.

The following morning Dan was up at 02:00 am, ironing his uniform and making sure that he looked his best. Whomever he was meeting in Colorado must be very important, and he wanted to look his best. His jacket and trousers were immaculate, and you could see your reflection in his shoes. He looked as if he was about to meet the President of the United States.

Dan packed his small bag with some personal belongings and some civilian clothing, as he was unsure what the mission would be and, perhaps, he would need to blend in with the locals. He boarded the express bus, which had him in the Atlanta airport two hours before his flight departed.

He checked in for his flight and sat waiting in the departure lounge. A young boy of no more than eight years of age walked up to Dan and tugged on his lower trousers. Dan turned as the young boy held out his hand like an adult looking to shake his hand at the outset of a business meeting.

'Thank you for your service to our country, sir.'

Dan knelt down and shook the boy's hand. Without saying a word, the boy nodded and quickly ran back to his Mother. It was a surreal moment for Dan, as if the boy was running in slow motion. Dan found it strange being thanked for his service to the USA when he had yet to do any foreign service, let alone prove himself in battle.

The flight to Vail was turbulent and bumpy, especially as the plane descended through the snow-filled clouds before landing on time in Vail airport. Dan walked into the arrivals hall, which was small in comparison to international airports such as Atlanta or Dublin. A handful of men stood holding paper signs with names printed, and a few kids walked along in ski clothing. It was only then that Dan realised he was dressed inappropriately for the snowy weather of Colorado. However, this thought was quickly removed from his mind when he heard a loud female voice shouting his name.

'Daniel!'

Dan glimpsed at a young blond lady running towards him with her arms outstretched and wide open. It took him a split second, which seemed much longer as if time was moving in slow motion, to realize that it was Sandy.

'Sandy... Oh my God, Sandy!'

He instantly dropped his bag and held out his arms as Sandy sprinted towards him like a young child running to her father. She jumped and landed firmly in Dan's arms, and they embraced and kissed passionately. Dan completely lifted Sandy off her feet into his embraced arms while swinging her around.

'Oh, Daniel, how wonderful it is to see you. This is going to be the best Christmas ever.'

Putting Sandy back on the ground as she pulled him towards a tall man who was standing at the back of the arrivals hall.

'You said you were going to Barbados!'

'I know. It was torture, but I didn't want to spoil the surprise. Come on, I want you to meet my Daddy.'

'Your Dad.' Dan slowed his walking pace and tried to fix his shirt, which had come out of his trousers with the motion of lifting Sandy.

'Dad, this is Daniel.'

Dan looked at the man, who was tall and slim with dark hair and a moustache. Dan put out his hand to shake

'Hello, Mr. Evans, I am Daniel Flynn.'

'Nice to meet you, Dan. Cut the Mr. Evans, makes me feel older than my years. Call me Chuck.'

'Ok, Chuck.'

Chuck looked Dan up and down.

'You're dressed for Miami. This is cold up here in Colorado.'

'Em, oh yea, I guess I got it wrong!'

'It's Ok, you can borrow some of my ski clothes. You like skiing, Dan?'

'Skiing, no, never tried it, sir'

'Well, there's always a first. Come on, we have a room booked for you at the Cascade Hotel, here in Vail, really nice spot, and the food sure is good.'

All three walked from the airport and got into Chuck's open back pick-up truck, which was parked directly outside the airport.

'Dan, you sit up front next to me, so we can talk man to man. Sandy, you're in the back, dear.'

With all three in the truck, Chuck drove away in the snowy weather. There were minimal cars on the road as there had been a recent falling of snow.

'So, how you finding the military, Dan?'

'It's hard going, but so far, so good.'

'Can I ask you a question... Chuck?'

'Sure.'

'How did this happen? Sandy told me she was going to Barbados for Christmas. I thought I was going for a work assignment?'

'Daniel, one thing you need to keep in the back of your mind is that contacts make things happen. Remember this in your military career.'

'So, you got me here, sir, I mean, Chuck.'

'Did you not want to see Sandy?'

'Yea, of course, thank you, Chuck, this is great.'

Dan started to relax as he reached back and held Sandy's hand. They drove along the highway, through the snow covered mountains and on to the hotel.

'It's so beautiful, Sandy, reminds me of Donegal.'

You know, Daniel, that's just what I was thinking. Do you get much snow in Ireland?'

'No, a little in December or January, but not much, only on the high ground.'

'Well, you're on the high ground now, Dan. Vail is rather high. You will enjoy Vail. It's similar to Aspen, only smaller and less commercialized. Do you know of Aspen, Daniel?'

'Yes, Aspen, saw that in the *Dumb and Dumber* movie!'

Sandy giggled from the back seat of the car as they pulled into the car parking space of the Cascade Hotel.

'Come on, Daniel, I have you booked in and have your key. Wait till you see the view from your room.'

Dan and Sandy ran into the hotel and onto the first floor. Sandy quickly opened the door to room 215 and pulled Dan into the room, almost jumping on him, kissing him passionately. Dan responded with similar eagerness, and before long, his hands were exploring the female parts of her body. Just as things were about to get interesting, there was a loud knock on the bedroom door.

'Oh shit, that's my Dad!'

Quickly they made themselves look decent. Dan opened the double doors that led out onto a small balcony consisting of two chairs, a table, and a spectacular view. Dan stood in awe with his mouth open as he looked out at the splendor of the mountain in front of him. There was the innocent, beautiful, and pure sound of a stream running along the side of the hotel at the bottom of the mountain. This was Colorado at her best, pure and beautiful nature supreme, only interrupted by a couple of jocks drinking their beers sitting in the hot tub.

'It's a great view, Dan. Looks a bit like Ireland, doesn't it?' sounded Chuck.

'It's amazing, wild and pretty and yet so spectacular. Have you ever been in Ireland, Chuck?'

'I have had a stop or two in Shannon and Dublin. Got to see your Cliffs of Moher in Clare. Very nice, a little like our Grand Canyon. You ever been in the Canyon?'

'No sir... I mean, Chuck.'

'Maybe we will go there sometime,' said Chuck as he put his hand on Dan's shoulder. He whispered in a stern tone, 'You better be nice to Sandy, or I will kill you, do I make myself clear?'

'Yea… sure, Chuck.'

'Oh, and no screwing in this room. I might be picking up your check, but I sure ain't going to let you screw my daughter in a room I'm paying for!'

'You boys having fun?' said Sandy as she walked onto the balcony.

'Oh, there you are, honey,' said Chuck as he put his arm around Sandy.

'Just getting to know Daniel a little better.'

'Well, there will be plenty of time for that, Dad.'

'Sandy, why not let Daniel get cleaned up and join us for dinner?'

'Yes, Daddy, Daniel will join us.'

'I will call for you. Come on, Sandy, let's give Daniel some time to breathe.'

Chuck walked out of the bedroom with Sandy following. She quickly turned and gave Dan a quick kiss.

'I hope you're hungry, Daniel. Make sure and leave some room for dessert!'

Dan showered and stood looking out at the mountain view. Although it was cold, with plenty of snow, the air was still crisp and clear. It was comfortable enough to stand on the balcony in nothing more than a bathrobe. Dan's mind wandered back to Ireland and his dad's place in Donegal. He recalled the snow-covered mountains and the fun in the bar. However, the serenity and beauty of the Vail mountains was like nothing he had ever seen before. By now, the jocks had retired from the hot tub, and the only sound was of the stream running by the hotel, along with the occasional unnerving howling noise coming from the mountain.

Dressed in his Levi jeans, boots, and shirt, Dan looked smart and was ready just as there was a knock on the door. He heard the sweet words of Sandy from behind, 'Hurry up Daniel, it's me.'

Opening the door, and before him stood Sandy, with her beautiful long blonde hair, dressed in tight black jeans, boots, and leather jacket with a furry collar. No sooner had Dan got the door open, she pushed him back into the bedroom, and they both fell wilfully onto the bed, kissing passionately. Once again, Dan's hands started to explore her body as she groaned with his every pleasurable touch. Dan was starting to enjoy himself when he suddenly recalled the words of Sandy's father. He quickly jumped up in front of the bed.

'Time is moving on. We better make a move. Don't want to be late for your Dad.'

'Daniel, what's wrong with you? Don't you want to have some fun?'

'Yea, sure, but look at the time. We've got to go meet your Dad.'

'Oh you're right, come on.'

Dan and Sandy quickly ran downstairs to the restaurant, which was very upmarket and not what Dan had become accustomed to, especially since joining the army. A large, orange-flamed open fire blazed in the corner of the room, creating a warm, homely feeling in the restaurant.

'Here they are!' sounded Chuck.

'Dan, this is my wife, Shirley. Come on in and sit down, guys.'

Dan shook Shirley's hand. She was at least fifty-five years of age, blonde hair and blue eyes, with a slim figure. A slender lady who took good care of herself.

'Nice to meet you, ma'am.'

'Oh, how nice to meet you, Daniel. I have heard so much about you from Sandy and Jo. You are so handsome.'

Dan, felt a little uneasy as if Sandy's mum was flirting with him, but he then thought it may just be the friendly Texan charm.

'Sit down, guys. Dan, will you have a beer? None of this wine lark for you, or would you like a pint of Guinness?'

'No sir… sorry, Chuck, a bottle of Miller would be great, thanks.'

'So, where is your sister Jo?' enquired Dan.

'She is back home in Dallas, studying for her exams,' responded Shirley.

'So, Dan, take a look at the menu. What are you having, son?' asked Chuck.

Dan looked at the vast menu, but more importantly his eye caught the price of the food. Dan looked a little uneasy. Chuck picked up on Dan's uneasiness from all his years of training surveying people.

'Dan, order what you want. This is on me.'

Dan still felt a little uneasy, especially with Sandy rubbing her foot on his leg, which was going higher and higher up his leg. Thankfully, the tablecloth draped down onto the floor and covered her foot and his manhood, which was getting rather stiff.

'Come on, Dan, what will it be? Tell you what, let's go with a couple of Colorado steaks. How do you like yours cooked, Dan?' asked Chuck.

'Steak, yes, well done, please.'

'Well done. Waiter, give me two steaks, better be good ones now, one well done and one rare, very rare, and make sure they're good steaks,' bellowed Chuck.

The two ladies ordered salads and light pasta dishes with a bottle of white French wine.

'So, Dan, you looking forward to your first deployment overseas?' asked Chuck.

'Yes, I guess so, a little anxious, but we are a good team, and we have been trained well.'

'I remember my first deployment. Well, it's still classified, but you always remember your first deployment and your buddies. You know, you fight for the guy beside you.'

The food arrived at the table. Dan couldn't believe how tender his steak was; he didn't need a steak knife. The taste was amazing and the texture really soft and tender. Dan gazed over at Sandy. She was still playing with Dan underneath the table. Chuck cut into his steak, and the blood flowed from the meat.

'I love a tender steak. Really good. How's your steak, Dan?'

'Very nice, Chuck, thanks.'

'Two more beers and more wine for the ladies,' shouted Chuck at the waiter.

'So, what part of the army were you in, Chuck?' asked Dan.

'Started in the Rangers and ended up in Special Forces.'

'Are the Rangers not Special Forces?'

'Yes Dan, they are, but I went a step higher than the Rangers.'

'Is that Delta?'

'Alpha, Bravo, Delta, call it what you will, Dan, but I call it Special Forces.'

Dan looked a little confused, but he continued to eat his steak and to try to control himself as Sandy continued to rub his manhood, which was now bursting to break free from his pants.

'So, Dan, do you miss Ireland?' asked Shirley.

'I don't miss the rain, but I do miss my Mum and Mickey.'

'Mickey, I wonder how he is doing, and my favorite was Billy... Dad, you have to take Shirl to Donegal, it's such a wonderful place,' Sandy said.

'Your parents own a hotel?' enquired Shirley.

Dan slightly coughed on his food, thinking of his parents' small hotel in comparison to the hotel in which they were staying.

'Yes, a small hotel and bar.'

'You have to see it, Shirl, it's so amazing, and the land is so green. Do you remember when we went on the boat to the islands, Daniel?'

'How could I forget?' responded Dan as he thought of the night he became a man on the Arran islands, his first night of passion with Sandy. He was excited about what lay ahead in Colorado, but he equally thought of the spine-chilling words of Sandy's Dad.

'So, Dan, you up for a bit of skiing tomorrow?' asked Chuck.

'I have never skied before.'

'Sandy will show you what to do. It will be great craic as you Irish say. I have arranged for some ski clothes to be delivered to your room. Should be there when you get back.'

'Thank you, Chuck. I can't thank you enough for all you have done for me.'

'You make Sandy happy… Continue to make to her happy, and we will get along just fine, Daniel Flynn!'

Dan felt uneasy at Chuck's words as he slurped down the remainder of his beer. Chuck uttered the words 'Daniel Flynn' as if he had a run a background search on him and most probably had. Dan wondered what connections Chuck had, especially in the military, and what his murky past held. Chuck, although friendly and a true American Gentleman, had a coldness in his eyes, a killer look with a dark history.

'Come on, Shirley, time for us to take our leave and let these love-birds have some time together.'

'We will see you in the morning.'

All stood and said their goodnights, leaving Sandy and Dan at the table. By now there was only a few other couples in the restaurant. Dan and Sandy moved over to the open fire and sat on a sofa, with Sandy resting her head on Dan's shoulder. Dan gazed at the open fire, thinking of his Mum back home in Donegal.

'Look, Daniel, it's snowing out.'

'I have never seen snow so heavy before.'

The snow blew down from Vail Mountain: heavy snowflakes, almost like small birds landing on the ground. Dan put his arm around Sandy as she snuggled into his chest, both warm from the blaze of the open fire. The two kissed while sitting on the sofa, getting ever more passionate as the seconds passed. Dan broke the kiss and embrace and said: 'Shit, Sandy, I have just realized, tomorrow is Christmas Day, and I don't have any presents for you or your parents!'

'Daniel, don't worry. Just being here with you is the perfect gift for me.'

Sandy pulled Dan towards her, continuing to kiss him.

'Let's take this upstairs,' whispered Sandy.

Dan could feel himself getting more and more excited, but at the same time, he could still hear the words of Sandy's dad.

Dan quickly jumped up. 'Let go outside, Sandy, in the snow.'

'But it's cold outside.'

He grabbed Sandy and pulled her out into the night sky. The ground was thick with snow, and the night sky was lit up by a silver moon that reflected off the snow on the mountain. The only sound was the stream flowing and the crunch of the snow under their feet. Sandy pulled Dan toward her and kissed him, exploring his mouth with her tongue. Dan responded with great excitement, only to be interrupted by Sandy's dad.

'Goodnight, guys,' said Chuck as he walked past the two of them.

Dan felt very uneasy and broke from the kiss.

'What's wrong, Daniel?' asked Sandy.

'Your Dad. I feel awkward.'

'Daniel, I am not a child.'

'Yes, but not in front of your mam and dad.'

'Daniel, don't be silly. Anyway, Shirl is not my mum, she is my step-mother.'

'Sorry, I didn't realize your parents were divorced.'

Sandy looked sad, and a tear built up in her left eye. 'Daniel, my mum died while giving birth to me.'

'Sandy, I am sorry. I didn't know.'

'That's OK, Daniel, I like Shirl, but she is not my Mother. You can only ever have one Mother and Father, but I guess you know that!'

'That's true, Sandy.'

Dan pulled Sandy toward him and gave her a strong hug, holding her in his arms.

'Daniel, I feel so safe in your arms and warm, even though the Colorado air is so cold tonight. I just wish this night would last forever.'

'Me too, Sandy, me too.'

'Let's go up to your room, Daniel.'

'Em…Ok. What room are you in, Sandy?'

'I am next door to my Dad. Don't think we could make much noise,' Sandy said, laughing.

'My room then, but what about your Dad?'

'Daniel, I told you I am an adult. Anyway, I have got something to show you.'

Dan, still feeling uneasy, walked back into the hotel and towards his bedroom with his arm around Sandy. The two entered his bedroom as

Sandy kissed him passionately. Dan's inexperienced lovemaking hands fondled awkwardly at her breasts. Things were looking good for Daniel when there was a sudden knock on the door.

'Ignore it,' said Sandy.

The knock grew harder and louder.

'I better get it.'

Dan opened the door, and in walked Chuck. Thankfully, Sandy still had her clothes on and looked decent.

'Dan, I had a great idea. Why don't the two of us go shooting tomorrow?' suggested Chuck

Shooting? Dan thought to himself, thinking of shooting something else as he looked at Sandy, who was fixing her hair.

'Yes, shooting. I will get some rifles, and you can show me how good a shot I hear you are!'

'OK, that sounds good.'

'Sandy, come on with me. I need you to get some things for me,' stated Chuck.

'Things, what things?'

Chuck took Sandy by the hand and slightly pulled her from Dan's bedroom.

'Say goodnight to Dan.'

Sandy winked at Dan as she walked from the bedroom. Dan fell back on his bed, exhausted, but in a way relived that Chuck had not arrived a few minutes later, as maybe he would have been sending for a rifle earlier than expected.

CHAPTER 21

The following morning Daniel walked into the reception and was greeted by Sandy with the usual hug and kiss.

'Merry Christmas, Daniel!' said Sandy as she reduced her hugging hold on him, well, at least enough for him to breath.

'Happy Christmas to you, Sandy! I just wish I had time to get you a present.'

'Stop worrying about that, Daniel. You will get your Christmas present later,' whispered Sandy as her dad and Shirley walked over to Daniel, exchanging Christmas greetings and good wishes.

'Looking forward to some shooting today, Dan. Should be some good old American fun!'

'What will we be shooting?' enquired Dan.

'Anything that moves is fair game up in the mountain forest, good elk and deer to be had around this area.'

'Elk and deer, seems a little cruel,' wimped Dan.

'Nonsense, this is America, home of the gun. Be ready to go in an hour. Did you get the ski suit in your room, Dan?' asked Chuck.

'Yes, it's a good fit. Thanks, Chuck.'

'See you in an hour in reception.'

With that, Chuck and Shirley walked off in the direction of the outdoor swimming pool.

'Isn't it a little cold for swimming,' asked Dan?

'The pool is heated. It's very nice. We can have a swim later, Daniel. Just make sure and keep your energy up for me!'

'Better go and get some breakfast then, seeing as you need me fit for later,' said Dan with a cheeky grin.

'Ok, I need to go get changed. We are going skiing, so I will meet you in reception with Dad in an hour. Enjoy your breakfast.'

Dan sat in the breakfast room, having consumed a large breakfast and about five large cups of coffee. He felt alive and happy, ready for the day ahead. His mind started to think of his buddies back in the army camp, especially Jelly, who was really starting to miss Ireland. Dan was his only contact with back home, and the two had become close buddies during the training.

He put on his ski suit and boots, standing waiting for Sandy and her dad in reception. After a couple of moments, Dan felt the impact of a snowball bouncing off his head, accompanied by the sweet laughter of Sandy. Dan paused for a moment as he gazed at Sandy, with her long blond hair glowing in the bright sunlight, which was extra bright as it reflected on the snow-covered ground. Sandy was wearing a gold colored ski suit. She looked hot, amazing, just like she'd stepped out of a James Bond movie.

'Wow, Sandy. Wow is the only word that comes to mind!'

'Why thank you, Daniel, but if you think this is nice wait till you see what I have for you tonight!'

'Come on, guys, jump in the truck,' shouted Chuck as he drove up in a large 4x4 truck. Dan had not seen such a large truck before. It was equipped with snow chains on the wheels. Both Sandy and Dan jumped into the back seat of the truck, and Chuck accelerated hard.

'So, where are we heading, Chuck,' asked Dan.

'Dropping the girls at the ski lift, then you and me are heading for some shooting. Picked you up a .338 Winchester Magnum rifle, should be powerful enough to take down a small elk or two.'

Chuck drove into the parking area of the ski lifts and let Sandy and Shirl out of the truck. 'See you back at the hotel later on girls,' shouted Chuck.

'Come on, Dan, ride up front with me.'

Dan sat in the front seat of the truck and fixed his seat belt. No sooner had he closed the door than Chuck accelerated fast, skidding out of the car park. There was an uneasy silence for a couple of minutes.

'So, Dan, you enjoying Colorado?'

'Yes, thanks, Chuck.'

'Are you enjoying my daughter too? Shame if there was an accident with one of those rifles, especially now that we have invested in all that army training!'

'Chuck, I really do like Sandy and would never do anything to hurt her.'

'Just remember what I said, Dan. You hurt my girl, I will hurt you.'

Dan felt uneasy especially with the tone of Chuck's voice and with him staring at Dan directly in the eyes while still driving.

'And if I take good care of Sandy, then I will be OK?'

Chuck smugly responded, 'You take care of Sandy, and I will take care of you. I guess it's a type of karma, Dan. You believe in Karma?'

'I guess so.'

Chuck drove off the highway and up a narrow country road that was completely covered with deep snow. The truck wheels struggled to get a grip on the snow, but managed it with the powerful V8 engine roaring as Chuck pushed down hard on the gas pedal. Finally, at the top of the snow covered lane, the truck came to a stop.

'Grab your things, Dan, we are going shooting.'

Dan stood out into the snow, which was crisp and dry. The air was fresh, cold, easy to breath, but yet low in oxygen levels due to the height of the mountain range of Colorado. The view was spectacular, almost taking Dan's breath away as he looked out into the forest that dropped down to the side of the mountain.

'Some view, isn't she?'

'Yes, Chuck, it sure is.'

'Plenty of elk out here to be hunted. Just keep away from the bears, and they will leave you alone.'

'Bears, you're kidding me, Chuck?'

'No, Dan, we have plenty of bears in Colorado. This is their home, so remember that and let's respect them by keeping clear of them.'

'Chuck, are they killer bears?'

'Yes, they are, but if you're lucky enough to see one, they will most likely keep clear of you.'

The two walked into the forest, which was thick with pine trees. It was difficult to see more than twenty feet. The further they went into the forest, the darker it got and quieter, with sounds of birds and other sounds unfamiliar to Dan.

'It's a little like Hansel and Gretel, Chuck. Sure hope you know your way back to the truck?'

Chuck pulled open his jacket pocket and showed Dan a compass that looked old, as if it had seen some better days.

'Never leave home without my lucky compass. This was my grand-daddy's. He was on Omaha beach on D-Day. Kept him safe, and it has kept me safe.'

'I guess it's like a lucky charm,' stated Dan.

Chuck grabbed Dan by the upper arm, squeezing it tightly. 'There is no such thing as luck. In battle you either kill or be killed. If it's God's will that you die, then you will die. Never forget that, Dan.'

'No... No, Chuck, I sure won't.'

Chuck stared at Dan for a moment, again with his killer eyes staring right through Dan. Finally, he let Dan's arm go and returned to slowly walking. Again, there was an uneasy silence as Chuck removed his rifle from his bag, checked it was loaded, and hitched in over his shoulder. Suddenly, he stopped and motioned his left hand behind him, making Dan also stop. He then waved his hand downwards, indicating for Dan to get on the ground. Dan felt as if he was in a movie like *Platoon*, and Chuck was the sergeant leading his troop through a Vietnam jungle, except this was not Vietnam, it was a cold snow-covered Colorado mountain.

'Unzip your rifle, Dan.'

Dan lay on the ground beside Chuck and pulled his rifle from its bag. He checked the sight and rested it on a log in front of the two of them.

'Do you hear it, Dan?'

Dan could hear nothing other than the singing birds and the sound of a small river flowing in the distance.

'Hear what, Chuck?'

'Shush now . . . . there they are down by the stream. You can just make them out, two elk. Be quiet now and follow me.'

Dan looked out in front of him and could see nothing other than the trees and the snow-covered ground.

Chuck moved slowly and quietly on his hunkers through the shrub with Dan, trying to be as quiet as possible as he followed.

'Walk on the balls of your feet, Dan, makes you quieter.'

After walking a distance in this uncomfortable manner, Chuck stopped and pointed out the elk, who was about 200 meters away. It was just about possible to make out the elk in the distance, but the trees obscured the view. Chuck lay down flat on the ground, and Dan followed his lead.

Once again, Chuck looked down his rifle using his scope and beckoned Dan to do the same with his rifle. Dan looked down his rifle and adjusted his scope, just like he had been trained in army training school. He could now clearly see the elk, which was standing in an opening beside the river.

'You should have a clean shot, Dan. Aim for the head, it's a clean kill.'

Dan took off the safety catch of his rifle and aimed down his scope. He had a perfect shot. He could feel his own heart beating with the anticipation of making the kill, his first kill as Dan had never killed anything before. Dan was the sort of guy who would open a window to let a fly out rather than smash its guts on the window. Dan moved his index finger onto the trigger and stared at the elk, which slightly moved to reveal a baby elk drinking from the river. Dan jerked backwards at seeing the young elk.

'Great, I will take the little one, Dan.'

Dan's heart beat hard, almost out of his chest, and he started to perspire with sweat dripping down onto his rifle.

'You shoot first, Dan.'

Dan froze for a moment, thinking of the Lord's commandment, 'Thou shalt not kill!' and here he was, in God's garden, about to take life.

'When you're ready, Dan, in your own time.'

Dan aimed to the left of the ear at a tiny branch of a tree and pulled the trigger of the rifle, which rang out loud. He then quickly moved to his right and bumped into Chuck, who let off a shot from his rifle that also missed its target. The two elk quickly ran away out of sight.

'What the fuck, Dan,' shouted Chuck. 'You did that on purpose.'

The two stood up, and Chuck punched Dan in the stomach, making him wince to the ground in pain.

'You made me miss, Dan, you thick Paddy fuck.'

Dan got back up and walked down to the river, which was a beautiful, picturesque, flowing stream.

After some moments, he turned and could not see Chuck. Feeling a little panicked, he shouted out Chick's name, but there was no answer. Quickly, Dan walked back up the mountain, stumbling and fretting but trying to keep his composure. The thick forest obscured his view, so he tried to follow his footsteps in the snow. Out of nowhere, Chuck suddenly appeared.

'Are you yellow?' squawked Chuck.

'No, no, I am not. Why did you hit me?'

'Get your ass back to the truck. Soldier my ass. If you can't shoot an elk, how the hell you going to shoot a terrorist?'

'The elk is innocent. The terrorist is evil and must be stopped,' responded Dan as he clambered back up the mountain, trying to keep up with Chuck.

'So, you're telling me in battle you're going to be a Judge? I would not want to be in combat with you. Now get your ass in the truck. Better still, get in the back of the truck.'

Dan climbed into the open back of the truck as Chuck put his rifle on the back seat. Chuck started the engine and skidded as he accelerated out of the parking area into the deep snow. The truck struggled to get grip in the snow as Chuck revved the engine more and more. Eventually, the truck picked up grip, and Dan bounced around the rear of the truck, bruising himself as his body slammed against the sides. Before long, they were on the open road, with Chuck driving at crazy speeds. Dan thought to himself, *If I fall out of this truck I am a goner, or if I get injured, how am I going to explain myself to Sgt. Bell and Sgt. Vickers?*

The truck pulled back into the set down area of the hotel. Chuck jumped out of the driver's seat and threw the keys at the concierge. Dan said nothing, just climbed out of the rear of the truck and walked into the hotel and into his bedroom. It was still early in the day. Changing into his shorts, he braved the cold air as he walked to the outside pool. Even though the pool was heated, the water was still cold, so he decided on sitting in the hot tub, which was unusual for Dan as it had started to gently snow, was about -5 degrees, and he was sitting in his shorts in a hot tube. Dan stared down at the stream that flowed past the rear of the hotel. It was possible to see people in the distance skiing down the mountain, which was really surreal for Dan as he sat in the hot tube contemplating what was to come when he shipped out for the Middle East.

Once again, Dan questioned himself on pulling a trigger and taking a life. If he could not kill an elk, how was he going to kill another human. In his mind he had built up a picture that he would be killing terrorists, but how do you determine who is a terrorist when looking down a rifle scope. Dan started to think of his home in Termon, Donegal, and yearned to see his Mum and Dad and have a pint of Guinness in his Dad's bar. He called home every week and spoke to his parents on Skype, but it was not the same, he truly missed Ireland.

As he continued to sit, his mind wandered and wondered what his soldier colleagues were up to back in Georgia. His thoughts were interrupted as Sandy shouted his name and ran towards him.

'Daniel, there you are. Did you have fun with Daddy?'

'Em, well, sort...'

'Great, let me quickly slip into my swimsuit, and I will be down to you.'

'I was getting...'

Dan couldn't finish his sentence before Sandy had run away towards her bedroom. Quickly, he jumped out of the pool and stood beside an outdoor fire. Although it was snowing and below zero, the heat from the flame kept his exposed body comfortably warm. As Dan sat beside the fire, he remembered that it was Christmas Day. He smirked to himself as he thought of Mickey back home in Donegal, eating Christmas dinner and trying to get his hands on Sgt. O'Brien's daughter Naomi. This had to have been the most unusual Christmas Day he'd had in his short life, but he was truly thankful as he sat back enjoying the tranquillity and beauty of Vail, Colorado.

'Are you getting back into the tub Daniel?' said Sandy as she slipped off her bathrobe, revealing her perfectly formed, beautiful, sexy, young, firm body, hidden only by her skimpy bikini. On seeing her, Dan jumped over the railing and splashed into the hot tub, splashing Sandy as she climbed into the tub and into Dan's open arms. The two kissed passionately and embraced tightly in the tub. An elderly couple, seeing their passion, decided not to enter the tub and walked the other way.

Sandy climbed up ono Daniel, straddling him and gripping his now firm and erect manhood. She managed to remove it from his shorts and slid her bikini bottoms to the side before letting him sink deep into her. Sandy started to move up and down while kissing Daniel passionately and letting her tongue explore his open mouth. Just for a moment, Dan forgot where he was and felt as if he was James Bond in a hot tub with a beautiful woman. To be fair, he was, but that changed when the manager of the hotel coughed with a loud, 'Hmm hmm, excuse me!!'

Sandy stopped kissing Dan, and the two of them looked up an angry and somewhat embarrassed hotel manager. He was fat and round, grossly unfit looking except for his large, well-used jaws, muscular from chomping on food.

'There are other people in the hotel. If you would kindly like to take this to your bedroom, we would certainly appreciate it!'

'Oh, sorry,' exclaimed Dan as he managed to shift Sandy off him to the side and quickly pulled his shorts up. The manager walked away as Sandy giggled in the pool. Dan also had a cheeky smirk on his face.

'Sandy, come on, we have things to do,' shouted Chuck as he glared at Dan from the side bar area. Dan's cheeky grin was instantly removed when he saw Chuck, who was standing over by the fire.

'I will call you in an hour,' Sandy said as she exited the pool, adjusting her bikini and putting on her robe. Chuck stared at Dan as he continued to stay in the hot tube. Even if he had wanted to get out, he couldn't, at least until his manhood stood down from attention. Sandy and Chuck walked back towards the hotel with Chuck's protective arm firmly around her shoulder. It was only when they started to walk that Chuck removed his killer staring eyes from Dan.

Dan exclaimed a sigh of relief as he put his head back to the side of the tub and looked at his hands, wrinkled from being in the water too long. Once Chuck was out of sight, Dan exited the tub and walked back the short distance to his room.

It was Christmas day, and Dan felt sad at the fact that didn't have a gift for Sandy. He decided to take a walk in the reception area, which had a few small shops, all closed of course as it was Christmas Day. It was at this point that he noticed a small silver chain and locket in the shape of a heart, the type of locket that you would place a photograph of your loved one in and wear it around your neck. Dan just had to get it, but the shop was closed and not due to open until midday the following morning. His Delta Airlines flight left for Atlanta at 12:35; there was no way he was going to be able to make the purchase. This was rather disappointing for Dan, so he decided to plead his case to the receptionist, who was rather taken by Dan's romantic attitude and good looks, not to mention his muscles, which were bursting from under his Ralph Lauren Polo top. However, the receptionist needed to get permission from the manager to open the shop.

'Ah, hello again. I didn't recognise you with your clothes on,' said the fat manager as he growled at Dan.

'I would appreciate it if I could make the purchase for my girl.'

'That's very romantic, but sadly the shop will remain closed until tomorrow at midday.'

'Look, sir, I ship out to Iraq, and I sure would appreciate your assistance,' pleaded Dan.

'Oh, and I guess you won't see your sweetheart for a long time. What a shame. The answer is no, lover boy. Now, thank you for your custom. Good day, sir.'

Dan took a twenty-dollar bill from his pocked and placed it in the top jacket pocket of the manager.

'Maybe this will help change your mind.'

'Why, thank you for the tip, Sir, but the answer is no. Now, good day, Sir.'

The little fat manager walked away laughing to himself, muttering under his breath. Dan walked from the reception area, feeling somewhat deflated. He entered the bar and sat drinking a bottle of Budweiser. A shadow cast over Dan as he stared down into his bottle of beer.

'What do you want to buy?'

Dan looked up and saw the receptionist staring down at him.

'I was looking to purchase the silver locket for my girl before I ship out. May not see Sandy for some time as I head back to Atlanta tomorrow.'

My sister owns that shop. I phoned her, and she told me to sell you the item.'

'Thank you, that's great, thank you.'

Dan and the receptionist quickly walked into the shop via the rear entrance. He was surprised at the weight of the locket.

'So, what's the damage, how much?'

'Let me see, that's $700.'

'$700, OK... I, em... didn't think it was that much.'

'You're military, aren't you? Well, let me see, how about an even $500. Would that be OK for you?'

'Yes, thanks, that's great, thank you,' said Dan as he handed over his credit card.

'Let me wrap that for you.'

'No, that's OK. I have something to put in the locket. Just the box is fine. Thank you, thank you so much.'

'Ah, you're welcome, and take care of yourself.'

Dan quickly ran back to his bedroom, delighted with his gift for Sandy. Now all he had to do was give it to her. It was looking like it was going to be a nice, romantic evening. As he opened his bedroom door, he noticed that there was a note on the floor, which had been slipped under the door.

Meet me in the foyer at 6.30pm, Sandy xx.

Checking his watch, it was almost 6pm, with just enough time for a quick shave and shower before meeting Sandy. Dan got an idea. He reached into his bag and took a small container from it. Opening the small container, he poured some of its contents, Garten clay, out onto a table. The whitish grey substance resembled cooking flower. He opened the locket and rubbed some of the powder onto the glass part of the locket, pushing the clay into the locket where normally a small photograph would go. It looked good. He then placed the locket back in its holder and left it on the bed. After his shower he put on fresh jeans and a long-sleeved polo top and leather jacket. He placed the locket in his jeans pocket and left the room, heading for the reception area. Dan walked into the reception area, and there was Sandy standing in a tight, flowing low cut black dress, with her long blonde hair blowing as the cold breeze blew in from the mountain.

'Wow, Sandy, you look great!'

'Thank you, Daniel. Let's go for a walk before dinner.'

Dan and Sandy walked out of the hotel and down the snow-cleared path to the river, which was flowing gently. Although only early in the evening, there was already a full moon lighting up the dark sky. The two young lovers walked arm in arm along the path. Danny tried not to shiver in the cold as he had placed his jacket over Sandy's shoulders.

'So, how did you and Daddy get on today?'

'Well, OK, it started OK, but not so good towards the end. What did he say to you?'

'Not a lot, which is unusual for Daddy. Tell me what happened?'

'I had an elk in my rifle site, and I just couldn't pull the trigger. I pushed your dad, so he also missed his shot.'

'You pushed Daddy!'

'Well, just a soft push.'

'Why didn't you shoot, Daniel?'

'It just didn't seem right, killing an innocent animal, and it is Christmas Day, Sandy.'

'Daniel, you're all heart.'

The two embraced and kissed passionately. Dan tried his best, but in vain, not to shake with the cold, which Sandy realized. It had also just started to snow again, only this time the snow was heavy and starting to block the path. The two quickly ran back to the hotel, stopping again to kiss along the way. The fat manager looked at the two of them with disgust, coughing while trying to get their attention.

'Oh, leave it out fat boy,' exclaimed Dan as he stuck out his tongue at the manager while ushering Sandy into the restaurant.

The two lovers sat at a table in the restaurant beside a blazing orange-flamed open fire, giggling and laughing about silly things, without a care in the world.

'So, where is your Dad tonight?'

'Shirley and Dad are gone out to dinner, so it's just you and me tonight, Daniel.'

Dan jumped as he felt Sandy's toes once again exploring his manhood under the table. He felt a little embarrassed but, all the same, was enjoying the moment.

'Daniel, tonight is my Christmas gift to you. Let's have dinner together, a drink or two, and then some desert... upstairs.'

'Christmas gift. I almost forgot, Sandy, Happy Christmas, darling.' Dan pulled the locket from his pocket and handed it to Sandy, who quickly opened the box.

'Oh, Daniel, it's so beautiful. Where did you get it? And look, a photo.'

'It doesn't matter how I got it. I have given you something better than a photo. That's Gartan clay.'

'Gartan clay, what's that?'

'Do you not remember, Sandy, back in Donegal in the field with the Priest, Mum, and Dad?'

'Yes, I do, Daniel. This is so much better than a photo. It will protect me while you are away.'

Daniel slumped back in the chair, reflecting on the word 'away,' which was a reminder of the uncertainty of what was to come for him. His eyes froze for a moment as he thought of his buddies back in Georgia preparing to be shipped out. In only a few hours he would be joining them.

'You look sad, Daniel, what's wrong?'

'Nothing, Sandy, let's enjoy tonight,' said Dan as he pulled himself forward in the seat. The two young lovers sat eating dinner, reminiscing about Sandy's holidays in Donegal, and Danny told old stories and jokes about his home, which was going well until Sandy's dad arrived at the table.

'Sandy, we need to be up early in the morning. Gotta catch an early flight back to Dallas.'

'How early, Dad?'

'Be in reception at 0800 hours.'

'Aren't you going to say hello to Daniel, Dad?

Chuck simply stared at Dan, making a slight murmur or growl like a dog growling at another dog over a bone.

'0800 Sandy. Goodnight honey.' He bent down and kissed her on the cheek without taking his eyes off Dan. He walked away, out of view.

'What happened between you guys today?' asked Sandy.

'Maybe I should have just pulled the trigger on that dam elk.'

'Daniel, you are so caring. It doesn't matter. Don't mind my dad. Thank you so much for this gift. Here, help me put it on.'

Dan stood up and walked to the rear of Sandy, who remained sitting. Her long blonde hair flowed over her shoulders, revealing a beautiful neck. He felt a like a vampire about to take a bite from a young virgin's neck. He could feel his masculine blood pumping through his veins. He wanted Sandy in a most manly way. Having fixed the chain around her neck, he gently kissed her neck.

'Oh, Daniel, it so beautiful. Thank you so much, I will never take it off.'

'You're welcome, Sandy.'

'Let's go upstairs, Dan, to your room.'

'OK, let's go.'

Just as Dan stood up, the fat manager walked in accompanied by two police officers. 'There he is,' sounded the manager as he pointed out Dan.

'Sir, please stand up and place your hands behind your back.'

'What's this all about?' asked Dan as he stood up and was immediately manhandled by one of the officers, who bent him over the table and pulled his hands behind his back, fixing them in handcuffs.

'Daniel, I will get Dad,' said Sandy as the second officer shouted at her, 'Sit down, miss!'

'What have I done?' asked Dan.

'You know what you have done, son. Narcotics are illegal in Colorado. You're facing some time here. Hope you like our state,' shouted the fat manager.

'I don't do drugs.'

'In your room, we found your cocaine and lots of it. Snorting your lines of coke in my hotel,' shouted the fat manager.

'Cocaine? I don't have any Cocaine. Never. No, I don't do drugs. This is a set up.'

'Ok, son, let's go to your room. You come along as well, miss. Cuff her, Joe,' said one of the officers.

Sandy started to cry as the officer placed her hands behind her back and put on the cuffs.

'Right, let's go to your room then, son,' said the officer.

'This way, officers,' said the fat manager as he led them towards the stairs. The few other guests in the room stood up, some with shock on their faces. As they walked towards Dan's bedroom, with Sandy crying and Dan getting agitated and upset over the false allegation, Sandy's dad suddenly appeared.

'Daddy, help me!' cried Sandy.

'What the hell is going on here, officers? Why is my daughter in handcuffs?'

'Drugs, sir,' responded one of the officers.

'Drugs? My daughter does not do drugs.'

'It's that Irish fellow. I knew he was wrong from the moment I saw him in my hotel. We found the drugs. Cocaine, sir, cocaine in his bedroom,' sounded the fat manager.

The two officers continued to manhandle Dan and Sandy as they walked to his bedroom, with the fat manager leading the way along the narrow corridor.

'You'd best be prepared for a lawsuit,' said Chuck as he quietly walked behind.

The manager opened the bedroom door, leading them all into the room, including Chuck, who stood alongside Sandy.

'Now, there you are, you see, cocaine, discovered by room service, who came in to simply turn down the room, and there is a lot of it,' said the manager as he pointed towards the table.

Dan started to laugh with a smirk on his face as one of the officers looked at the white powdery substance on the table.

'Joe, give me one of your tester kits?' asked one of the officers, who then scooped up a small amount of the powder and placed it in the kit.

'If this turns blue, then its narcotics, but I don't think its cocaine,' said the officer.

Sandy looked at Dan, who winked and smiled at her, which made her feel a little more comfortable.

'I know what that is. That's not cocaine. It's Gartan clay,' explained Dan.

'Gartan clay, what's Gartan clay?' asked Chuck.

'I don't know what Gartan clay is, but it's certainly not turning blue, which makes it not an illegal substance,' said one of the officers.

'Release my daughter,' said Chuck in a commanding voice.

'Yes sir. Joe let the young guy go too,' responded the officer.

'What, let them go? But they are doing drugs in my room,' demanded the fat manager.

'Sir, we apologize for our actions. If you want to make a complaint against us here is a card and our details,' said one of the officers as he handed a business card to Dan.

'No, officer,' responded Chuck, 'you only did what was asked of you. Dan take Sandy downstairs. I want a word in private with this nice manager.' With that, Chuck pushed Dan out of the room.

'Sandy, I am so sorry,' exclaimed Dan as they walked from the room.

'Let me go to my room, Daniel. I need a little time to myself.'

Dan felt bitterly disappointed as Sandy walked away along the narrow corridor. Dan then re-entered his bedroom. As he opened the door, Chuck was leaving the room with the manager profusely apologizing for his actions.

'I will take care of this, Dan. Go to bed, son,' said Chuck as the fat manager walked with a pale white face as if walking towards his own execution by firing squad. Dan sat on his bed for a few moments, then wiped up the Gartan clay, which to be fair, did look like cocaine. He thought to himself, *Gartan clay is supposed to protect me not cause me problems.* He lay back on his bed, with the doors open to his balcony. It had stopped snowing and was a cold crisp night with the moon illuminating the night sky. Dan phoned Sandy's room, but there was no answer. It was getting late, and he was fretting that he might not see Sandy before a quick goodbye in the morning, but there was nothing he could do. He climbed into bed but was unable to sleep. Dan looked up at the bright silver moon and thought of his friend Mickey back home in Ireland. He slowly drifted off to sleep with the cold Colorado mountain air making him extra sleepy.

Daniel, Daniel, are you there... Dan opened his eyes forgetting where he was for a moment, then quickly jumped up to the sound of a shallow knocking on his bedroom door. He quickly ran and opened the door. Standing before him was Sandy, wearing a bathrobe and slippers, with her long blond hair shining in the hallway light.

'Sandy, Sandy.'

'Can I come in, Daniel?'

'Of course.' Dan held the door open as Sandy walked into the room. Dan was standing in his boxer shorts, revealing his muscular toned body.

'So, Daniel, would you like your Christmas present?'

'Christmas present... what?'

Sandy slipped out of her bathrobe, revealing sexy white silk lingerie, consisting of white silk panties and bra complete with hold ups and shiny stockings. She looked amazing, every young man's dream. Dan's mouth dropped wide open at this sight of Sandy. He had only ever seen such beauty in a Playboy magazine or adult TV show.

'Well, are you going to just look at me, Daniel?'

Daniel was awestruck for a moment at the pure beauty of Sandy. He had never seen anything as beautiful. She looked like a Playboy pinup. He stood silent for a moment.

'Daniel,' sounded Sandy.

On hearing his name, he was removed from his transfixion and back to reality. He leapt forward and embraced Sandy. He kissed her passionately and she openly responded. Her body felt amazing under the silk lingerie. Dan's hands explored her curves and ravished her body as he kissed and explored her every crevice. Sandy did not try to stop him as she also responded to his openness. The shyness Dan had previously displayed was gone. With his Sandy he was a professional love maker.

Looking on, you would think that he was a porn star with his bulging muscular body.

The two fell onto the bed with Daniel inserting himself into Sandy, who let out a slight groan with pleasure. He started to move back and forwards, thrusting himself into her with lovemaking applied with gentle force. Sandy continued to groan with pleasure and started to hear Dan make climactic noises.

'Oh, Daniel, I love you,' sounded Sandy.

'Oh, oh, Sandy, I am cumming, Ohhh,' exclaimed Daniel as he pumped himself into Sandy without attempting to withdraw. Sandy openly accepted Daniel, clinging onto him and pulling him into her as if trying to get even closer to him, which was not possible.

'Oh, Sandy, that was amazing.'

'Yes, Daniel, but let's go again.'

'Again.'

The two young lovers made love for the next three hours in every position imaginable. Daniel was now an expert at making love, and Sandy was showing him a few moves and positions, but always in a lovemaking capacity: erotic and sexy but always in a loving method. The two finally fell asleep in each other's arms, well, with Danny's arms wrapped around Sandy, who snored in her sleep rather loudly, which was unusual, to say the least, for such a petite lady.

The following morning, Dan awoke at 07:00 to the sound of his alarm. The two had been asleep no more than a couple of hours and looked a state, but greeted each other with large banana smiles.

'You have to meet your dad at 0800.'

'I know, I just don't want this moment to end, Daniel. When will we see each other again?'

'I have a tour of duty to complete, but I will make it back to you, Sandy, I promise.'

'You will have to come see me in Dallas. You would love Dallas, it's a wonderful city. We can go horse riding.'

'I was thinking of a different type of riding, Sandy.'

'Daniel.'

With that, the two once again made love, with Daniel climaxing no less than five times and Sandy the same.

'I have to go. Meet me in reception in twenty minutes,' said Sandy as she kissed Daniel and ran from his room, clutching her smalls and wearing nothing but her bathrobe.

Time passes so fast when you're having fun, and Dan had had his fill of fun and frolics with Sandy, but sadly it was once again time to say goodbye. Dan walked into the reception area of the hotel. Shirley was already in the truck, and Chuck was settling the room account at the reception. Sandy stood wearing her jeans and cowboy boots with a tear in her bright blue eyes. The two embraced with a longing hug as Chuck walked over and put out his hand to shake Dan's.

'You're OK, Dan. Good luck in Afghanistan, son, and remember, pull the trigger first.'

'Yes, Chuck, thank you. I will remember that, but Iraq is my destination.'

'Maybe... Sandy, let's go.'

Dan hugged and kissed Sandy one last time, and Sandy clung to him like a child clinging to her mother on the first day of school.

'I love you, Daniel. Please don't do anything stupid and come back to me.'

Sandy walked to the truck, climbing and waving as Chuck drove away from the hotel. Dan brushed a tear from his eye as he caught the last glimpse of the truck as it exited the car park. He knew in his heart that he loved Sandy, but he also knew that it was going to be a long time before seeing her again. Dan was heading into the combat zone.

CHAPTER 22
AFGHANISTAN

'Welcome back lover boy,' laughed Coffee as Dan walked back into his troop. The guys all sat around chatting about their Christmas. There was tension in the air as the guys would be shipping out the following day. Dan could feel the tension mixed with fear of the unknown and the trepidation or feeling of being helpless to make any changes now; it was too late for the guys to back out.

'Attention,' shouted Sgt. Bell as he walked into the troop's quarters accompanied by Sgt. Vickers. The two sergeants were dressed in formal military uniform, smart looking, and their shoes, well, you could almost see your face in their shoes. All the men quickly stopped what they were doing and stood to attention at the end of their beds.

'Men, stand easy,' said Sgt. Bell.

Sgt. Vickers addressed the men: 'You men are now qualified United States Army soldiers, the finest army in the world, and it has been a privilege to train you men. Tomorrow morning at 0500 you will be shipping out for your first tour of duty. You will be supporting the U.S. marines and most likely will not get involved with direct combat, which I am sure to you is a disappointment. Sgt. Bell will be coming along with you on your tour. Sadly, I cannot travel, and no, it is not because of my age, it is because of my need to train the next bunch of trainees who arrive tomorrow. So when you leave in the morning, leave this room the way you found it and be proud of what you have achieved and proud of your comrades, but most of all be proud to be American Soldiers. Congratulations, men and welcome to the United States Army. Do you have any questions?'

'Sir, what part of Iraq are we travelling to,' enquired Adams.

'That is classified information. You will get your orders tomorrow. Make sure you get some sleep, men, you have a long flight tomorrow.

'Thank you and goodnight, gentlemen.' The two sergeants then exited the room, leaving the soldiers to return to what they were doing. Dan sat on his bed and looked at the photograph of Sandy that he kept in his wallet. He lay back on his bed slightly grinning at his private thoughts of the previous few days and winced in pain as he thought of how long it was going to be before he would see her again.

'Well, boy, did you bury the baldy lad?' enquired Jelly.

'That's a very personal question, Patrick.'

'Oh, so its Patrick now. A couple of days ago it was Jelly. Give us a look at the photos.'

'I didn't take many photos. Well, just a couple.' Dan showed Jelly the photo of Sandy from his wallet.

'Bloody hell, she's a fine bird, Danny. I wouldn't have been taking photos either, I'd have been riding her in the bed all night, boy.'

'Yea, yea, Patrick.'

'Are ya blushing, Patrick?'

'Feck off, Danny boy.'

All the guys checked their gear and then double checked it again, as they had been taught by the two sergeants. That night was a sleepless night as the guys spent most of the night talking about personal lives and what might or might not lie ahead of them. The men felt in some way like the 101st Airborne troops on the night before the D-Day landings in France. Either way, they were trained, ready, and hungry for combat.

'All right, men, get up and get ready to ship out in 30 minutes,' shouted Sgt. Bell as he switched on the lights. The men quickly jumped out of their beds and made ready, again checking their equipment before standing in the parade ground before Sgt. Vickers and Captain Larmon.

'Men, I wish you every success on your tour of duty. God be with you, and good luck,' said Captain Larmon.

The men quickly boarded the coach and before long arrived at Atlanta International Airport. Dan felt a little strange, as did some of the other guys, walking around the airport in military combat clothing while mixing with civilians.

'Let's go get a McDonalds, guys, it will be a while before we get some good old American food,' sounded Coffee.

Dan, Jelly, and Coffee stood in line along with Chico, Tango, and Clarke.

'It's a bit early for Big Macs,' said Sgt. Bell.

'Never too early for food, Sgt.,' responded Clarke.

'You fat fuck, Clarke.'

'Sgt., we are a team now. Don't speak to Clarke like that... even if he is a fat boy,' responded Dan.

'You're right, Flynn, sticking up for Clarke as well. I think you will become a Private first class.'

'Thank you, Sgt.'

'Just don't get all mushy on me.'

'No, Sgt.'

The guys approached the counter and all ordered Big Macs with fries and large Coca Colas. However, when they went to pay, the lady at the cash register told them that it was covered.

'Who paid for us?' enquired Coffee.

'I did,' said a man standing nearby. 'You boys have some chow on me.'

'Thank you, Sir, can I know your name?'

'Dave Finney, son, and thanks for your service, guys.'

'I can get used to this,' responded Coffee.

'Times have changed, guys, since Vietnam. At least now the civilians respect the U.S. Army and our efforts to protect them,' responded Sgt. Bell.

The guys soon boarded their flight into the unknown on a Boeing 767 300 chartered aircraft with leather seats. That was about it; there was no inflight entertainment, seat back TV screens, or music, just a basic aircraft and no inflight magazine. Still, the guys settled into the seats, which for a charter aircraft were reasonably comfortable. Once the guys were finally boarded, the aircraft doors were closed, and they started on pushback, with the intercom providing a scratching sound as the captain made his announcement.

'Good morning from the flight deck, this is Captain Sean Dwyer, and I am joined in the flight deck with fellow Captain Philip Courtney. Our aircraft call sign is Pixie 45, and we are taking off momentarily from runway 35. Our flight time today is estimated at 7 hours and 20 minutes to Shannon Ireland, where we will stop for an hour, and then onto Bagram airbase, which is about a further 9 hours. Sit back and enjoy your flight, gentlemen.'

'Do you hear that, Dan? We're stopping in Shannon, home soil. Didn't think we would be back home that soon,' sounded Patrick.

Within a few moments, the engines roared on full power as the aircraft picked up speed before pulling back and lifting off the ground. There was an eerie silence on the aircraft as the guys seated at the windows peered out at the last views of America before it was obscured by the clouds.

'We're on our way, boys,' said Coffee.

Before long, the boredom of the flight set in, with Jelly fidgeting and annoying Dan, who was busy typing a letter to Sandy. The inflight food had been served and devoured by the guys, who had drunk their two beers each and now sat reading or talking. The atmosphere was upbeat even though the guys were heading into the unknown.

'What are you reading, Coffee?' asked Jelly.

'*Helmet for My Pillow*, by Robert Leckie. He was a marine in the Pacific against the Japs in World War Two.'

'Glad I am not in the Marines, they get all the hard jobs and seem to pick up the most casualties.'

'Not in Iraq or Afghanistan. It's the Army that is picking up the most casualties with the IEDs,' said Coffee.

'What are IEDs?'

'Improvised Explosive Devices… or roadside bombs.'

Jelly took a gulp of Coke as his brain digested the thought of roadside bombs exploding beside him. Before long, the captain came back over the intercom.

'Gentlemen, Captain Sean Dwyer here again. We shall shortly begin our descent into Shannon Airport. Once we arrive at the gate, you can depart and stretch your legs. We had a tail wind, and we crossed the Atlantic rather fast, so you guys will have an hour on the ground. Make sure and get yourself a pint of Guinness.'

The plane erupted in a roar of excitement and claps as the guys realized that they would have a little time in Shannon to get off the aircraft and grab a beer or two or maybe even a shot of Jameson Irish whiskey.

The aircraft descended over Co. Clare, with an excellent view of the Irish coast, green grass, and mountain ranges. It was as if God had removed all of the clouds and hazy mist of Ireland for Dan and Patrick to get a view of their home... Ireland. The aircraft touched down in Shannon with a gentle bump before arriving at the gate. Sgt. Bell made a quick announcement, warning the guys to have a single drink and to be back at the aircraft in no more than forty-five minutes.

Dan and Patrick walked from the aircraft and into the transit lounge, which did not permit them to access duty free, but there was a bar with plenty of alcohol, and there was no problem in accepting U.S. dollars. All the guys quickly ran to the bar, with the barman panicking at the sight of over 200 guys dressed in U.S. Military uniforms all looking for Guinness. Thankfully, an extra two barmen were on hand to deal with the extra business.

Dan was not interested in drinking Guinness, which the guys found strange, as surely an Irishman would want a pint of his country's renowned beverage after having been away for so long. No, Daniel was looking for a telephone, as he wanted to phone his Mum and Dad in Donegal. He managed to find a payphone and quickly placed a single Euro coin into the slot and dialled his parents' phone number.

'Hello, Flynn's Guesthouse.'

'Hi, Mum.'

'Daniel, is that you? Where are you?'

'I am in Ireland, Ma, Shannon Airport.'

'Oh, Daniel, are you coming home so?'

'No, Mam, I am on a flight to Afghanistan, with the guys, Mum.'

'Oh... Afghanistan, that's an awful dangerous place, son.'

'It's Ok, Mam, I am with my brothers. They will take good care of me.'

'Will ya stop, Billy, it's Daniel on the phone,' said Dan's mum, who was trying to get Billy away from the phone. He was drunk as usual.

'Hello, Dan the man, 'tis Billy. How ya getting on with the wee Texan lassie?'

'Grand, Billy, grand. How is Mickey doing?'

'Oh, will ya stop, Dan. Didn't Sgt. O'Brien catch him riding wee Naomi again, only this time he was riding her in the back of the police car. There will be murder yet.'

'Good old Mickey, tell him I said, hello.'

'Dan, its Mam again. I am worried about you going to Afghanistan. Will you look after yourself and don't do anything stupid.'

'I told you, Mum, I will be fine. I have to go, Mum.' The phone went dead as all the credit had been used. Dan walked away thinking and laughing to himself at the idea of Mickey being caught with Sgt. O'Brien's daughter in the police patrol car.

The guys boarded the flight again, with some of the guys having consumed more than one or two pints, which made the atmosphere on the aircraft somewhat jolly and boisterous. Even Sgt. Bell had had a couple of beers, and his snoring on the flight kept the boys both entertained and awake.

'Gentlemen, this is Second Captain Phil Courtney, we are about to begin our descent into Bagram airfield. This is a combat zone designated airport, although we don't expect any problems. Please close all window blinds and keep your seat belts fastened. We will be going in hot, so we will have you on the ground shortly.'

'What does he mean by hot?' Dan enquired.

'It's a straight dive in landing, just in case of any small arms fire or RPGs,' responded Coffee.

'RPGs, Rocket Propelled Grenades. If one of them hits the plane, it's curtains for all of us,' replied Dan.

'Hold on tight, gentlemen, here we go,' said the captain over the intercom.

The aircraft began a steep approach, descending rapidly. It was a scary experience for the guys and disorientating as the window blinds were closed. It was not possible to see how close they were to the ground. The engines also made strange noises along with the flaps, not your normal landing. After a few moments, the landing gear deployed making everything sound louder. A few moments later, and with a sudden impact, the aircraft hit the ground. The men were thrown forward in their seats as the engines roared in reverse, slowing the aircraft.

'Gentlemen, welcome to Afghanistan. I hope you enjoyed your flight with us and sure do hope to see you all on board again. The outside temperature is 10 degrees.

'Wow, that's cold,' stated Jelly.

Dan was thinking about the captain's words, 'hope to see you on board again,' and was pondering how many of the guys on the flight would become casualties of the conflict. A sad reality of war, a heavy price for peace and freedom.

'Well, here we are, boys, Afghanistan. I wonder if the Taliban are waiting for us, guys,' said Coffee.

'No need to wonder, Mr. Roberts. I can assure you they are here watching our every move, looking for a weak link in the chain to strike at us. Be on your guard, guys. Even in the base, this is their turf, and they know it better than any of us yankees,' said Sgt. Bell in an almost father-like, caring way.

The men walked from the aircraft and were quickly loaded onto trucks that carried them the short distance to the arrivals hall, which was rather similar to a civilian airport, with the one exception that all staff were U.S. military. After collecting their baggage and personal belongings, the guys were walked back to the trucks and driven to a hotel-like structure within the base.

'Alright, guys, off the truck. Get your room. Three men to a room and no bickering like a bunch of women, just move it,' shouted Sgt. Bell.

Jelly quickly ran first into one of the rooms, which had three single beds and an en-suite bathroom consisting of a toilet, shower, and sink. Although basic, it was comfortable and a big improvement on what the guys had become accustomed to in Fort Benning.

'Dan, quickly in here. You too, Coffee,' sounded Jelly as he led Dan and Coffee into the small bedroom.

'This is good, I like this place,' stated Coffee.

'I wonder how long it will be before we begin combat duty,' said Dan.

All three men stretched out on their beds. Within a few moments, the three of them were sound asleep. The only sound from the room was Coffee's loud snoring, which did not seem to bother Danny or Jelly.

'Well, would you look at the sleeping beauties. Get your asses up and assemble outside... now,' shouted Sgt. Bell The three guys quickly awoke and ran outside, half dressed, and stood to attention with the other newcomers. Dan tucked his shirt into his trousers while Jelly and Coffee also tried to make themselves look presentable.

Sgt. Bell was now dressed in full traditional uniform and looked very smart. He stood up front, alongside another two Platoon Sergeants and two Lieutenants, who also looked smart.

'Attention!' shouted one of the Lieutenants. A tall, slender, but fit looking man in full army uniform walked out in front of the men. 'Welcome to Afghanistan, gentlemen. I am Colonel Clive Brooks, and I am responsible for this airfield and base, along with your safety. No matter where you are on the base, you should always keep a weapon with you. Although the base is relaxed, we are at war with the Taliban and others, and this is their turf, so don't you ever forget that this is a combat zone. That being said, I like to think that this is a small U.S. city. Hell, we even have a cinema, internet stations, and Green Beans coffee, and once we Americans have our coffee, well that ain't so bad. Be safe, gentlemen, and look out for one another, and we will get along just fine. Break the laws of this town, and you will end up in front of the MPs.'

Dan looked on and thought of Col. Brooks as some sort of a sheriff of an old Texan town, friendly but laying down the law. Dan was just pleased to hear there was internet as now he could make contact with Sandy.

'The food around here is not so bad, and there are plenty of things to keep you guys occupied. Just don't venture outside the camp unless on patrol. You will hear on news channels that the war in Afghanistan is coming to an end. Well, gentlemen, it ain't. We are still losing soldiers to

IEDs, snipers, and organised attacks, so stay sharp and focused and work together as a team. Now go get some rest and report back here at 06:00 for assignment. That is all, gentlemen.' The colonel walked into a small office and one of the lieutenants shouted, 'Dismissed!'

It was now just after 7 pm, dark and cold, surprisingly cold as Dan had always thought of Afghanistan as being a warm, desert location. All the guys walked back towards the rooms. Dan checked his computer but was unable to get a broadband signal. Within a few moments, all three of the guys were back snoring tucked up in their beds.

CHAPTER 23

❦

'**A**lright men, get your asses out of bed,' shouted Sgt. Bell as he entered the room and switched on the lights. Bell was togged out in full military clothing, mean looking and ready for combat.

'What time is it, man?' enquired Coffee.

'It's 3:30 am. This is way too early,' responded Dan as he squinted at his watch, the bright glowing fluorescent light hurting his eyes.

'Get your asses up, full gear in the yard, five minutes.'

It was possible to hear the groans of some of the other guys from the other rooms as Sgt. Bell continued along the corridor shouting at the guys.

In just over ten minutes, the troop of some 40 guys stood in the main yard, dressed in full combat gear, including helmets and protective glasses. The only item missing was their weapons, which Sgt. Bell had purposely not yet passed out to the men. The early morning air was cold and crisp, with little moisture in the air. The guys stood shivering together in the dark, cold, early morning, with only the airfield lights giving off a luminous glow.

'Well, guys, isn't this nice. Here we are now in cold Afghanistan. I thought you would all like to warm up with a nice little run around Bagram airfield. Wouldn't that be nice and a good way of getting familiar with our surrounds... Move out!'

Sgt. Bell broke into a fast-paced jog, and the guys ran behind him, with most, as usual, just barely keeping up. Running with full gear, helmets, and body armor is much harder than running in a polo shirt and shorts. The guys looked on as aircraft of all shapes and sizes were landing. The airfield appeared as busy as JFK airport, with multiple military and civilian type aircraft landing and departing. The Sgt. made the guys run for just over an hour before returning them to their rooms.

'This is pure punishment,' sounded Jelly as he collapsed in a heap on his bed, soaked in sweat.

'Why did Sgt. Bell have to come to Afghanistan?'

'Good to have some experience with us Patrick,' stated Dan.

'Oh, there you go with your Patrick. Wake me in 30 minutes. I need more sleep.'

'Come on, guys, let's go and get changed and get some breakfast before the 06:00 parade,' responded Dan.

After a quick breakfast the guys stood to attention in the parade ground. There was an eerie silence that was only broken by the roar of aircraft jet engines. Col. Brooks walked onto the parade ground and addressed the men.

'Good morning, gentlemen. Today you will be broken into teams within the unit. Normally that will consist of about eight of you. Guard duty is a requirement for the airfield, and some of you will move out North to another advanced field base. Collect your weapons and remember what I said, keep a firearm with you at all times. This is a warzone, and don't you forget it. Dismissed, gentlemen.'

Colonel Brooks saluted the men and walked off into the distance with a familiar face for Dan; it was Major Robert Redmond, who looked stern and was fully dressed in desert camouflage gear. He appeared to be having an argument with Col. Brooks, or at best a disagreement. It was a heated exchange of words as the troop looked on and tried to hear what was being said.

'That's enough, men. Get your asses to the armory, collect your weapons, and get on the range. Now, men, move it!' barked Sgt. Bell.

The guys quickly ran towards the armory and stood in line, waiting to collect their rifles and ammunition. Each man was given their Colt M4 and 210 rounds of ammunition. However, as today was target practice, they were given another 210 rounds, and some of the men dropped their magazines as they exited the armory.

Dan stood in front of the issuing sergeant and handed him his credentials. 'I was wondering who this baby was for,' stated the sergeant as he handed Dan his M107 50 caliber sniper rifle.

'That's some rifle, son. You be sure to keep her well-oiled, as she will get all dried up out here.' Dan smirked as he thought of Mickey back home in Donegal, trying to get Naomi oiled for his sexual pleasure.

The guys walked onto the shooting range as Sgt. Bell shouted orders and reminded the guys of the importance of looking after their rifles like the way they look after their women back home. Each of the guys emptied the magazines at the targets, most of them hitting the targets, but like back in Fort Benning, Jelly was missing everything, not even getting close to the targets, which was evident from the shots embedding themselves into the sand bunker at the rear of the targets.

Dan set up his rifle, cross checking every little component, as if he was inspecting a child before their first communion. He then loaded the magazine, which consisted of ten rounds of ammunition, and adjusted his scope. Dan squeezed the trigger, which pushed the rifle back into his shoulder with the force of the mini explosion as the bullet exited the rifle. The target was annihilated as the 50mm round exploded on impact.

'Hold your fire, Flynn. Why are you using that gun on this range? Get onto the sniper range,' shouted Sgt. Bell.

Dan foolishly realised that he was on the wrong shooting range and quickly manoeuvred to the sniper range. He was the only one on the range and quickly set up the automatic targets before letting off round after round. He didn't see a couple of the guys who stood behind him, watching him take out the furthest target with ease. Dan emptied magazine after magazine, hitting almost every target with relative ease; at least, he displayed no apparent signs of difficulty or strain.

'Flynn, you are a damn good shot, son,' shouted Sgt. Bell as he stood behind Dan.

'Thank you, sir.'

'OK, men, you're free for the afternoon. Tomorrow morning, 05:00, we leave for patrol, so gather up your equipment and make sure you have all your gear ready. Get new ammunition and get an early night. Tomorrow is action day.'

The guys quietly walked from the shooting range. There was a sombre feeling amongst the men, as they knew they would soon see action.

The words 'action day' echoed in their minds. Quietly, Dan, Jelly, and Coffee returned to their room.

Dan grappled away with his now fully charged laptop. The Wi-Fi signal was good, and he tried to Skype Sandy. It rang out for several rings, but there was no answer.

'She is probably in bed with some yank, Danny boy,' laughed Jelly.

'Fuck off, Patrick.'

'Ohhh, serious Dan, will you relax, man!'

Dan's Skype rang, and he quickly answered; it was Sandy.

'Hi, Daniel.'

'Sandy.'

'Ah, look at the sexy Texan girl,' scoffed Jelly and Coffee while peering over Dan's shoulder at his laptop.

'Guys, will you have some respect for Sandy,' shouted Dan.

'Who is there with you?' asked Sandy.

'Ah, my two roomies, Patrick O'Kelly and James Roberts.'

'Hello, gentlemen,' responded Sandy.

'Are you in your pajamas, Sandy?'

'Daniel, its only 5:15 am here in Dallas, and yes I am still in bed.'

'Come on, Coffee, let's give the two lovers some privacy,' said Jelly as he exited the room, leaving Danny alone with his laptop and Sandy.

'What's Afghanistan like, Daniel?'

'It's cold, Sandy. I haven't been outside the base yet. Going on active patrol duty tomorrow morning, so I guess I will get a look then.'

'Be careful, Daniel. Don't want you getting hurt on me. I just don't know what I would do if you got killed on me,' said Sandy in her soft, southern, sexy Texan accent.

'I won't, Sandy. I will be safe. Sure, haven't I got my Gartan clay with me?' Dan checked his watch, which had some of the clay glued to the back of it so that it was always in contact with his skin. He had also placed some in his shoe, as he had hoped that this would protect him from stepping on a booby trap or triggering a roadside explosion from an IED, which had already caused so many horrific injuries and deaths to the U.S. troops in Afghanistan and Iraq.

'Daniel, I am starting back at medical school tomorrow, so don't call me so early. Just mail me, and I will call you.'

'OK, Sandy. By the way, how is your dad, Chuck?'

'He is fine, Daniel. I think the issue with the Gartan clay and the cops in Colorado has made him a bit more relaxed towards you.'

'Colorado, it was only a couple of days ago, Sandy, and it feels like a lifetime away. It was such an amazing place, and I still have not skied.'

'Would you have preferred to go skiing than doing what we did?'

'No, of course not, but maybe not shooting with your Dad!'

'Well, we did have fun, Daniel, didn't we?'

'Yes, Sandy. I wish I was with you now.'

'Me too, Daniel, in my bed. It's so warm and toasty in my bed.'

The lovers were interrupted as Major Redmond barged into the room. Dan quickly closed his laptop aside and jumped up to attention.

'You looking at porn on your laptop, Flynn?' asked the Major, who had a stern look in his eyes. His tone was like a head teacher asking a child if they were eating sweets in class.

'Sir, no sir, I was talking to my girlfriend in Texas, sir.'

'Texas. Nice women in Texas. At ease, son.'

'Sir.' Dan breathed out and tried to relax, or at last show that he was relaxed.

'Flynn, I am going on a reconnaissance exercise tomorrow, and I need a second man, with a good aim. You with me, son?'

'Sir, yes Sir.'

'Cut the Sir shit, Flynn, this is combat. Don't like being called Sir in the field as some terrorist may think I am important and try to take me out. Be ready for 04:00. We travel light. Just take ammunition, food, and water. Oh, and Flynn this is a classified mission, so not a word to Sgt. Bell or your room buddies.'

'Yes sir... I mean, Major.'

The major walked towards the door, then stopped. 'I guess you can call me Robert or Bob in the field. Only use Major or Sir when we're with the other guys.'

As soon as the Major had exited the room, Dan quickly logged back onto Skype.

'What happened, Daniel?'

'Sorry, Sandy, the Major entered my room. I had to cut you off.'

'Is everything OK?'

'Yes, fine, just wanted to talk to me about tomorrow, but all is good.'

'Daniel, I have to go and get ready. I am going out with my Dad, going shopping this morning, may even get you a present.'

'Present. I wish I could get you something, Sandy.'

'I have my pendant you gave me right here. I keep it beside my heart.'

'Will ya hurry up in there,' shouted Jelly, who was banging on the door.

'OK, Sandy, I got to go. Will call you soon.'

'Call me soon and write me. Love you, Daniel.'

In barged Jelly and Coffee, who were eating burgers and drinking cans of Coke. Jelly threw a burger at Danny, which in mid-air flight somehow became loose from its paper covering and bun, causing the burger and red ketchup to splat on Dan's bed.

'Oh, sorry man.'

'Patrick, for feck sake, man.'

'What did the Major want, Dan?'

'Nothing, Patrick, just wanted to compliment me on my shooting today.'

'You're a mean shot, Danny boy. You know your shooting is going to get you out of the infantry and into Special Forces.'

Danny put the burger back together as best as he could and lay back on the bed, pondering his future and what tomorrow would bring. He was keen to work with the Major and knew that he could learn a lot from the major's shooting skill, but at the same time, he feared the unknown and that night prayed that he would return safe from his tour in Afghanistan.

CHAPTER 24

Bleep Bleep, Dan's beside alarm clock sounded his wake up. However, he didn't need the alarm as he was already awake and had hardly slept during the night. He quickly grappled at his clothing and his bag of killing equipment and then walked slowly towards the door as he did not want to wake the guys who remained sound asleep.

He walked into the night sky, which was clear with bright stars flickering as if winking at him. A large oval-shaped moon broke the darkness, and the silence was only broken by the sound of his boots crunching the sand below. As he stood in the yard area holding his bag over his shoulder, his memory raced back to his first day of school as a young child waiting on the school bus in Donegal with his Mother clutching his hand.

'Morning, Dan,' sounded the Major as he silently walked up behind Dan, which caused him to jump in surprise.

'Morning... Bob... so how are we getting to our destination, sir?'

'I told you, no more Sirs or Major. Follow me, son.'

The two walked along the parade ground and down a narrow lane to an open area located near the main runway. The area was littered with military aircraft of various shapes and sizes, including airplanes, small helicopters, and Apache attack helicopters.

'This is the Little Bird AH 6 helicopter and your best friend in the field. When in a fix, these babies will get you out of trouble.'

Dan walked around the small helicopter and looked at every detail with some amazement. It was Dan's first time to see a helicopter up close, let alone fly in one.

'Major Bob Redmond,' sounded a tall man, who walked towards Dan and the Major, holding out his hand shaking the Major's hand with a warm greeting.

'Why if it's not Emerald Five. Brian Wilson, good to see you again.'

'Dan, climb aboard. This is Emerald Five, your pilot in the sky and friend in the field.'

'Nice to meet you, sir.' Dan saluted the pilot.

'Less of the saluting. Now get in, we got some flying ahead of us,' sounded the pilot.

Dan climbed in the back of the helicopter with the major, handing him two bags and two rifles, along with an MP5 machine gun. Dan packed all the gear into the helicopter while the Major got into the front and Wilson started the helicopter engine. Quickly the blades rotated, and within a few seconds, the aircraft started to lift off the ground. Dan put a small headset on, which permitted him to communicate with Wilson and Redmond, who sat up front.

'Emerald Five to control, request immediate departure on Vector Five.' Although a request, Wilson sounded as if he was demanding the authority to make an immediate departure. This was especially true considering the helicopter was already at least two feet off the ground and starting the climb into the night sky.

'Emerald Five, clear to go, good luck!'

Wilson pulled on the control stick, and the helicopter quickly pulled to the right while climbing into the night sky. Dan held onto the seat and double checked that his seat belt was secure; the helicopter moved like a roller coaster ride as Wilson manoeuvred it without any concern for the comfort of his passengers.

'So, where are we heading, Bob,' asked Dan via the headset.

'Heading North, son, into the mountains around the Kush region, which borders with Pakistan. We have reports of Taliban Al Qaeda activity in the area.'

'Any idea how many?' asked Dan.

'Don't worry, son, I brought extra ammunition, so we will have plenty of bullets for the guts of those terrorist bastards.'

'But there are only two of us,' sounded Dan.

'Two U.S. soldiers, son, is more than enough and we have Emerald Five here as backup, so relax and get some shut eye. We got another seventy minutes to our destination.'

Dan sat back in his seat and checked his equipment, making sure that his gear was well secured to his belts and double checking that his handgun was loaded and holstered on his hip.

'You got a green boy there, Bob. Have to break him in with a few kills,' said Captain Wilson.

'You're right there, Brian.'

Before long, Wilson started to reduce altitude by diving steeply towards the ground of a mountainous region, just as daybreak started to light up the sky.

'Make ready. It will be a quick departure,' said Wilson.

They landed with a bump, and Dan and Bob jumped from the helicopter. No sooner had their feet hit the sand than Wilson was climbing into the morning sky.

Bob opened the carrier bag and handed Dan his rifle and a small supply bag, which contained food, water, and ammunition. He placed his own sniper rifle over his shoulder and affixed the MP5 machine gun over his chest.

'Quickly, Dan, let's get out sight.'

Bob ran in the direction of a ridge of mountains with Dan trailing behind. As they approached the mountains, Bob dropped to his knees and then to his chest, lying flat on the ground. Dan copied his manoeuvre. Looking toward the mountain, Dan couldn't see any other people. There were just mountains, sand, rock, and some grass, nothing like the sprawling Irish mountains of Donegal.

'Stay down and silent,' whispered Bob.

There was still no people to be seen. However, it was possible to hear an engine noise, which grew louder as it got closer. A Mitsubishi pickup truck passed within 100 feet of them. Two men sat in the rear, with balaclavas covering their faces and dressed in Arab attire. One of the men held an AK47 in his arms, which Dan was accustomed to seeing in training and also recognized from the many movies and news reports from the area.

'OK, they're gone. On your feet, son. Follow me.'

Bob jumped up and took off running at a fast pace, faster than jogging, towards one of the mountains. Dan quickly followed, and the cold air was quickly replaced by Dan's sweat as they both approached the mountain. Although a mountain, it was not steep, and it was possible to hike up with relative ease. But Dan still found it difficult because of the amount of the gear the guys were carrying and the constant fear-infused adrenalin he had from being in a combat zone with the ever present threat of an attack.

Reaching near to the summit of the mountain, Bob pointed toward a ridge with at least a 50 ft. cliff to the front and good foliage to the rear, which gave natural camouflage and protection from any individuals who might approach from the rear. Dan looked down from the ridge and observed some white tents and two open backed pickup trucks, which had machine guns fitted to the rear. It was possible to observe the movement of individuals near the tents.

'This is an Alpha training base for Al Qaeda terrorists, supported by the Taliban. Try using your scope, son.'

Dan knelt down and pulled his rifle scope from his bag and looked towards the training camp. This was up close and personal. Dan had a perfect view of the camp and the individuals who sat about the place, not like the training he had received courtesy of the U.S. military.

'I count 42, which includes six guards. What have you got?'

Dan quickly counted and decided to agree with Bob's count. 'Looks about right.'

'OK, son, this is our vantage point. We will be staying here for some time, so make yourself comfortable and break open some chow. I'm hungry.'

Hungry? Dan couldn't think of food with the excitement and thought of what might lay ahead. Eating food was the last thing on his mind.

'Ya gotta keep your energy levels up. Take some energy bars and drink plenty of water. Set up your rifle, lock and load, and make sure your second gun is by your side with one in the chamber at all times. You never know what may happen, so stay sharp and ready for action.'

The two sat on the ridge, with Bob crunching on bars of high-protein chocolate and sipping cold coffee. Dan simply sat, saying nothing, observing Bob and the guys down below. Bob suddenly leaned forward, pointed his rifle towards the camp, and silently adjusted the scope.

'Well, at least when the shit happens, these guys are in perfect range for some killing.'

Bob sat back up and spat out the remains of one of the chocolate bars.

'So, tell me Dan, how did a young Irish lad like you end up in the U.S. Army?'

Dan smiled with a cheeky grin as he thought of Sandy but simply said, 'I guess it was a calling.'

'Calling my ass. Ireland has a decent army, especially the Special Forces. What's that they are called? Oh, yea, the Rangers, why not join them?'

'Yes, Ireland has an army, but it's small, and there is not much chance of seeing action,' responded Dan, who was sitting easy, almost relaxing as if sitting out on a picnic with a friend, except he had a large sniper rifle over his knees.

'Action. Well, you joined the right army for action. Everybody wants to pick a fight with the yanks. Quiet now and get down,' said Bob as he pulled Dan down onto the ground until he was flat on his chest. Bob fixed a suppressor, or silencer, to his MP5 and aimed it away towards some foliage. Dan could hear or see nothing of an immediate threat as he lay face down in the sand with his heart beating fast. A few moments passed before he could hear a foreign voice, which he quickly recognized as being Arabic. Dan glanced up briefly and could see two men no more than twenty feet away wearing traditional Afghan clothing. His eye fixed firmly on the AK47 one of the men was carrying. The second man was unarmed but was carrying a small holdall bag. The two men stopped and looked in the direction of Bob and Dan, and the guy holding the AK47 pulled the strap so that the gun was moving towards his hands. However, before he could grasp the rifle, Bob squeezed the trigger of his MP5, which, although fitted with a silencer, still rattled and clicked as it released several rounds, hitting the guy with the AK47 in the upper torso and head, instantly killing him. The second guy also got hit in the upper torso, with blood splattering the sandy ground. Both men fell to the ground, and the second man winced in agony as Bob quickly squeezed off another two rounds as if mercifully putting a dog out of its misery that had just been run over by a car. Dan was shocked at how effortlessly Bob had killed the two men, without a second thought. Dan stared at the two guys who were now bathed in a pool of red blood and blue intestines, which had initially pumped from their bodies and now trickled onto the ground, soaking their white clothing. Bob walked around the two men and beckoned Dan to come over. Dan somewhat timidly stared in shock at the warm corpses.

'Are they dead?' asked Dan in a childish tone.

'Sure are, son. A dead terrorist is now a good terrorist. Remember that, son.'

'You killed them so easily.'

'Better them than me. That's two less to worry about, Dan. Get back to the ridge and keep an eye on the base while I dispose of the bodies. It won't be long before they are missed.'

Dan returned to the ridge, somewhat in a state of shock at what he had just witnessed, but equally thankful that it was not he and Bob lying in a pool of blood. He sat pondering his thoughts of being back home in Ireland and was thinking of his Dad serving in the bar and also of Sandy and what she was up to in Dallas. His mind was racing; seeing two men killed, gunned down before his eyes, was almost too much to take. He then thought of Sandy's Dad and his preparing to kill the elk in Colorado and how easy it was for Chuck. But then, if you kill a man, you become hardened, and taking the life of an animal would be much easier with this type of conditioning.

'Any movement?' asked Bob when he returned to the ridge.

'No, just the same as before. How did you know they were near us? I didn't hear them approaching our position.' said Dan.

'I didn't hear them. I smelled them. The dirty smell of sweat out here gets in your nose.'

'Do you think they knew we were here?'

'Nope, but still couldn't take any chances.'

Dan sat back onto the ridge as Bob took out a satellite phone and adjusted the numbers to the correct frequency.

'Charlie Base, we have contact with local forces. Two KIA and at least 40-50 insurgents in the field at the base. Request air support to neutralize base.'

'Negative, Delta One, we have a coalition negotiation team enroute. Can you confirm if there are hostages at the camp?'

'Negative, cannot confirm either way.'

'Roger that. Maintain surveillance and report on observations... out.'

Bob put the satellite phone back in his backpack and reloaded the MP5 with a fresh magazine clip. He then sat back and thought for a moment before moving closer to Dan.

'OK, Dan, I need to get closer to the camp. Need to check if there are any hostages. Otherwise we can't call in air support and neutralize the camp. Now we will switch to radio coms. Your call sign is Emerald One, and I am Delta One, you got that?'

'Yea, Bob. Is that like Delta Force?'

Bob didn't answer, just glared at Dan for a moment and then continued on picking up some basic equipment.

'You're not going down there, are you?' asked Dan.

'Gotta check for hostages, son. Check your side arm. Is it loaded?'

'Yea, with one in the chamber.'

'Good, lock and load your rifle. If I get into trouble and shooting starts, take out as many of these terrorists as possible before calling for backup, which is Emerald Five. Brian will get you out of here. You got that?'

'Yea, Bob… Emerald Five.'

With that, Bob jumped up and ran a short distance to the side of the cliff. He quickly scrambled down the cliff and out of Dan's view. Dan peered through the scope of his rifle but was unable to see Bob; it was as if he had simply vanished into the mountainous terrain.

Dan sat back and double checked his side arm and rifle, cross checking the sight and making sure that he was all set up to fire his weapon. His mind was racing as he thought about killing another man, but he knew that he had no option. He thought back to watching TV and the 9/11 terrorist attacks. This would be his chance to get revenge for the innocent people who had died. The time passed slowly as Dan constantly peered through the sight of his rifle and also glanced around him as he was afraid that a terrorist might sneak up on his position and that his throat would be slit. He scanned the area but was unable to locate Bob, who was somewhere in the open ground between him and the terrorist base. A crackle came across the radio with the whispering sound of Bob, who did not bother with the Delta/Emerald call signs.

'Dan, are you receiving me,' whispered Bob.

'Yes, Bob.'

'We have a positive on the hostages. Not sure how many. Will need to check. Sit tight.'

The radio went dead as Dan quickly scoured the area. After a few seconds, he caught sight of Bob, who was up close near the base, within no more than fifteen feet of a terrorist who patrolled the perimeter with an AK47. Dan then observed two white men dressed in raggy civilian clothes, possibly Europeans or Americans, being removed from one of the tents and walked over to a second larger tent. Dan looked back towards Bob, who was again out of sight. However, the guard that was fifteen feet from Bob was also missing. Dan adjusted the sights on his rifle but was unable to locate Bob. He then observed one of the open back trucks with a machine gun being driven from the base in the direction of his vantage point. Dan felt a large lump in his throat as the truck stopped at the bottom of the cliff and the driver shouted something in Arabic in his direction.

'Dan, are you receiving me… over?' called Bob on the radio.

'Ya, but I have company over here.'

'Stay still and quiet. I am on my way back to you. They can't see you and can't scale the cliff, so just stay quiet.'

Dan now knew what the words 'eat dirt' meant as he buried himself into the ground, face first, as he tried to stay out of sight of the two terrorists below him. The two continued to talk to each other in Arabic and shouted out the names of the two colleagues who were now missing.

'I am coming up close on you, Dan, so stay quiet, it's me,' stated Bob quietly over the radio.

Dan was somewhat confused on how fast Bob had returned from the base but was pleased to hear he was near as the terrorists below got back into the truck and drove back towards the base.

'Twenty feet away. Stay down, Dan.'

After a few more minutes, Bob approached Dan, who was lying flat on his chest and peering over the ledge towards the base.

'You're sweating there, Dan,' sounded Bob, who unzipped his jacket and made himself comfortable on the ridge.

'Going to have to call this in... Charlie Base, you hearing me?'

'Go ahead.'

'We have a positive on the hostages. Sighted two and possibly another two in the base. Requesting support to take out the base.'

'Hold tight one moment... please.'

What seemed like an eternity was only a few minutes of waiting. Both Dan and Bob stayed silent, waiting for the orders and decision from control.

'Bob, this is Colonel Brooks. We only have the rookies, who are one hundred clicks southwest of your position. Need to hold off until we can get a Navy Seal team in place.'

'Negative, Colonel. By the looks of my observation, they are getting ready to execute the hostages. We need to go in now.'

On hearing the words 'go in now,' Dan shook with fear. Deadly assassin as Bob was, taking out fifty armed terrorists would be simply impossible. All Dan could hope for was that a Navy Seal team would be operational and in place to attack the base.

'Hold tight, Bob. We will divert the rookies to your position, but do not attack. That is an order.'

'Yes, Colonel, we will hold the line until the rookie reinforcements arrive… out.'

'OK, Dan, make ready for combat, son.'

'But there is only the two of us!' exclaimed Dan.

'We are American soldiers, Dan, the best army in the world. Now it's time to kick some ass.'

Once again, Dan checked his rifle, sidearm, and ammunition. All was as before, nothing had changed. His equipment was ready for action and only required a finger to pull the trigger. Bob also checked his equipment and viewed the enemy, aiming down his rifle with the scope.

'Oh, yea, time to kill me some terrorists. Plenty of bullets for this scum,' sounded Bob, who was only itching to pull the trigger on his rifle.

CHAPTER 25

T he two sat on the ridge overlooking the terrorist base. The sun was now high in the sky, and a slight breeze blew. There were no clouds, just pure blue sky. Dan's nerves were on edge as he checked and rechecked his equipment. He tried to drink water and eat some chocolate bars to keep his energy levels high. He knew that Bob was only itching to get into a fight and to get back to killing, as Bob was a highly trained professional killing machine that was oiled and ready for action.

'How many rounds you got in your magazine, Dan?'

'Eight rounds.'

'OK leave it at eight and set up your second and third cartridges beside you so that you can quickly reload. When the shooting starts, keep your sidearm beside you and your knife at hand. I don't think we will get overrun, but you never know. Always best to be ready.'

'Have you killed many people?' blurted out Dan as if asking his older brother if he was still a virgin. Bob smirked to himself and then looked at

Dan with a stern look in his eyes. He didn't need to answer; Dan already knew the answer to his question.

'Killing is what I do. Not murder, as that would be against the Bible, but killing terrorists is what I do best, and yes, I enjoy shooting those bastards.'

Dan thought for a moment of the Bible and the Ten Commandments, and whispered, 'Thou shalt not kill.'

'What did you say, Dan, thou shalt not kill? Well, don't you think it's a little late for that? Here we are facing off an army of terrorists and you're quoting the bible. Are you in the wrong profession, son?'

'No… I was just…'

'Listen to me, Dan Flynn, these are lowlife scumbags who believe that if they kill innocent Americans they will go to heaven and be greeted by seven virgins. Well, it's my job to introduce them to the virgins. Can't think of anything more annoying myself than seven women, one does me just fine… Now, it's time to kill me some terrorists.'

'Delta One, are you receiving, over?'

'Go ahead,' sounded Bob.

'This is Romeo One, Sgt. Bell inbound. We have three Humvees with the Rookies twenty clicks from your position.'

'Roger that. Be advised we have 50 bad guys in the camp with possibly four captives. Suggest you hold short maybe five clicks while we plan our attack… over.'

'Understood. Will hold short.'

Bob looked out from the cliff at the base using his scope. This was an army training camp that needed to be annihilated. Normally, an airstrike would be called in to destroy the camp, but as there were hostages, the strike needed a surgical approach to kill the terrorists and extract the hostages.

'You ever done this before, Bob?'

'Once or twice, but no two situations are the same. That's why we train and train so that we are ready for any eventuality within the field.'

Dan thought of his training back in Georgia and how hard Sgt. Bell and Vickers had been on him. Maybe this hardness would help him with what he was about to face.

'Delta One, this is Romeo One. We are at the holding pattern now, over.'

'Roger that… OK, here is the plan. Two Humvees will carry out a straight line attack, with the third Humvee picking up the hostages. I will be in the camp and will show you the way. Emerald One will be on sniper duty, taking out the targets.'

'Roger. Understood, Delta, starting our approach.'

Dan looked a little scared at the thought of being a sniper and finally taking lives. He reached into his pocket and checked that he had some of his Gartan clay, which he hoped would keep him safe from the response fire.

'Romeo One, what Rookie troop are you with, over?' asked Bob.

'We got the fresh boys who arrived yesterday… over.'

'That's your guys, Dan, so remember when you're taking aim that those are your brothers down there that are being shot at, and shoot to kill. Go with chest shots.'

Dan realised that his two pals Jelly and Coffee were in the Humvees, preparing to attack the base, and that he could make a difference in protecting them. He bent down and aimed his rifle at the camp, checking that his scope was within range.

'Don't shoot yet, son. Wait till I give you the signal and keep your radio on.'

'Where are you going, Bob?'

'Same as before. I like the MP5. It's up close and personal. I will need to show the guys the location of the hostages. Hold shooting until I give the order. Good luck, Emerald One.'

No sooner had Bob finished his sentence than he was away and out of sight again, making his way back towards the enemy base.

Dan took off his watch and placed it beside his sidearm, rubbing his hands and making sure that he was ready to take the action needed, that is, pulling the trigger. He peered through his scope and observed two terrorists standing together holding AK47s. Dan checked his range again and thought how he would have to kill the two soldiers. He paused for moment, thinking of the word 'soldiers.' This was not World War Two, and he was not shooting at German soldiers in a war declared by Nazi Adolf Hitler against humanity. No, this was worse. These guys he would be shooting at were not soldiers of a country; they were terrorists with the sole aim of killing innocent Americans, British, French, and other innocent people. Killing these guys should be easy, but Dan kept recalling the commandment of 'Thou shalt not kill.' Dan's thoughts were interrupted with a crackling on the radio.

'Delta One to all units. We need to move now. They are going to kill the two hostages in front of the large tent.'

'Romeo One received, we are two clicks out.'

'Emerald One, take out the guard on the right. I got the guy on the left... in 3... 2...'

Dan's heart raced as he took aim, leaning into his rifle and pulling it into his arm pit, with his finger on the trigger. He was going to cross the line and kill a man.

'1... fire.'

Dan looked at the guard to the left, who shuddered and rattled as the bullets from Bob's MP5 ripped into his flesh. Dan's heart raced as he aimed to the right and pulled the trigger. Instantaneously, he saw the guard spin and fall to the ground, but he was not dead. Dan had aimed at his upper arm, and the large round had effectively amputated his arm and part of his shoulder. The man lay on the ground screaming in agony as blood pumped from the wound, turning the brown sandy clay into a dark red mush. Almost immediately the terrorists started shouting as Bob ran into the camp and shot another terrorist straight in the head. The contents of the man's skull splattered on a tent to his rear. Bob then threw a flash bang grenade at the terrorist who was holding a large sword above the heads of the two kneeling hostages, as he was preparing to kill in a samurai-style execution. The flash bang caused immediate confusion.

'Emerald One, free fire. Take these assholes out, now!'

Dan aimed at another terrorist, who was running towards Bob, and fired. On this occasion he hit the terrorist just below the right knee, which instantly amputated the lower leg. Once again, the terrorist fell to the ground in agony, grasping at what was left of his leg below the knee.

Bob ran towards the terrorist holding the hostages and shot him almost point blank in the head. He then pulled the two hostages to their feet and shovelled them towards some cover, which consisted of water barrels and crates of food, located to the side of the camp. By now the element of surprise had been exhausted, and the terrorists began to reform and run towards Bob, who was holding them off singlehandedly with his MP5.

Dan observed two pickup trucks with machine guns fitted to their rears being manned by the terrorists and starting to drive towards Bob's position. Dan took aim and fired, hitting the guy in the rear who was manning the machine gun in the forearm. He fired again and hit him in the elbow, causing his arm to almost explode with the impact of the high velocity bullet. He then took aim at the driver of the car and fired, hitting him straight between the eyes. The shot caused an immediate imprint of red blood and brain tissue on the windscreen of the car, which slowly came to a stop. As the passenger exited the car, Dan shot him in the neck, which decapitated him. His legs bent, and he fell to his knees with his heart pumping blood from his neck where his head had been a second before. Dan quickly changed cartridges and put another round in the chamber. He had crossed the line and had taken life. There was no turning back now; it was kill or be killed.

'Romeo One entering the game,' sounded Sgt. Bell on the radio as two of the Humvees drove towards the compound at speed. One of the soldiers in the Humvee opened up from the machine gun turret with what sounded like a chain gun. It may have sounded like a chain gun, but it looked more like a chainsaw, as the bullets ripped the terrorists apart, simply making them fall like skittles being hit by a bowling ball.

'Dan, get your ass down here. I need support,' shouted Bob.

Dan quickly checked his rifle, grabbed his sidearm, and started to climb down the cliff before running towards Delta One, who was pinned down by about fifteen terrorists who were shooting at him from the other side of the camp. Humvee One entered the camp and continued to rattle off bullets almost non-stop into the terrorists, who continued to be ripped apart. The second Humvee also entered the compound, firing its machine gun, eating up the terrorists. It was very much a one-sided affair. The third Humvee came up alongside Dan, and the front passenger pulled him into the vehicle with the simple words, 'Want a lift, man?' as if he were a taxi driver offering someone a ride in New York City.

'Good to see you, Dan,' shouted Coffee, who was sitting in the rear of the Humvee.

Dan looked around at Coffee, who was dressed in full battle gear and holding his rifle across his chest. Dan was sweating profusely and simply said, 'Where's Jelly?'

'He is in Humvee Two, Dan.'

'Delta One to Romeo One, could do with some support over here.'

On hearing the request from Bob, Romeo One pulled in front of Bob, providing him with additional cover while Humvee Two pulled in front and opened fire on the terrorists shooting at Bob.

The third Humvee, containing Dan, entered the compound and drove over beside the first Humvee.

'Delta One, moving the hostages towards Humvee Three now. Open up, guys.'

Dan jumped from the Humvee with the other troops and helped Bob load the two hostages into the back of the third Humvee. Bullets crackled around them as Bob shouted at Dan and the Humvee driver, 'There are another two hostages in that large tent. Come with me, and we will go get them.'

Dan and Bob ran towards the large tent with the Humvee driving alongside them, providing cover from the dwindling number of terrorists, who continued to get ripped apart by U.S. bullets.

On entering the tent, a terrorist swiped at Bob with a large knife, cutting him deep on his upper arm. However, without hesitation and within no more than two or three seconds, Bob had the terrorist on the ground and the terrorist's knife plunged deep into his chest. The terrorist screamed in agony as he shouted, 'Allahu Akbar,' but grew quieter as his heart slowly stopped beating.

Dan quickly untied two hostages, who spoke in French with limited English. All four men ran towards the tent exit. The two hostages were also pushed into the rear of the third Humvee, which quickly exited the compound. By now the shooting from the terrorists had died down and almost stopped. The reason was simple; they were nearly all dead.

Bob and Dan stood beside the two Humvees, both exhausted and exhilarated from all of the action.

'You did well, son. I like the way you took out the terrorists with your shooting. Taking off a limb causes a painful, slow death, son. Good call, great job,' said Bob. He patted Dan on the back as he fixed a bandage to his injured arm.

Jelly came walking up to the two men. 'There you are, Dan. Who would have thought, our second day in Afghanistan and we would see all this action, ah boy.'

Dan was delighted to see Jelly, who was hopping around with excitement at the action, even thought he had not fired a single shot from his rifle. Dan was exhausted but felt miserable at the words of Bob. It was not his intention to kill, but equally, it was not his intention to cause a more painful death.

As all the shooting had stopped, Sgt. Bell was checking the guys, making sure none of the troops were injured. Dan walked towards the entrance to the camp and over to the lifeless corpse of the terrorist he had first shot. He looked down in horror at the pool of blood and the amputated arm that he had achieved from a shot from his rifle. The body was motionless and pale from the loss of blood. Dan thought of his actions with sadness as he stared at the open-eyed corpse of a man who was no more than twenty years of age. One of the soldiers pushed Dan out of the way as he took photographs of the dead and dying terrorists.

Dan heard the words, 'Water, water…' and he caught the eye of a dying terrorist who was lying on the ground, missing his legs and his intestines and the contents of his bowels on the ground beside him. Dan walked over and poured some water on his dying dry lips. Although the sight was deplorable, and in the past such a sight would have caused Dan to puke his guts, he felt an immense sense of compassion for the dying man. He no longer saw the man as a terrorist but as a fellow human in his last minutes of life. The man murmured the words, 'Thank you,' in a strong British accent.

'You're English,' said Dan.

'Yea, from London.'

'I'm Irish. How the hell did you end up out here?'

'Irish. It's a long story. Would you do something for me?'

'Sure,' muttered Dan.

'Find my wallet and contact my mother and tell her… I love her and… sorry.'

With that, the man grew faint, and he held up his hand. Dan knelt down and held his hand as the man looked at him muttering his last words, 'Life's only the…'

His hand grew limp, and he breathed out his last breath with the word 'beginning.'

Dan closed the man's eyes and made the sign of the cross on his forehead. Standing back up, he looked around for the man's wallet, which was not in sight. All he could see was his legs detached from his torso, blood and guts spattered around the ground. However, as he walked away from the man, back towards the main camp, he spotted a small leather purse. He quickly searched it and found that it contained a university photo identity of the man and his name and date of birth. Abdul

Jabaar. He was 22 years of age. *What a waste of life*, Dan thought to himself.

'All units prepare to move out,' Sgt. Bell sounded on the radio.

Dan walked into the camp and looked over at Bob, who was talking to familiar faces from his troop. Jelly and Adams waved at Dan and saluted at him as he climbed into Humvee Two along with some of the other guys and Sgt. Bell. Obviously, Adams had improved and was no longer anti-Irish or black. War and killing has a way of changing a man's outlook on life.

'Come on, Dan, we're moving out. We need to pick up our stuff from the ridge before we leave.'

'RPG!' shouted one of the guys.'

Dan turned and looked as an RPG hit the second Humvee, causing an immediate flash and explosion of flames. Dan realized with horror that Jelly was in the vehicle.

'Patrick!' shouted Dan as he ran towards the vehicle, which was engulfed in orange flames. The guys from the first Humvee dived on the ground along with Bob as pieces of the Humvee blew into the air. Bob looked at Dan, who was now at the Humvee, battling the flames and trying to open the door. Bob jumped to his feet and ran towards Dan, who was now pulling a wounded Sgt. Bell from the vehicle. Dan returned and pulled Jelly from the vehicle, not paying any attention or notice to the bullets bouncing off the ground as the terrorist who'd fired the RPG had now opened up with an AK47. Bob pulled at Dan's waist as Dan carried Jelly's body from the burning vehicle, taking his sidearm and shooting back at the terrorist who had now simply disappeared.

Dan dropped Jelly's body on the ground and took off his jacket, using it to cover Jelly's badly burnt body. He then turned and ran back towards the jeep, which exploded and was now completely engulfed in flames. Dan felt a sudden thump and a sharp pain in his side, which knocked him off his feet. He tried to stand up, but his legs would not move, and he fell back to the ground. He looked down and saw his own blood coming from the side of his torso, yet he still tried to stand.

'Stay down, son,' shouted Bob, who ran to his aid and put pressure on the wound.

'Delta One to base, urgent medevac required. I say again, urgent medevac required!' shouted Bob into his radio.

'Emerald Five to Delta One, I am close. Will take the medevac call.'

'Just relax, Dan, and stay with me, man,' shouted Bob.

'I got shot, Bob. I fucked up.'

'You did good. No, save your energy. Defend our position,' shouted Bob at the remaining troops from the first Humvee. Within a couple of minutes, Emerald Five was landing in the compound, and Dan, Jelly, and Sgt. Bell were loaded into the rear of the Little Bird. It was a bit tight because Bob also climbed into the front as the helicopter lifted into the sky. Brian saw some terrorists climb into a pickup truck and drive from the compound. Quickly, Bob encouraged Wilson to fly over them as he aimed his MP5 out the window and let off a full clip, which ripped the vehicle apart, killing the terrorists. The helicopter then climbed into the sky at full speed.

CHAPTER 26

✺

'Stay with me Dan, stay with me,' shouted Bob, who was half sitting in the front and rear of the helicopter. Sgt. Bell moaned in pain, while Jelly was out cold, which was just as well as his body was badly burnt.

'Brian, how far to base?' enquired Bob.

'We're about ten minutes out.'

The Little Bird struggled, as Brian was travelling at full speed and no more than fifty feet off the ground.

'Emerald Five to base, we're coming in hot. I got three wounded men on board who need urgent medical assistance.'

'Roger that, Emerald Five, you're clear to land. Medic team is standing by.'

'You hear that, Dan? Medics are standing by, just stay with me.'

Dan's mind drifted in and out of consciousness. Losing blood, he was shivering with coldness. His mind was racing back and forth, thinking of Sandy in Dallas, his Mother in Donegal, and Christmas in Colorado. He was dying. He could not feel any pain, and all he could see was a bright blueish light above him. Suddenly, he was looking down on his body with an immense sense of love, laughter, and happiness. He could hear his name being called by a man with a soft angelic voice.

'Daniel, Daniel, it's not your time. Go back.'

'Who are you?' asked Dan, without opening his mouth, as if speaking with his mind.

'You know who I am.'

'Jesus,' said Dan.

Then a sudden bolt, blackness and pain.

'He has lost a lot of blood, Doctor, we're losing him,' sounded a nurse.

'Once more,' stated a doctor.

With another jolt of electricity on his chest, Dan opened his eyes.

'Welcome back,' said the surgeon as he took the defibrillator away from Dan's chest.

'Keep him sedated for forty-eight hours. He needs rest, blood, and fluid,' responded the surgeon.

'The other guy is dead. Time of death, 16:45,' sounded a doctor.

Dan turned his head to the right and saw Jelly's lifeless body stretched out on an ER gurney with a doctor and two nurses standing over him.

Dan started to cry upon hearing the news that his friend Jelly, aka Patrick O'Kelly, had died. He drifted in and out of consciousness as the medication removed all pain from his recovering body.

Dan awoke in bed. He was attached to a heart monitoring machine, which beeped away, and a drip containing fluid, which fed into his forearm.

'Oh, my head.'

'Welcome back, Daniel,' said a nurse who was standing over his bed.

'What, where am I?'

'You're at Landstuhl Hospital in Germany, now relax.'

'Germany, how did I get here? When did I get here?'

'Relax now, all is fine. You've been here twelve weeks now.'

'Twelve weeks.... Oh, my head hurts!'

'You have been in a coma since the surgery.'

'Surgery, what surgery?'

Dan panicked and quickly checked his body over, making sure that everything was still in place. Thankfully it was, other than having a large scar on his stomach. He tried to get up and was successful in moving his legs, but all of his body ached. A few moments later, a doctor arrived in the room and checked Dan.

'Well, son, you're very lucky. I think that with some time, you will make a complete recovery. We almost lost you!' said the doctor.

'What happened?'

The door to the private ward opened, and in walked Major Robert 'Bob' Redmond, who was dressed in full military uniform, immaculately dressed as if about to parade in front of a general.

'Well, how's the patient?'

'Sir, I have been better... What happened out there... I remember the Humvee on fire and then nothing.'

'You were running back towards the Humvee, there was an explosion, and a piece of shrapnel got stuck in your side. You tried to get back up, fell back, and banged your head. Wilson flew you and the other injured guys out to base. They patched you up as you died on the op table from blood loss, before shipping you to this place.

'Jelly… Patrick.'

'Sorry, he didn't make it.'

'Your actions under fire saved the life of the Sgt., who you pulled from the Humvee. He has already been shipped back Stateside.'

'The Sgt.?' asked Dan.

'Yes, Dan, you saved the life of Sgt. Bell. You're a hero, son.'

'I am no hero,' responded Dan.

'Yes, you are, son, and I am proud to have served with you.'

With that, Major Redmond stood up and saluted Dan, who saluted back, and then the Major walked from the room.

'Major,' shouted Dan.

'Yes, son.'

'I need to get a message home to Ireland and to Sandy in Dallas.'

'What do I look like, a fucking carrier pigeon?' hissed the Major. 'Use the phone.' The Major darted his eyes towards the phone beside his bed. He reached over to the bedside locker and pulled the old fashioned dial phone towards him. Dan quickly dialled Sandy's home phone number in Dallas, but there was no answer. He tried again and again but still no answer. Dan was starting to get frustrated and would have been happy even just to talk to Sandy's Dad, but nothing, no answer. He hung up the phone and lay back in bed, pondering his vivid memory of the explosion and the raging battle that to him felt as if it had lasted for hours when. In reality, it had been over in no more than twenty minutes. He closed his eyes and tried to get the dark thoughts of death from his brain and replace the thoughts with happy memories of his life in Ireland. He thought of Mickey chasing Naomi around and her dad chasing him in the police car, which made him smile, but still his mind came back to the fighting and killing in Afghanistan.

Dan didn't hear the bedroom door open, but quickly opened his eyes when he heard his name being called in an instantly recognisable voice: 'Daniel.'

He looked up and saw Sandy standing before him. She quickly ran over to his bedside and embraced him, squeezing him so hard that she hurt his stomach wound.

'Sandy, are you real? How did you get.... here?' said Dan, who was finding it difficult to breath, let alone talk, as Sandy squeezed and kissed him. Eventually Sandy stopped and sat beside him, holding his hand.

'Daniel, I just knew you would come back to me.'

'How long have you been here? How did you know I got injured?'

'Take it easy, Daniel, you will pull out your stitches. My Dad has contacts. You know that he was former military, well, sort of.'

'I know, I know, Secret Service. Just my luck my girl's Dad is fucking U.S. Secret Service.'

'You have been in for a long time. Things have happened outside, but all will be fine, Daniel.'

'Is my Mum Ok? I need to talk to my Mum.'

'Yes, Dan, she is fine. I have been talking to her every day since I got here.'

'When did you get here?' enquired Dan.

'The day after you arrived. You had two surgeries, and they repaired you real good, so with some time you will be 100%.'

'Oh, Sandy, it was terrible, horrible, the blood, killing endless killing. I don't think I can go back.' Dan started to cry, and quickly Sandy embraced him, holding him in her arms as he cried.

'Shush now... shush, you won't have to, Daniel. You need time to heal. You have done more than the average American for our country. I don't know how you got hurt. Did you not have your magic clay with you?'

'It's not magic clay, it's Gartan clay, and yes, I did have it with me, but I guess it didn't work.'

'As you soon as you're strong enough, Daniel, we will get you out of here. I have some news for you!'

'Ha, what news?'

A Doctor entered the room and informed Sandy that they needed to run some checks on Daniel and that she should come back in the morning as he needed rest and no shocks to his system. Dan kissed Sandy.

'News, will tell you tomorrow.' Sandy quickly ran from the room.

'You picked up some nasty wounds, son, but it looks like you will make a good recovery. Is your eyesight OK?' enquired the Doctor.

'Yea, Doc, I am fine. Body aches… Wait a minute, you said wounds, Doc. I only have my stomach wound.'

'No, Dan, when we checked you over we found some shrapnel lodged in the back of your skull, so you needed surgery on the back of your head.'

Dan reached around and felt a large plaster on the rear of his head. 'Maybe that's why I have a damn headache.'

'We didn't know if your brain would be affected, but the test results are positive, and seeing you today makes me think you will make a full recovery. Now, I need you to get some rest, and your little lady friend will be back in the morning.'

The Doctor gave Dan a relaxant that put him back to sleep. Although asleep, Dan was thinking, and his mind was racing back to the battle scene and the killing, the explosion, and seeing his pal Patrick 'Jelly' in the burning Humvee. Although asleep, he was talking out loud: 'I didn't have it on my person. Yes, I had the clay with me, and I was fine, but I left it my jacket pocket, which I placed on Patrick to keep him warm. It was after this that I got injured.'

'Mum, I had the clay with me... I just forgot.'

'The clay.'

When Dan awoke it was early morning, and he had slept all night. Feeling a little stiff but relaxed, he decided to get out of bed, slowly putting his feet on the ground and standing, which hurt at first as his muscles got used to working again. He made it across the room to the bathroom and back to the bed and was tired. This was going to take some time and some physiotherapy before he would return to normal movements that he had previously taken for granted. He longed for a shower but was not so sure that he would make it on his own. Then again, he did not want to ask Sandy or some nurse to help him; he was too proud for that treatment. Then again, he was sure that some nurse must have given him a bed bath when he was in the coma.

The door opened, and in walked Sandy, beaming with a big smile, her perfect white teeth glistening and sparking in the reflection of the light.

'Good morning, Daniel, how are you today?' said Sandy as she pecked him on the cheek.

'Much better, Sandy, but I would love a shower.'

'Well, that can be arranged.'

Sandy helped Dan into the shower, which he managed to take on his own. The feeling of the fresh hot beads of water on his skin was amazing. The hot shower improved his healing process by at least a week. Dan put on a bathrobe and returned to his bed, which Sandy had made to her perfection. Sandy started to laugh.

'What's so funny, Sandy?'

'I was just thinking back to wearing a bathrobe on the Aran islands. What was that lady's name? Remember, she owned the hotel on the Aran islands?'

'Hotel... more of a guesthouse. Mrs. Murphy.'

'Yea, that was the lady. She was funny.'

'Do you want the good news, Daniel?'

'News... yes, you said you had some news!'

'Oh, that, well, I spoke to the Doctor, and he said you will be released soon, but you will need to take it easy!'

'I know, I know... I just want to get out of here and back to Ireland... May sound a little boyish, but I really want to see my Mam.'

Dan sat back on his bed. As much as he was delighted to see Sandy and to have her with him in Germany, he really wanted to see his family and, in particular, his Mother. He had witnessed such turmoil, killing, and had been away from home for so long that he was ready to return to Ireland for his Mother's love. Once again, the Doctor entered the room. This time he motioned for Sandy to stay in the room.

'How soon can I get out of here, Doc?'

'Dan your body has suffered major trauma. You need to rest and take it easy.'

'I can do that back home in Ireland. I just want to get home.'

'OK, OK, maybe in a few days. We will see how you are doing.'

'Thanks, Doc.'

'Well, good to see you looking fit again, Dan,' sounded Major Redmond as he walked into the bedroom, once again with an immaculate uniform.

'Sir.' Dan went to stand up, but the major waved at him to stay sitting.

'How's he doing, Doc,' asked the Major as the Doctor wrote on his clipboard.

'Excellent, Major Redmond. He is making excellent progress and will be out of here soon, but he'll need to rest for a month or two.'

'Good to hear that, Doc. Well, Dan, you're very lucky, son.'

'Yes sir.'

'So, what are you going to do for a couple of months?'

'He wants to go to see his Mom in Ireland,' responded Sandy.

The Major nodded and played with his hat as he stood looking at the Doctor's notes on Dan. Patient privacy had no place in the Major's mind; he looked on Dan as his property.

'OK, home to Donegal, Ireland, sounds like a plan. Take care, Dan. I am heading back to the States. We'll be in contact soon.'

'Sir, can I have a word with you in private?' asked Dan as he stood up and ushered the Major to the bedroom door and into the hallway. By now his walking had improved significantly. Once in the hallway, Dan closed his bedroom door.

'What is it, son?' asked the Major.

'I need to get out of this place and back to Ireland. Can you make it happen?'

'You need rest, Dan.'

'I will get that in Ireland, at my Mom's place.'

'Does your mom make apple pie, Dan?'

'Apple pie…Yes sir, the best.'

'I just love homemade apple pie. Leave it with me, Dan,' said the Major as he walked away. Dan re-entered his bedroom and sat talking to Sandy. To Dan's surprise, the Major kept his word, as later another Doctor examining Dan gave him some painkillers and informed him, 'You're free to go tomorrow morning, Dan,' and handed him two airline flight tickets to Dublin.

'Do you want me to go with you, Dan?'

'Damn right I do, Sandy. I am going home and so are you.'

CHAPTER 27

❦

Sandy and Dan arrived in Donegal, having flown from Germany and taken a bus and taxi from the airport, and stood outside his parents' hotel. It was early afternoon, and the neon light advertising his parents' hotel was not lit, which now reflected Dan's feelings on America and the first-hand experience of the killing he had witnessed in Afghanistan. The place looked dreary in the misty rain, but it was home. They had not phoned ahead or emailed, so walking in on his parents was going to be a big surprise. All was quaint, quiet, and relaxed, so different from the war-torn battles and their hectic life styles of North America.

'I'm a little nervous, Sandy, walking in like this.'

'Come on, Daniel, your Mum is going to be so excited to see you.'

The two walked into the small bar, which was silent other than the clock ticking away on the wall. Nobody was in the bar, but everything looked the same to Dan since he had departed. Dan stood dressed in his

U.S. Army uniform, complete with cap and shiny shoes, which looked like mirrors reflecting the light.

'There will be two British gentlemen arriving later along with a young girl, so we will have to make them feel welcome. They will take two of the rooms,' said Dan's Mum, who was talking on the phone in the kitchen. Dan stood behind her, placing his bag silently on the floor. His Mother turned and, on seeing Dan, simply and silently hung up the phone, walked over to him, and hugged him while crying, shaking, and yet remaining totally silent. Dan responded by putting his arms around her.

Eventually, she broke the silence. 'My boy is back, thank you, God. Sandy, thank you for bringing him home and welcome back, dear,' said Dan's Mum as she tried to compose herself and wipe away the tears. She put her arm around Sandy and pulled her into the now three-way hug.

'Look at you, Daniel. What happened to my boy? You are so strong and full of muscles.'

'Ah, will you stop, Ma? You're embarrassing me now… Where's Da?'

'He's taking Billy into Letterkenny hospital for an appointment.'

'What's wrong with Billy?' enquired Sandy.

'Oh, nothing much, other than drinking too much Guinness and whiskey.'

'Daniel, it's wonderful to have you home. I have missed you so much, son. Are you OK? You're injured. I didn't hear from you in such a long time?'

'I'm fine, Ma, nothing that a few of your dinners and apple pies won't sort.'

'Dinner! Now Daniel, we will have to fatten you up some!'

Dan walked into the bar with his arm around Sandy. He was happy and content to be home, back in Donegal with his two ladies.

'We will have to organize a bedroom, Sandy!' exclaimed Dan with a hint of excitement.

'You mean bedrooms, Daniel. You need your rest; no fun for you till your back fit again. Wouldn't want you to hurt your wounds.'

Dan kissed Sandy in the bar and was exploring her body with his hands, getting carried away to the point that he did not hear the bar door open as his dad and Billy walked into the bar. Dan's Dad was delighted to see his son, but not as much as his mother. There is an exceptional bond between an Irish son and mother that is unbreakable, similar to that of a father and daughter.

'Well, would ya look at that. If it isn't the wee Texas Rose. Come here till I give you a kiss,' requested Billy.

Billy pushed Dan out of the way and gave Sandy a kiss on her lips while giving her a bear hug, almost squashing her.

'Quick, Martin, call Barney and Jimmy. We will have a hooley night tonight!' requested Billy.

Dan's mum responded in a stern mother-like mode: 'There will be no hooley tonight, Billy Carrick. Daniel needs his rest, and anyway, Barney and Jimmy are playing tomorrow, Friday night.'

'A drink', suggested Dan.

'No thank you, Daniel, and you're not having one either with your medication,' hissed Sandy as she intervened, displaying a motherly authority.

'Sure, you two can have an argument, and I will drink your two drinks!' suggested Billy.

Dan was feeling tired, even though it was only early in the evening. It was only 60 hrs ago that he'd been in a coma. He needed sleep and rest, and that is what he got. Even Sandy stayed away from him that first night back in Donegal.

The following morning Dan awoke early and entered the bar having slept for sixteen hours. As usual, his Mother was in the kitchen preparing breakfast and lunch while washing clothes at the sink. Dan was delighted to be home and was already starting to feel himself, come back to a sense of reality.

'There you are, son. Now, what are you doing today?'

Although a question, it may have been more of a hopeful recommendation from his mother for Dan to stay at the hotel.

'Was thinking of catching up with Mickey, Ma, how has he been?'

'That rascal is still canoodling with Sgt. O'Brien's daughter, Naomi.'

'Well, if he's canoodling with her then things must have improved.' Daniel laughed out loud, thinking of Sgt. O'Brien chasing down Mickey's antics.

'What was it like, son, in Afghanistan?'

The question immediately wiped the smile off Dan's face, and his eyes went cold and distant looking.

'I don't want to talk about it!' responded Dan as he stood up and walked towards the back door and into the early morning misty air. The clouds appeared to be clearing, and there was every chance that it was going to be a nice, pleasant day. Dan stood outside, pondering in particular about his friend Patrick Jelly O'Kelly. He was so deep in thought that he did not hear Sandy approaching him.

'Good morning, Daniel.'

'Hi, Sandy. Sorry, I was deep in thought.'

'Penny for them… your thoughts.'

'Ah, it's nothing, just thinking of Afghanistan and the senseless killing of such young guys. You know, Patrick was only in his twenties.'

By now, Dan would only ever refer to Jelly as Patrick, as a mark of respect to his friend; it didn't feel appropriate calling him Jelly.

Suddenly, Dan burst into uncontrollable sobbing,

'It's OK, Daniel.' Sandy hugged Dan as he regained his composure. 'I remember when Dad used to come back from operations, he was always different.'

Dan thought of Chuck and knew he had an interesting history and background. Sandy put her arm around Dan and rested her head on his shoulder. The two stood motionless, simply enjoying the moment, while Dan wiped his eyes.

'Daniel, can I ask a favour?'

'Sure, Sandy, anything.'

'Will you take me to that beach we went to last year, Port something. Remember, with the white sand.'

'Port Salon, sure, let's go now, Sandy. Da's car is here, and I could do with a walk on the beach.'

Sandy ran off into the hotel and back to her bedroom, leaving Dan outside pondering his thoughts. His mother walked out to him and put her hand on his shoulder, having being discretely watching from the kitchen.

'I don't know what you witnessed, son, and you're all grown up now, but to me, you're still my boy, wee Daniel.'

'Thanks, Ma. Can I borrow Da's car today?'

'Of course you can. Are you OK for money as well? Here, €100, buy Sandy some lunch.'

'Ma, thanks, I am fine for cash. Sure, I am on the U.S. government's payroll now.'

Although Dan was only partly joking, he was still a serving soldier in the U.S. Army who was on an extended leave of absence from duty as he was recovering from some serious wounds. Dan didn't know what the future would hold in his career, and he was aware that he would have to return to the Army when they called for him.

Dan quickly changed and got dressed into his civilian clothes that he had left before departing to the USA. His Levi jeans were now too big for him. He had toned up from all the training in Fort Benning so much that he had lost two notches on his jeans belt. Waiting in his Dad's car for Sandy, tooting the horn, he was growing impatient and quickly realised that he was getting aggressive in his behaviour. Maybe he was suffering from post-traumatic stress. He realized that he might have a problem.

'What's the rush,' shouted Sandy as she climbed into the passenger seat of the car.

Dan drove away along the narrow country roads, with no Bee Gees music on this occasion, only his Dad's collection of Daniel O'Donnell.

'Sorry about the music, Sandy!'

'I do recall you saying that to me previously, Daniel. I like this country music. Remember, I am a Texan gal... Is this Irish Country Music?'

'Ya can't get more Irish country than Daniel O'Donnell. Why, he is not far from here in the same County of Donegal.'

They drove along the scenic route until they arrived in the car park of Port Salon beach. It was a windy day, which caused big white and blue Atlantic waves to crash against the shore, creating a beautiful white mist of water on the beach that reflected in the sunshine. Both a surfers' and lovers' paradise, it could have been a postcard from the Atlantic coast of Barbados, except with a backdrop of glorious green mountains. To Dan, it reflected his mind's view of Hawaii. Except, in true Irish form, it was still a little on the chilly side as it was not yet summer. The two young lovers walked along the beach, arm in arm, without any immediate cares, although Dan was aware that he would have to return to the U.S. Army at some stage and that Sandy would have to return to Dallas. However, for the time being, he was going to try and live in the present, which was at home in Ireland with his Sandy.

'Daniel, I have some news for you,' said Sandy in a soft and quaint voice while they walked at a slow pace along the beach.

'Yea, Sandy, I know you have to go home to Dallas soon, I know, but let's just live in the moment.'

With that, Dan stopped walking and stood in front of Sandy, pulling her to him and kissing her. Sandy broke the kiss and embrace and walked off in front of him.

'What's wrong, Sandy, what did I do... slow down, stop, what's wrong?'

Dan grabbed hold of Sandy by her arm and stopped her from walking.

'Daniel, I am pregnant!'

'What... when?'

'Come on, Daniel, you're not stupid. Vail, Colorado, at Christmas!'

'How long are you gone... when is it due?'

'How can you refer to our baby as an it? I knew you would freak out when I told you.'

Sandy ran towards the water's edge, stopping as a large wave crashed onto the shore, wetting her feet and jeans. Dan paused for a moment before running after her and stopping in the water in front of her. The water covered his shoes and ankles, but he did not notice as he was caught in the moment.

'Sandy, I am not freaking out. It's just this is some news, a lot to take in, give me a few moments!'

'How do you think I feel, Daniel? I have to carry and give birth to our child.'

'What did your Dad say?'

'He doesn't know… Jo knows. I told her, and I got an extended leave from college, but Dad does not know… yet.'

Dan swallowed a gulp of nothing as he thought of the reaction that Chuck would have to the news. Chuck's rifle came to his mind and the Elk in the scope, only this time it would be Dan in the riflescope as Chuck took aim. Dan wrapped his big arms around Sandy, offering her as much physical comfort as he could give.

'All is going to be fine, Sandy, I love you. This is great news. We should celebrate. Let's tell everybody!'

With that, Dan picked up Sandy in his arms, falling over in the process onto his back, completely submerging himself in the cold water and Sandy partly. He quickly got up and rubbed his stomach, which ached from picking up Sandy. The two lovers dried off as best as possible before returning to the car and driving back towards Termon.

'There's Mickey,' shouted Dan, stopping the car as he spotted his old pal Mickey Flynn standing outside the local shop.

'Mickey!'

'Well, would you look who it is, Danny boy and Sandy. Should you not be over in America boy?'

'Ah, it's a long story, Mickey. What happened your face? You look like you did five rounds with Mike Tyson. You're still fighting with Joe McGuirk!'

'If only, Dan. Ah, it's a bit of a problem like!'

'Go on, Mickey.'

'I got Naomi…pregnant. The Sgt. did this to me!'

'Ah ha, good man, Mickey, he did some job on you!'

'Battered me, Dan, battered me good. Look, I have to go. I will be up later for a few pints. We will catch up then.'

Danny found it hard to concentrate on the road as he drove back to his parents, somewhat scared, laughing, and crying all summed up in mixed emotions, but as a man he was delighted that Sandy was pregnant and expecting his child.

Upon arriving at his parents, he ushered Sandy into the kitchen, where, as usual, his Mother was making more food than was required to feed the entire family while Billy was eating a large ham sandwich and sitting at the family table.

'Ma, we have some news!' blasted Dan.

His Mother turned from the cooker, holding a large hot apple pie. She put a smile on her face and simply said, 'Let me guess, you're getting married!'

'No… well, not yet,' responded Dan. 'Sandy is going to have a baby!'

'A baby, well, isn't that great news… Young Dan is going to be a Daddy,' laughed Billy.

'Shut up, Billy, this is no laughing matter. Pregnant, you say, Daniel!'

'Yes, Ma, you're going to be a Grandmother!'

Dan's mother had to sit down at the table, putting her head in her hands.

'What's Fr. O'Shea, going to say? You had best go to confession, and you too, Sandy!'

'Confession? I have done nothing wrong. Anyway, I am a Protestant, not a Catholic,' said Sandy.

'This calls for a drink,' called Billy.

'Oh, so that makes it all right then, little Ms. Texas,' hissed Dan's Mum.

'Ma!'

Sandy ran out of the kitchen and into the bar, with Billy running after her.

'What's wrong with you, Ma?'

Dan walked after Sandy, who was being comforted in the bar by Billy. Well, he had helped himself to two glasses of whiskey and had one in front of her at least for cosmetic viewing.

'It will be OK, Sandy. Ma will come around, I promise.'

'I am so scared Daniel, just so scared. What is going to happen?'

Dan hugged Sandy while Billy downed Sandy's whiskey and patted her on the back, at the same time filling another glass at the bar. Sandy sobbed into Dan's arms.

'Sure, isn't it only a baby that you're having,' suggested Billy.

'I am sorry,' exclaimed Dan's Mum as she entered the bar and hugged Sandy, who broke from Dan's large, hugging arms. 'Come on into the kitchen with me, Sandy, for a little chat and a cup of tea. Dan you stay with Billy and have a drink.'

Sandy and Dan's Mum left the bar. Billy did not require a second invite for a drink; by now he had already downed half the bottle of straight Jameson whiskey. The two sat silently in the bar, both looking at the closed kitchen door like two dogs waiting in anticipation of what food would be served.

After no longer then ten minutes, which felt like ten hours, the door opened and Sandy and his mother entered, laughing and joking while smiling from ear to ear. Dan and Billy looked at each other in amazement. It was as if the two ladies had been best friends for years.

'That's a woman's prerogative for you, Dan!'

'Everything is going to be just fine, Daniel,' said Dan's mum as she stood in the kitchen doorway with her arm around Sandy.

Dan smiled as Mickey Flynn walked into the bar, with his face looking even worse than earlier on. One of his eyes had now completely closed and was bright black and blue, as if he had been polishing his eye.

'That's some shiner on ya, Mickey.'

'Come on Sandy, lets you and I go for some girlie time and leave the boys to catch up,' suggested Dan's mum in a friendlier but more controlling motherly tone. The two returned to the kitchen, leaving the two old friends in the bar, along with Billy and the remaining contents of a bottle of whiskey.

'What happened, Mickey?' enquired Dan.

'Sgt. O'Brien caught me in the act with his beloved daughter. He gave me a bit of a kicking, but Joe McGuirk was saying bad things about Naomi, so I gave him a few slaps. He paid rent-the-thug Frankie Downes and his two buddies to beat me up. They got me a few days ago.'

'The bastards! We will have to sort them!

'Fuck them, 'tis not worth it.'

'So what's the story with you and Naomi?'

'Ah, man, I love her to bits. She's not due until September. We're still together like. I think that fat bastard Dad of hers is coming around to the idea.'

'That will be the day, Mickey!'

'Mickey, I have news for you too!'

'Go on, Dan.'

'Sandy is also expecting a baby!'

'Oh, man, wow, that's great news. We will have to get locked to celebrate. So how was the U.S. Army?'

Instantly, the mood within the bar changed from one of pals catching up on times past to a seriousness, almost like the atmosphere within a courtroom when the judge enters and the words 'all rise' are shouted.

'The Army training was tough, but Afghanistan was really bad. I killed a man, no two, maybe more, I can't be sure, Mickey!'

Dan looked sad, and his eyes seemed to sink back into his head. This was the first time he had spoken about Afghanistan and in particular killing. On seeing the two guys deep in conversation, Billy continued to take advantage of the open bottle of whiskey while sitting at the bar.

'Did you shoot them, Dan?'

'Yea, with my rifle. First, I aimed for their limbs as I didn't want to kill, but the high caliber round we use instantly amputated the limb, causing them to bleed to death.'

'Fuck me!'

'It's not a good feeling, Mickey.'

Mickey was somewhat shocked at listening to the confession of his friend whom he had known since they'd started together in the local school when they were four years old.

'It's a hell of a thing to kill a man, that's what John Wayne used to say,' said Mickey.

'It was Clint Eastwood, in the movie *Unforgiven*, ya thick Mickey,' bellowed Billy from the bar while downing another glass of golden malt whiskey.

'Dan, I have to head up to Dublin. Naomi has to have some check-up in one of the main hospitals.'

'Can they not look after her in Letterkenny hospital?'

'No, man, don't ask me why. Listen, let's catch up in a couple of days when I am back,' sounded Mickey as he walked from the bar.

Dan sat down on a bar stool, peering into a clear glass of whiskey that Billy had poured him. He simply stared at the whiskey, its golden brown color bringing his mind back to Afghanistan and seeing his friend Jelly lying on the ground dying before his very eyes. Jelly was not just a friend, a fellow Irishman, but a brother united in the blood while wearing the United States Army uniform. The vision of Patrick haunted Dan, and he needed to figure out a way of clearing it from his mind.

CHAPTER 28

ℐℛ

T he days turned into weeks. Nearly eight weeks had passed since Dan and Sandy had returned to Donegal. Sandy, although in contact with her Dad, was set about making a life for herself in Ireland. At this stage she still hadn't mustered up the courage to tell her Dad that she was pregnant, but had decided not to return to Medical School in Texas. Dan was working in the bar and had been in contact with the U.S. Army, who had agreed to an extended leave of absence in order for him to recover from his wounds of battle. By this stage, Dan had made a full recovery and had returned to running and staying fit. This was not the only thing he had returned to. By now he was an expert in the bed, and let's just say that Sandy and Dan had more than their fair share of enjoyable fun in the bedroom, with Dan taking full advantage of having a beautiful young woman like Sandy staying in the hotel. His parents were also pleased. For a Mother, having your son at home after him having been away at war is wonderful and makes you appreciate the little things.

Martin, Dan's Dad, was also happy as Sandy helped out at the evenings in the bar and had increased the business turnover and profit.

You see, Sandy was really good looking, sharing not just her name but good looks and sexiness with Olivia Newton John's character *Sandy in Grease*. The word had spread of the Texan babe working at Flynn's Bar to beyond the townland of Termon. Many lads would just come to have a look and admire her beauty, even though now her pregnancy was showing and it was obvious she was expecting a baby.

'Another hooley tonight like last weekend and we will have to invest in a bigger bar!' said Martin as he rubbed his hands at the idea of at last making a good profit from the bar and guesthouse.

'You're exploiting Sandy,' responded Dan.

'No, no, not at all, Daniel. Sure, she needs to slow down with the baby on its way.'

Dan sat in the kitchen, responding to emails on his computer. Coffee was still out in Afghanistan with the other guys. However, after their baptism of fire at such an early stage they had pulled back to guarding duties away from the frontline action. As much as Dan was happy to be home and enjoying his time with Sandy, he did miss his army pals and stayed in touch as best that he could, mainly with Coffee, who had also been close to Jelly. The three had joined up together, suffered the pain of training, and had bunked together in Afghanistan, if only for a couple of nights, before Jelly was killed in action. It is difficult for civilians to understand the sense of brotherhood that military personnel share with each other. Although not related in the technical sense of the word, losing a buddy in combat is difficult, and the loss is shared by all. Dan realised that he had changed and that his temper would activate at the least silly mistake, such as a verbal disagreement. He would feel that he would want to strike out with his fists to take revenge.

'There is some American man in the bar looking for you Daniel,' said Betty, who was busy cleaning. On hearing the word 'American,' Dan jumped from the kitchen chair and ran into the bar. Standing before him, dressed in civilian clothes and smoking a cigar was Major Robert 'Bob' Redmond.

'Major!' sounded Dan with excitement mixed with nervousness, as he was delighted to see him but also curious as to what he wanted.

'Good to see you, son... Well, are you going to offer me a drink?'

'Sure, what will you have, whiskey or beer?'

The Major looked out the window at the sun and glanced at his watch. 'Bit early just yet, black coffee is good.'

Dan poured a fresh coffee, which was brewing behind the bar, and the Major sat at the bar. 'So, how have you been, Dan? You enjoying your life?'

'Yes sir, I mean, Major.'

'Bob, it's just Bob.'

Sandy walked into the bar, looking as radiant as ever, while rubbing her ever-expanding stomach.

'I see you have been busy, Dan,' exclaimed the Major.

'Sandy, this is Major Robert Redmond, who was in the area and dropped by. Say, why are you here, Bob?'

'We need to talk. We can talk later.'

'Nice to meet you, Major Redmond. Phew, Daniel, I am puffed. This has to be a boy. I am so tired. I think I will go back to bed and lie down. Sorry, Major, I don't mean to be bad mannered.'

'Ma'am, nice to meet you,' said the Major, and he stood up as Sandy exited and walked back to her bedroom.

'Oh, I have something for you,' said the major as he pulled a medal from his jacket pocket and handed it to Dan. 'It's a purple heart, Dan. You got it for being wounded in action. I think you deserve a better medal for what you did out there, saving Sgt. Bell's life while under fire!'

Dan peered down at the medal, which he held in the palm of his hand, while his mind once again raced back to Afghanistan and Jelly lying on the ground surrounded by gunfire and explosions.

'Haunts you, son, doesn't it?'

'Yea, Bob. Every time I close my eyes I see Patrick dying in front of me. Wish I could have saved him.'

'It's the price of freedom.'

The Major slurped down his coffee while chewing on the butt of his cigar.

'How is Sgt. Bell?'

'He is doing OK from what I hear. Won't be back training guys for a while, recovering from the burns, but from what I hear he will make a good recovery.'

'So, what are you doing in Ireland, Bob?'

'I came to see you, Dan!'

Dan's Mother walked into the bar from the kitchen. She had been busy cooking, as usual, and washing clothes. As all good Mothers know, the kitchen is the office that never closes and comes as the price for accepting the name of Mother.

'Ma, this is a friend of mine. Major Redmond.'

'Pleased to meet you, Major Redmond.'

The major jumped up and shook Dan's Mother's hand. 'Please call me Bob, Mrs Flynn. It's such a pleasure to finally meet you, Ma'am. Your son Daniel is a credit to you.'

'Oh, thank you,' responded Dan's Mum in somewhat of a flirtatious tone as she was impressed with the Major's good manners.

'Are you on a holiday?' enquired Dan's Mum, wondering just why the Major had decided to call on her son.

'Well, just dropped in to see Dan and some other business.'

'Are you staying local?'

'I just arrived this morning. May be in the area for a couple of days. Can you recommend a hotel?'

'Oh, no need for a hotel. You're a friend of Daniel's' so you will stay with us. Sure, we have plenty of free rooms, and it will be nice for Daniel.'

'No, Ma'am, I cannot put you out like that, sniff… sniff…'

The Major sniffed at the sweet aroma of home cooking that wafted from the kitchen, bringing him back to when he was a child and his mother was cooking. 'What a beautiful smell!' he said.

'Nonsense, you're staying with us, and that is that, I have spoken. Now, what you're smelling is an apple pie I have just taken out of the oven. Would you like a slice?'

'Apple pie.'

'Sit down. Daniel, get more coffee for Bob.'

Dan's Mother placed a large slice of apple pie in front of Bob, which was still hot, fresh from the oven, and covered in sweet sugar. The smell was divine, and Bob devoured it like a child eating candy for the first time. Dan's mother was thrilled and immediately placed a second, larger slice in front of Bob, as she relished the idea of someone appreciating her good food like a starving man having just come in from the wilderness.

'This sure is good pie, Ma'am.'

'Well, there is plenty more where that came from. Eat up now!' sounded Dan's Mam as she went back into the kitchen, leaving the two to talk.

'So, what you looking for, Bob?'

Bob finished devouring his second slice of pie before gulping down half a cup of coffee, wiping his mouth, and lighting up a fresh cigar.

'OK, I will be honest with you. I am heading back out tomorrow evening. Have a flight picking me up in Belfast.'

'Heading back to Afghanistan?' enquired Dan.

'Yea… you recall how your friend Patrick died, don't you?'

'From the explosion in the Humvee!'

'Caused by?'

'The terrorist who fired the RPG!'

'Correct. The CIA have picked up intelligence on that guy. He is one of the leaders of Al Qaeda based out of Iraq. His name is Iyad, a Syrian national, training fresh recruits in a larger camp in southern Afghanistan.'

'Is it a big camp?' enquired Dan.

'Sure is, twice the size of the one you were in, at least 60 bad guys.'

'So why not just send in aircraft and torch the place?'

'They have hostages and intel. If we raid the place, we will get intel on their operatives in Europe.'

'I see, so why me, Bob?'

'I need a sniper. I need a guy I can trust, who will have my back, but most of all, I need someone who's a good shot. Next to me, you're the best I have seen in years.'

'I am sure the Navy Seals have some good snipers, and what about your Delta pals, can they not spare a sniper?'

'Navy Seals will stick it on CNN. This is a Delta mission. We go in, do the business, get the result, and leave. Nobody will know we were there... What about it, Dan...?'

'I don't know, I've got to think of Sandy!'

'What about Patrick...? Revenge, Dan. You can take the shot on Iyad, kill that evil bastard, and avenge your fellow mick.'

Dan clenched his fist, and his pupils dilated at the thought of revenge. He could feel his blood starting to boil and the aggression build within him, which was something that the U.S. Army had installed into his system, controlled aggression. Unknown to Dan, the Army had turned him into a controlled killing machine.

'So, what about it, Dan?'

Dan didn't need to think too long. He wanted revenge for Patrick.

'I'm in.'

'Good, but remember, this is a top secret mission. Nobody can know. Tell your girl you're heading to Iraq and will be back in a week. Not a word. Our lives depend on utmost confidentiality.'

The two shook hands as the band started to set up their instruments, getting ready for the hooley night. Bob went to his room and agreed to leave for Belfast Airport at 16:00 hrs the following day.

Walking up the corridor to Sandy's bedroom, Dan paused before knocking on the bedroom door, which was something he had not done in a long time. He knew that his departure was going to hurt Sandy and his parents, but he had a burning sensation within his gut. He needed to return and above all, avenge the death of his friend.

'So what does the Major want, Daniel?' Sandy, displaying a sense of intelligent intuition, knew that a Major from the U.S. Army would not be visiting Dan for a catch up meeting or just happened to be in the area.

Sandy had grown up with her dad in Special Forces and the US Secret Service, she knew the drill and was aware that Dan would be leaving her again.

'I have been called back on a mission. Have to head out to Iraq, but I will be only gone a week.'

'When do you leave?'

'Tomorrow, 16:00 hrs.'

'OK.'

'Sandy are you not mad at me?'

'We both knew this day would come, Daniel, but why only a week… Is this a special operations mission?'

'It's classified… sorry.'

'Classified… that's a word my mother used to hate. She would hear Dad saying it, and then he would be gone, sometimes for a day, a week, or several months at a time. I guess this is the price of working for the U.S. Army!'

'It's the price of freedom.'

'No, Daniel, the price of freedom is me standing over your grave with our child, grieving for you. Can somebody else not go in your place?'

'No, I have to go.'

Dan walked from the room and to his bedroom. He readied a small bag, packing some fresh shirts and jeans, which he threw into the corner of his room in a rage of anger. He felt somewhat torn. He wanted to get revenge, to serve the USA, and to help his friends in uniform who were still out in Afghanistan. But he also felt the responsibilities of being a father to his unborn child, for loving Sandy and the pain this was going to cause his Mother, yet he knew in his heart that he had to do this one last mission. Iyad and his training camp had to be stopped before more American soldiers lost their lives. He had a skill, and this time he was going to apply his skill to killing terrorists.

Dan awoke to the sound of Barney and the guys playing their instruments downstairs. It was 8 pm, and he quickly ran down to the bar, which was already nearly full with the locals downing pints of Guinness. Sandy was pulling pints behind the bar, looking stunning as usual, and Mickey was in deep conversation with Naomi at a small table. On seeing Dan, his Mum quickly pulled him into the kitchen like she was scolding a young child.

'What do you think you are playing at?' crooked his Mum while pointing her finger in the direction of Sandy. 'You have responsibilities now, heading off on some hair-brained mission. Let someone else go!'

'No, Mam, I have to go, the Major needs me.'

'Tell him to fuck off!' Dan stood back in shock at his mother's use of the F word. He realised that this was not going to be easy.

'I have a job to do, and that is it, the decision is made!'

Dan walked back into the bar, where Fran and his three bully boy chums stood over Mickey, pointing at him and slapping him on the face. Mickey simply stood with Naomi, pleading with Fran not to start any trouble. Fran turned to walk away, then quickly turned back and head butted Mickey in the face, which knocked Mickey to the floor. Fran quickly followed up with a kick to Mickey's stomach, causing Mickey to crunch up with pain while Fran kicked at him again. Dan pushed his way over but was blocked by Fran's chum Tommy, who waved his forefinger at Dan as if telling him to stay out of it. Pausing for a second, Dan grabbed Tommy's finger and bent it backwards until it dislocated, and Tommy cried out in pain. Fran grabbed a bottle of beer from the table and swung it at Dan, who ducked, causing the bottle to fly through the air and hit Sandy directly on the side of her head. Dan jumped on Fran, pushing him to the ground, landing on top of him. Quickly, Fran's two thugs pulled Dan off him, holding Dan in an arm lock while Fran stood up.

'I'm going to enjoy this. You have had it coming for a long time,' said Fran as he prepared to punch Dan, who was still being held. All of a sudden, Fran fell on the ground, shaking from the impact of a punch to the side of his face and neck. As Dan turned to see who had delivered such a devastating punch, Major Bob Redmond came into vision and sent an uppercut into the nose of one of the thugs holding Dan, causing it to explode. The third guy simply let go and made for the door. Dan ran to Sandy and helped her up from the floor.

'I am OK,' said Sandy as she steadied herself back onto her feet.

'Aha, I knew there would be trouble once Dan Flynn was back in town,' sounded Sgt. O'Brien, who entered the pub in full Garda uniform, complete with cap.

'Fran started the trouble,' said Dan.

'Mickey Flynn, I might have known you would be at the centre of this action.'

'Dad, that's not the case, Mickey defended me from Fran and his thugs,' responded Naomi as she comforted the bruised and blushing Mickey.

'Right, right then all out. We will have to have an enquiry. Close the pub, I am revoking the license.'

'Hey fat guy, what's your problem?' asked the Major.

'Fat guy? I am Sgt. O'Brien. Who are you, some stupid yank?'

'That's Major Robert Redmond of the United States Army. I suggest you show some respect, Sgt.,' responded Dan.

'Respect. Listen to me boy, you have till midday tomorrow to get out of town, or I will lock you up!'

'For what am I being locked up… fatty?' enquired the Major.

'This is my town. I am the law, and if I say you're going to jail, then you're going to jail.'

'Midday, I need longer than that!' responded the Major.

'I will be back to check, and if you're not gone, yank, I will lock you up. Come, Naomi.' The Sgt. pulled at Naomi's arm and led her from the pub.

'I am sorry about this, Bob,'

'Nothing to be sorry about, Dan.'

'Yes there is, you bastard, taking my son away. How dare you, who do you think you are?'

'Mum,' shouted Dan.

'It's OK, Dan, I will take my leave. See you tomorrow.'

Dan spent that night with Sandy. The young couple cuddled in bed, without intimacy, yet there was a closeness and a sense of destiny in being together. On this occasion, Dan was not nervous about returning to Afghanistan, but he was worried about something happening to him and not being there for Sandy and his child. He got little sleep that night but knew he had made the correct decision in supporting the Major. The two lay in bed, whispering sweet nothings in each other's ears, before Dan finally got out of bed and went to his room to make ready for the 16 hrs departure.

Before long it was midday. The Major sat at the bar drinking coffee and sucking on the end of his cigar. As usual, Dan's Mother was baking in the kitchen, and Sandy was helping Betty to clean the tables. Martin was busy restocking the shelves, and Dan was itching to get on the road to

Belfast. The door opened, and in walked the rather well-nourished Sgt. O'Brien, once again in full Garda uniform.

'Well… well… well, I don't believe it. The yank is still here, and it's let me see now, 12:07 pm. I hope you will find our jail comfortable… boy.'

Major Redmond remained sitting at the bar, calmly taking out a fresh cigar and striking a match.

'Oh, now you're trying me boy, smoking in a public place of work is illegal in Ireland and carries a €500 fine.'

The Major ignored the Sgt. and inhaled deeply on the cigar, blowing smoke into the atmosphere, causing the Sgt. to cough and splutter.

'That's it now, boy, I am arresting you…'

'Sgt., just go. You're making an eejit of yourself. You're an embarrassment. Just go,' sounded Dan.

'I will not. I will call for backup, and we will lock you up, Mr. Major!'

Bob smiled as he drank the last drop of his coffee and stood up.

'You got me, Sgt. Dan, the keys for my car are in my room. Pick me up at the cop precinct at the agreed time.'

'There will be no picking up. You're going to jail, boy,' exclaimed the Sgt. as he led Bob to the back seat of his police car and drove away.

'God help Sgt. O'Brien!' smirked Dan.

CHAPTER 29

ↄ℗*

1 5:30 hrs., time to go and pick up Major Redmond and on to Belfast. Dan grappled at his small holdall bag and went downstairs to the bar. Both his Mum and Dad stood in the bar, alongside Sandy, who was rubbing her tummy.

'I guess it's time to go.'

Dan's Mam handed him two small bags containing Gartan clay and placed a small silver cross around his neck. She said nothing but just hugged him and then ushered Martin into the kitchen, closing the door. This left Dan and Sandy on their own in the bar.

'I won't be long, just a week or two, and I will return.'

'How will you get Major Bob from the Police station?'

'Don't you worry about Bob. Be more concerned about the Sgt.'

Sandy and Dan embraced and kissed each other.

Sandy wiped away a small tear from her eye. 'I now know how my mother felt, when Dad went to work.'

'Don't worry, Sandy. I will be back before you know it… I promise.'

Kissing Sandy once more, he exited the bar to the carpark, which only contained two cars: his dad's car and a brand new BMW. He pressed the key fob that he had found in Bob's room, which unlocked the doors to the BMW. Starting the car, the CD started to play loudly, Kenny Rogers greatest hits, *'Ruby Don't Bring Your Love to Town.'* Dan found it strange music for the Major, expecting him to be more of an AC/DC or Guns N' Roses fan, but Kenny Rogers may have been closer to the Major's age. Sandy stood in the doorway to the hotel, rubbing her visibly pregnant tummy, and gently waving as Dan drove from the car park.

The BMW was an amazing drive, nothing like he had ever driven previously. He drove the short distance to the Police station, observing the Major standing outside still smoking a cigar. Once he stopped the car, the major simply said, 'I'll drive,' and pushed Dan into the passenger seat. The Major accelerated quickly up to 100 mph along the narrow country road as they headed for Letterkenny and onto the small border town of Lifford before crossing the border into Northern Ireland.

'So what happened to Sgt. O'Brien?'

'Oh… fatty is just hanging around. He will be cool,' smirked the Major.

Before long, they arrived at Belfast Aldergrove Airport. Leaving the BMW with a Police officer, they were escorted into a private area of the airport used for visiting dignitaries.

'What airline are we flying with, and where are we flying to, Bob?'

'Classified.'

'Hold on a minute. Am I not part of the team?'

'Classified… Just sit tight.'

A young man approached the Major and said in a strong American accent, 'Gentlemen, your flight's ready.'

The three men walked from the terminal and were driven across the apron to a large aircraft that looked in pristine condition, at least on the outside. The Major and Dan climbed up the stairs and entered the aircraft, which consisted of several guys working on computers. A flight attendant escorted the two of them to a row of business-class-style seats and suggested that they fasten seat belts for an immediate departure.

'This is a nice plane, Bob.'

'Boeing 777, used by the CIA and military intelligence for covert operations.'

'So, where are we heading?'

'Classified… I'm kidding ya. Heading back to Afghanistan, so sit tight and try get some rest.'

The flight attendant returned and handed the guys a couple of beers

'Make yourselves comfortable. We have an immediate departure. Once we level out, I will serve dinner. We have a couple of steaks. You OK with that?'

'Thank you, Ma'am,' responded Dan.

The plane pulled away, lining up on the runway before the engine roar sounded, and within a few moments they were airborne. Although the guys were sitting in the equivalent of business class seats and service, this was no commercial flight. There were no announcements from the captain or movies on board, although the seats and food were excellent. As promised, the flight attendant returned with two large steaks, sweetcorn, and potatoes, along with more beer for the guys. Dan enjoyed the meal and was adjusting his seat for a nap when another guy with a familiar face approached them.

'Good to see you, Bob.'

'Well, if it isn't Emerald Five himself, Brian Wilson.'

'Good to see you alive and breathing, Dan. Last time I saw you... well, let's just say you didn't look so good.'

'Thanks, Brian!'

'Did you get my request?' asked Bob.

'Follow me.'

Bob nodded at Dan to follow them as they walked towards the rear of the aircraft, which had several guys sitting at computers and a few private meeting rooms. It was like being in the office of an insurance company, except they were cruising at 35,000 feet and all of the passengers wore military uniforms. Brian opened a rear door leading into a small cargo holding area, which consisted of crates and ammunition. Brian lifted a box up onto a crate and pulled two large bags from the box.

'Ah, there she is... my MP5.'

'And one for Dan,' continued Brian as he handed Dan an MP5 machine gun.

'This is an old gun, Dan, but she won't let you down in any climate. It was always my weapon of choice. Can do some real damage with one of these old ladies.'

'I know. I already seen you and the old lady in action,' responded Dan as Bob pulled at the loading mechanism and checked the scope.

'I also have something of sentimental value for Dan.'

With that, Brian pulled out Dan's M107 50 caliber sniper's rifle, which was a little dirty and covered in particles of sand.

'Is it my rifle? I thought I left it in Afghanistan.'

'Sure is. I went back and picked it up for you. I know how you guys are sentimental about your rifles.'

Grabbing the rifle, Dan immediately started taking it apart and cleaning all the parts. He also took a small container of oil from the bag and sat in the corner oiling and polishing the rifle.

'Kids with their toys, ah, Bob?'

'Guys, I have a question for you, and please be honest with me. I deserve some honesty!' exclaimed Dan as he stood up beside them.

'What do you want to know?'

'I want to know, are you guys members of Delta Force?'

Brian started laughing, but Bob remained stone-faced and stern looking.

'There are Special Forces and then there is Delta Force, or The Unit, which is the best of the best. Yes, Dan to answer your question, I am a tier one Delta Force operative, as is Brian,' responded Bob.

There was an uneasy silence for moment as Dan digested the information. Brian bit into an apple and crunched the apple in his teeth, having also changed his facial expression from one of friendliness to that of a fierce expression.

'Does that make a difference to you?' enquired Bob.

'Yes, it does actually. If you guys are Delta, then I also want to be Delta, part of the team.'

'Dan, the Emerald Delta operative, good one!' said Brian as he wiped apple juice from his lips.

'Don't see why not. He sure displays all the required characteristics, bravery or should I say stupidity, under fire and of course being a good sniper,' said Bob.

'What else do I need to do? What about training?'

'You're right, in normal times there is a selection process and training and more selection. Only 2% make the final grade. But these are extraordinary times. We are at war, gentlemen, and having observed Dan in action, I have no problem with issuing an executive order... Dan Flynn... welcome to Delta Force,' exclaimed the major as he saluted Dan, who responded by standing to attention and returning the salute. Bob then handed Dan a Delta Force emblem for his uniform. 'Always wear it with pride, Dan.'

'Welcome to the unit,' said Brian as he shook Dan's hand and patted him on the back. Dan looked at the badge with great pride and a sense of honor. He then returned to his rifle and continued to oil and polish the gun before putting it all back together.

'When you're finished with your rifle, best oil up these two MP5s and then go get some sleep, son,' said Bob, which was a request mixed with an order. Bob and Brian walked back towards their seats and requested some more beers from the flight attendant, leaving Dan to do the grunt but yet important work.

The aircraft landed with a thump, which awoke Dan, who had fallen asleep in the comfort of a business class seat provided by the US government. The aircraft slowed on the tarmac as Dan peered out the window. 'Welcome to Iraq,' said Bob.

'Iraq... Didn't you say we were heading back to Afghanistan?'

'Change of plan. Fresh intelligence enroute has put our guy in Iraq. Just be thankful it's not Syria. Good job on the equipment, Dan. Let's move.'

The aircraft stopped on the edge of the airfield, and Dan, Bob, and Brian were greeted by a local Iraqi Army officer who escorted them to a waiting car taking them to a secure military base. The three of them were shown to private bedrooms, which resembled that of a good three-star hotel, complete with private bathroom and shower, even a mini bar stocked with American beer and a mixture of Irish and Scotch whiskey. 'Think I joined the wrong army,' said Dan as he explored the mini bar.

The major had given Dan and Brian four hours for R&R before they were required to meet in a briefing room. Not wanting to waste time sleeping, Dan took his rifle and the MP5, as he had observed a shooting range supervised by an Iraqi officer on the way to his bedroom. He obtained ammunition for the MP5, but the Iraqi officer didn't have any for the sniper rifle. Loading the MP5, he quickly got to grips with the weapon, which performed well on semi-automatic when taking aim and excellent in automatic mode. The weapon was really comfortable. He understood why it was Bob's weapon of choice. Quick short bursts were perfect for clearing a room and close combat, and semi-automatic was perfect if adopting a more prone, distant position. Dan liked his new toy, like a kid with his new Christmas present and quickly used up the provided ammunition.

'Isn't she a lady?' shouted the Major as he walked onto the firing rage, carrying his weapon of choice.

'With a spit of death.'

Bob rattled off a magazine of bullets, hitting all of the targets with mainly body shots, but some head and face shots.

'She has been replaced by some new, more advanced weaponry, but for me she is the perfect fit.'

The Major handed over two magazines of bullets, correcting Dan and his stance and holding position, which improved his aim and hit rate. However, he was a natural, and although trained to use sniper rifles, he was equally good with the machine gun and pistol. The true skill of a Delta Force operative is to be skilled with any weapon including their hands and knife. If the President of the United States needs a job done, he calls Delta Force. The words of wisdom echoed in Dan's mind as he destroyed the range targets.

'Gentlemen, welcome to Iraq and our somewhat unofficial command post,' sounded the Major as he welcomed Dan and Bob into the meeting room.

'This is Izzi. He is one of our local agents based here in Iraq, an undercover specialist who has managed to infiltrate Al Qaeda and obtain valuable intelligence. Pay attention to him as he will be on the inside when we take them out. Over to you, Izzi.'

A small Middle Eastern looking man about thirty years of age stood up and walked over to a laptop that projected a map of Iraq onto the wall.

'Gentlemen, you're welcome, but not by everyone. This is a covert mission. We will carry out the operation, and you will leave within 48 hours if all goes according to plan. The individual you are interested in is Iyad, a terrorist commander responsible for many attacks on European targets. He has lived in Egypt and the UK, is involved with terrorist financing, but also, as we know, likes to get involved with killing U.S. troops.'

Izzi clicked the computer mouse, and up popped an image of Iyad. Dan clenched his fist, feeling the anger within him build at the thought of Patrick dying at the hands of Iyad and his RPG attack.

'We obtained this photograph from British intelligence MI6, who have been tracking his movements for some time. Iyad is currently based in a safe house in the city of Al Qaim, which is approximately 400 km from this location.'

'That borders Syria,' exclaimed Bob.

'Yes, it's a hostile city. If you get captured, shoot yourself,' responded Izzi.

'In ten minutes, we will move to a small British outpost located outside Haditha, which is a distance of 135 km. Iyad is expecting two journalists from Jordan tomorrow. However, the journalists will be undercover agents, and bang bang, the mission will be complete.'

'How many bad guys do we expect?' enquired Bob.

'Iyad has personal protection of 10 mercenaries, who are highly trained former military. At any one time he has two by his side. In addition, there is a garrison of terrorists here, not a training camp, but at least seventy of them, all armed and willing to die for the Jihad.'

'Thank you, Izzi. Brian, Bob, Izzi will be working undercover and will be in the area, so remember, he is one of us. Brian will fly Dan and me in his Little Bird to the British outpost in Hadith. We will equip up there with our gear. However, Dan, get some clips from the Iraqi store down below, as you never know what we will encounter enroute. Let's do this.'

'Sir,' responded Brian and Dan as they stood up and wished Izzi well before gathering some basic equipment and heading to Brian's Little Bird.

CHAPTER 30

❦

'Emerald Five cleared for departure,' stated the control tower, which was pointless as Brian was already airborne and climbing towards cruising altitude, having programmed the navigation direct to Haditha. Once again, Dan sat in the rear, with Major Redmond sitting up front with his MP5 close to hand, locked and loaded, ready for action.

'That reminds me. Got you guy's a couple of gifts,' said Bob as he rummaged in a holdall bag. The Major pulled out two new Glock .22 pistols and handed them to the guys.

'Happy Birthday, guys, from Uncle Sam. These are better for dealing with the climate we will find ourselves in, much better in sandy environments.'

On hearing the word 'sandy,' Dan immediately started to think of Sandy, back home in Donegal, and how he missed her. His face sank a little, and his eyes went distant with sadness.

'You thinking of your cute Dallas gal, Sandy?' asked Bob.

'Dallas gal. I love Texas women. Real cowgirls, real American women,' said Brian.

'How many times you been divorced, Brian?'

'Fuck you, Major!'

'Dan, look after that Glock and keep it with you at all times. Holds 15 and 1 in the chamber, semi-automatic, a real stopping gun.'

'Thank you, Sir.'

'Stop the sir crap, this is the combat zone. As before, Bob is fine.'

The guys settled into the smooth flight before they landed in the British outpost, which consisted of one main building, some United Nations supply trucks, and about twenty British soldiers in full battle uniform.

'Welcome, Major, to Stirling Base. I am Captain Michael Hunter. This is Sgt. O'Neil of the Regiment – Special Air Service. He will assist you with anything you need.'

'Thanks, Captain. Sgt. O'Neil, good to see you again, son. We need to gear up and get some ammunition,' responded Bob.

'Not a problem, Bob. We will get you sorted.'

'You know Sgt. O'Neil?' asked Dan.

'Yea, Sgt. and I trained and drank together. He's a good guy.'

Dan thought of how disciplined, gentlemanly, and respectful the British Army were in comparison to his buddies in the U.S. Army. His mind drifted back to Donegal and the British Major Terry O'Neil, who had called to the pub looking for directions for potential relatives.

In the British small armory, Major Redmond handed Dan three clips of ammunition for his Glock along with four clips of ammunition for his MP5.

'That's a lot of ammunition, 168 rounds.'

'You cannot count. It's a total of 214 if you include the two clips you already have!'

Scratching his head, Dan loaded the ammunition into his holdall bags.

'Do you have any 50 caliber for an M107?'

'Two clips are all we have,' said Sgt. O'Neil as they handed over the equipment, which also included military desert warfare uniforms.

'We won't be needing the British uniforms. Our jeans and shirts will do just fine, guys,' suggested Bob, and Dan breathed a sigh of relief. He had nothing against the British, but wearing a Union Jack on his sleeve was a bridge too far. Having got all equipped and ready for the mission, Dan managed to scab a few extra magazines of ammo and decided to get some more action in the small makeshift shooting range. He was itching to try out his new Glock handgun, which was the one gun that had plenty of ammo. He set up the targets, which were mainly old bottles of beer and some cans of Coke. With relative ease from a short distance, he took out all of the targets and really enjoyed how easy the weapon was to use. In no time at all he had mastered the weapon, which sat nicely holstered on his right upper leg. Brian and Bob walked over to Dan, throwing him a bottle of beer, sniggering at him as he stood like John Wayne with his gun holstered like he was in the Wild West.

'All you're missing is your horse and cowboy boots,' laughed Brian.

'OK, guys, we have a green light for tomorrow morning. We will leave at 03:00 hrs. via the Little Bird, which will have us at our target location for 04:30. We will base ourselves at Izzi's house, which is 115 metres from the targets. It has a balcony and a type of attic conversion that we will use for our surveillance vantage point. The target's house has one floor upstairs, which consists of two bedrooms and a roof area. The ground floor is open plan with a basement, which we think is a cellar for holding either ammunition or possible prisoners. The place is well guarded, both internally and externally. Dan, you set up a sniper position. Brian will hold off in the Little Bird until we call for extraction. Are we clear?'

'Yes sir, but why not just call in the Airforce?' enquired Dan.

'Too many civilians in the area. This is a simple mission with one objective, kill Iyad and take as many of his terrorist friends with him… Any more questions?'

'No… Sir.'

'Ok, go get some shut eye.'

'You can sit up front, Dan' said the Major as they climbed into the helicopter, shuffling the bags of guns and ammunition in beside them as Brian lifted into the pitch black sky. That night the moon was low with more than normal cloud cover, perfect for a covert mission deep into enemy territory. The Major appeared uneasy as he checked over his MP5, counting the magazine clips and other equipment. Brian slurped down a hot coffee from a drink canister provided free by garages to loyal customers. The atmosphere was tense and somewhat surreal, as though, rather than heading out on an assassination mission, they could just as well be three sales guys on the way to close a potential deal, only in a car not a helicopter.

'Coming up on Vector One,' said Brian as he flew towards the target zone.

'Make ready, Dan, Vector Two is our stop.'

Dan grabbed his bag, placing it on his lap. He readied his MP5, checking that the silencer was fitted, and rechecked his side arm, which was still holstered to his leg alongside a canteen of fresh water.

'Vector Two. Good luck, boys.' Brian hovered a couple of feet off the ground, permitting the guys to jump out, and then he pulled away into the night sky. There was nothing, just the blackest darkness and total silence.

'We're 1.5 clicks from the city of Al Qaim. We need to move fast before daybreak, or else we're fucked.'

Bob and Dan ran towards the city, feeling vulnerable in the open. Darkness was their only friend, but they needed to hike the 1.5 clicks before daylight. The city of Al Qaim is large in comparison to your average town in Ireland, with a population of 250,000. It borders Syria and sits along the Euphrates River, making it a perfect base for terrorist operations. Bob checked his satellite navigation, which indicated that they were close to the city and needed to move faster, as two western men dressed in jeans and carrying weapons would stick out in Iraq. While running, Bob put his arm in front of Dan, stopping him in his tracks.

'What's wrong?'

'Minefield. We need to stick to the main road.'

The two continued running along the road and eventually entered the city, which was quiet and resembled a deserted ghost town of Western America.

'It sure is quiet.'

'Wait for the call to prayer. This place will become lively!'

'Second house on the right, two blocks northeast,' said Bob as he checked his bearings and the map while walking along the deserted streets.

A local man appeared in the distance and walked towards the two of them, saying something in Iraqi.

'I think we're rumbled,' said Dan.

'If we were rumbled, we would be dead. It's normal to see American soldiers in town, but not dressed like two cowboys!'

Bob knocked on the door of Izzi's house. The door swung open, and Izzi pulled them inside. Izzi was not in any way relaxed, appearing extra stressed, which Dan thought was understandable considering the mission at hand.

'OK, OK, we need to move fast. The TV journalists have changed the plan. They will arrive at 09:30. Come on, the best vantage point is from the top floor.' All three of them climbed the stairs to the top floor of Izzi's home. Opening the window in the attic gave a bird's-eye view of Iyad's residence.

'I will go now, back to Iyad's, or I will be missed,' said Izzi in a scared tone, his voice shaking.

'Izzi, is there something you are not telling me?'

'No, Major… relax, all is good.

Dan and Bob set up an observation post in the attic, with a perfect, clear view of Iyad's home, which was getting clearer as the sun had started to rise. The rifle scope had been set on the house, and although they only had 16 bullets, all it would take would be one clear shot to complete the mission. The call to prayer was sounding, and the streets were busy with many of the locals attending prayer. There was little movement from Iyad's, with the exception of two men standing at the main entrance, holding AK47 rifles. One man was also on the roof and also holding a rifle and smoking a cigarette.

'Something's wrong,' said Bob.

'What?'

'I have a bad feeling about this!'

'Relax, Bob!'

BANG – a massive explosion blew up half of Izzi's house, and Dan and Bob fell to the lower floor. The attic had been blown off the house, and the floor collapsed to the floor below them. Neither of them moved, as they lay covered in parts of the house, while twenty armed terrorist stood over their bodies.

Coming to, Dan drifted in and out of consciousness. He could hear Arabic words, and he briefly glimpsed Bob, who was tied to a post on the other side of a dimly lit room and being shouted at by two men in broken English while one of the men punched him in the face. Dan realised that he was also tied to a post and relentlessly tried to free his hands, catching the attention of one of the bad guys.

'Ah, the other scum American is awake.'

One of the terrorists walked over to Dan and poured a bucket of water over his head, causing him to instantaneously regain consciousness.

'You scum American... shit.' He spit in Dan's face before walking back over to Bob.

'He is the Senior Officer, Major Bob Redmond. The other guy is a nobody,' said Izzi, who stood beside another tall Arab. Dan realized it was Iyad. Feeling his fists clench with anger, he wanted to kill Iyad with his bare hands if necessary.

Iyad walked over to Dan, who tried to free his hands in vain, but who stared directly into Iyad's eyes.

'You are not American, you are British,' said Iyad.

'Fuck you, ya terrorist bastard, I am Irish!'

'Ireland... but you are with the American.'

'Say nothing, Dan,' shouted Bob from the other side of the room.

'You America pig, shut up, you pig bastard,' shouted one of the terrorists as he repeatedly beat Bob around the head and face, causing blood to gush from his nose.

'I am Irish, but I enjoy my freedom, so I guess that makes me an American,' exclaimed Dan.

'So you will die with the American,' said Iyad, who pulled a large knife from his coat and placed it at Dan's throat, slicing it across his throat, cutting him enough to make him bleed but intentionally not enough to cause serious injury or death.

'Leave him alone, you terrorist fuck,' shouted Bob from the other side of the room.

The word 'terrorist' enraged Iyad. He ran to the other side of the room, driving his knife into the upper leg of Bob and causing him to grit his teeth in agony. But Bob did not scream out, even as Iyad twisted the knife in his leg before pulling it out, causing blood to spill onto the floor.

'You are not so brave now, Mr. American Major, are you?'

'Iyad… come closer… before I pass out…,' said Bob, whose head hung down so that his chin touched his chest.

'Yes… Mr. Major America, what do you want to say to Iyad?'

Iyad bent down, putting his right ear beside Bob's mouth.

'Iyad… I am going to stick that knife up your fucking ass,' Bob said, slowly and softly at first but getting louder and louder, until he opened his mouth wide, stretched his neck out to its full length, and bit down hard onto Iyad's ear, ripping off most of it before spitting it onto the ground.

Iyad, unlike Bob, screamed in agony and grabbed at his ear, dropping his knife onto the ground. He quickly ran from the room, leaving the two guards, one of whom hit Bob in the face with the butt of his rifle, causing Bob to fall unconscious.

Dan, although scared and in great fear for his life, sniggered to himself at the sight of Iyad running from the darkened room without his ear. Only the Major could give so much pain to a terrorist while being incapacitated himself.

Looking around the room, there was nothing Dan could do to release his hands from the large pole. The rope holding his hands had been well tied and ripped into his wrists each time he tried to wriggle free. He looked over at Bob, who was a pitiful sight and appeared to be dead. There was no movement from him other than the pool of blood on the floor, which was ever growing. His nose was also badly broken, and one of his eyes had completely closed.

'Bob, Bob, can you hear me?'

But it was hopeless; the Major was done, with his body only being held up against the post by his bound hands.

The time passed slowly, with Dan unsure when Iyad and Izzi would be back with the other terrorists to finish him off. He looked down at his shirt, which was now covered in dried blood. His back also hurt, and he could no longer feel his arms or bound hands. He thought of Sandy in Donegal and his unborn child growing up without a Father. He hadn't given much thought to being a Father, but now leaving Sandy and his child was the one factor that was hurting him the most. He had accepted that he was going to die at the hands of Iyad, and he hoped that it would be quick and that he would not be paraded on TV while having his head cut off. Even though the media and social media wouldn't show the video, he was sure that it would end up on the internet and that his Mother and Sandy would get to see the video. Dan started to drift into his memories of losing his virginity on the Aran Islands, walking on the beach, and trying the snow in Colorado. He thought of the

Gartan clay, which was still in his pocket, and although injured, he was still alive for the time being.

His drifting ended as he returned to reality with a terrorist standing in front of him, holding a knife. The guy looked exactly like what an Islamic terrorist should look like, complete with a long beard.

'I have good news for you, Mr. Irish... you are going to die a painful death, but it will not be on TV recording. First we will cut you by the neck, then hang you upside down so you will bleed out like a cow... like a...!'

The terrorist shuddered and turned, falling flat on his face with a knife sticking out of his back. Two men appeared in front of Dan wearing black military commando clothing, complete with balaclavas, holding machine pistols. One of them quickly cut the robe holding Dan's hands, causing him to slide to the ground and wince in pain. The second guy checked at Bob's neck for a pulse and then cut his hands loose, causing him to also fall on the ground.

'Who are you?' asked Dan as he looked up at the balaclava-covered face.

'I'm your nightmare.'

Just then, the door opened, and two terrorist guards walked into the room. Quickly, the second commando opened up two quick blasts of silenced machine gun fire, causing the two men to fall dead to the floor, with one just about saying the word 'Alarm' before having a round enter his head, splatting his brain onto the ground.

'Come on, we don't have much time,' said a commando, who by now had placed a bandage around Bob's leg. Bob was starting to come to, uttering the words 'water, water...'

A commando handed him a canteen of water, and Bob gulped it down like a runner who had just completed a marathon in the Sahara Desert.

'Can you shoot?'

Dan looked up at the commando's eyes. 'Damn right, I can.'

With the chance of getting away, the adrenalin had kicked in as he was handed a loaded Glock pistol.

'Let's go'

Dan shuddered to his feet, which hurt like hell, but he knew that if Bob was going to make it, the guys would need to give him more attention and carry him, leaving one commando and Dan free to fire.

'We're in the basement. We need to get to the top floor and onto the roof.'

'Understood. Let's go.'

The first commando led the way, with the second carrying Bob. Dan made up the rear, walking slowly while holding the Glock ready to fire. They opened the door from the basement and started to climb the narrow staircase up to the ground floor. As they got closer to the ground floor, it was possibly to hear Arabic voices. The first commando looked back at Dan and the second commando, and raised three of his fingers, suggesting three terrorists. He adjusted his machine gun, checking the silencer, before opening up with a hail of bullets on the three guys, who immediately fell to the floor. Quickly, the guys climbed the stairs and made their way to the second staircase. One of the supposedly dead terrorists let off a shot from an old pistol while lying on the ground, which narrowly missed Dan's head. Dan aimed at the terrorist and fired one shot, hitting him in the upper face, causing a trail of blood and brain to follow the track of the bullet as it exited the terrorist's head. Although the shot was a classic marksman shot, it had made a noise alerting the two guards outside the house, who ran into the main room.

As the first commando came to the top of the first staircase, a terrorist came out holding a familiar gun, Bob's MP5. The commando squeezed off a quick blast of three rounds, all hitting the terrorist, who fell dead to the floor. As Dan walked past the dead terrorist, he holstered the Glock and picked up the MP5. He then burst into the room in which the terrorist had come from, which was empty. However, Dan observed two magazine clips from the MP5, which he collected. Dan could hear the two terrorists coming up the first set of stairs from outside. As they ran in front of him to the second set of stairs, he cocked the MP5 and gave a quick whistle. The two terrorists slightly turned while Dan opened up on them with about 15 rounds, riddling them as they fell to the ground. He calmly stepped over their bodies and continued to follow the two commandos and Bob to the second floor.

'We need to get to the roof, which is via that hatch,' said the leading commando.

'OK, I will cover you.'

The commando opened the hatch and pulled himself through the small opening onto the roof. The second Commando lifted Bob and pushed him through the opening onto the roof before climbing through himself. Dan heard a noise coming from inside a room towards the end of the landing area.

'Come on,' sounded one of the Commandos as he leaned through the opening and reached towards Dan. At the same time, a terrorist opened up with an AK47 from down the bottom of the stairs, hitting the Commando in the arm. Dan ran towards the room and kicked open the door. Inside, Iyad was holding a gun to the head of a woman, who looked European and no more than twenty years of age.

Dan raised his MP5 and pointed it towards Iyad.

'No, no, Mr. Irish, or I will kill her. Now drop the gun.'

Dan thought for a moment, then dropped his MP5 to the ground.

'You stupid Irish man,' said Iyad as he pulled the trigger, instantly killing the young girl. Dan immediately drew his Glock and fired, hitting Iyad in the arm, causing him to drop his gun as he fell to the ground. Dan shot him again in his left foot and again in his right foot, causing him to cry out in agony. Calmly, Dan picked up his MP5 and exited the room, leaving Iyad in agony on the floor, grabbing at his wounds, trying to reduce the bleeding. As he exited the room, he opened up his MP5 as did the commando who was leaning through the attic opening, at the terrorist on the stairs. The terrorist's body rattled as he was hit by the barrage of bullets and fell to the floor.

Quickly, Dan climbed through the opening onto the roof and regrouped with the two commandos and Bob. By now terrorist rein-forcements had arrived and had begun shooting over at the roof. The guys crouched down behind the perimeter wall of the roof with bullets bouncing around them.

'Delta seven to all, we need an extraction asap,' one of the Com-mandos called out on his radio, to which there was no response. Bullets continued to hit the wall around the guys as a terrorist climbed through the opening onto the roof. Dan opened up, rattling off rounds into the terrorist until his MP3 ran out of bullets.

He quickly reloaded the magazine.

'We need to conserve our ammo. Delta seven, we need urgent extraction over.'

The guys continued to shoot back at the terrorists, making every bullet count as nearly every bullet found its target. The guys behind the balaclavas were the best shots Dan had seen next to the Major, who was also doing some damage to the terrorists even though he was half dead and in severe pain.

'You're a brilliant shot,' said Dan to the lead commando, who was hitting everything he aimed at, even though now they were down to their last couple of ammo clips.

'This fairer for you, Dan… the elk… shooting back?'

Dan looked at the commando in shock as he pulled off his balaclava, revealing a familiar face. It was Sandy's dad, Chuck.

'What the hell… How did you get out here?'

'More importantly, Dan, is how are we getting out of here,' said Chuck as he continued to shoot the terrorists.

'That's my last clip,' said Chuck.

Dan was shocked and amazed at Chuck being out in the field, but no time for thinking, they were all in a fight for their lives as by now there was at least fifty terrorists all armed with machine guns surrounding Iyad's house.

'Delta Seven, this is Emerald five inbound, over.'

'Emerald five, we have four on the roof of the Alpha building under heavy fire, requesting an immediate evacuation, over?'

'Roger that Delta seven, we inbound and hot, over.'

'Thank God, Brian. I forgot about Brian,' exclaimed Dan as he threw his Glock to the second commando, who was now out of ammunition. The second commando, who had now been shot four times, continued to fight and hit all the targets he aimed at as if shooting a toy gun at a carnival. He too pulled off his balaclava, also revealing a familiar face. It was Sgt. O'Neil of the British SAS.

'What the hell,' exclaimed Dan.

'Friends stick together. Never forget that, son,' responded Chuck.

From over the horizon, Brian approached in his Little Bird and let rip with some 50mm cannon fire, which opened up the terrorists, ripping them apart like a flock of birds hit with a shotgun at close range. The terrorists started to run as Brian hovered overhead, delivering and injecting hot lead into their bodies. A second, larger helicopter appeared overhead, with guys dropping to the roof via ropes while firing at the terrorists, who were now running away from the fire.

'They're my guys. SAS,' said Sgt. O'Neil, who was now being treated for his wounds by a medic who also assisted Bob. By now, the terrorist fire had all but stopped, other than the sweet sound of Brian's cannons occasionally firing at some remaining targets. The guys were winched aboard the British helicopter, and the medics worked on Bob, who was drifting in and out of consciousness. As the helicopters exited the area, there was a large explosion that ripped through Iyad's house. A medic treated Dan as Chuck approached him in the helicopter.

'Is his nose broken?' asked Chuck.

'No,' responded the medic.

Smack, Chuck punched Dan directly in the face, causing his nose to bleed.

'It is now... That's for getting my daughter pregnant!'

CHAPTER 31

ᏧᏑ

T hree of the guys shared a private hospital ward in the British
military hospital in Baghdad. The most severely injured was
Sgt. O'Neil, who had been shot several times but was expected to
make a good recovery. Major Bob Redmond looked like shit. His face
was badly bruised, and his leg had been stitched up. Other than his
ass swelling up from an allergic reaction to the tetanus injection, his
prognosis was that he would make a full recovery. Dan's nose had to
be reset, and his eyes were black and blue, but aside from his hurt
pride he had no serious injuries. The only guy not to sustain any injuries on the mission was Chuck, who had his own private room away
from the guys at the hospital. He had been admitted to be checked
over, his only injury being a sore wrist and knuckle from punching
Dan.

Two British officers walked into the room and saluted the men indi-
vidually, giving most of their attention to Sgt. O'Neil, who, to be fair,

was the only British soldier involved in the operation. One of the men then shook the hands of Bob and Dan.

'Well done, lads...'

'Sorry, my vision is not so good...Who are you, sir?' enquired Bob.

'I am the helicopter pilot who evacuated you.'

The pilot turned and saluted the men, who saluted back. Sgt. O'Neil tried his best to stand while the officer and pilot exited the room.

'He is not just a pilot.'

'He is Prince William, the future King of England,' said Sgt. O'Neil.

'Wow, rescued by a Prince,' responded Dan.

'Hey Sgt., how are you English with a name like O'Neil?' asked Dan.

'My ancestors are Irish, come from Donegal.'

Dan thought of the English gentleman who had been in his dad's hotel and pub and who'd had the same surname as the Sgt.

'Are you any relation to a Terry O'Neil?' asked Dan.

'He's my dad!'

'It's a small world,' responded Dan.

It wasn't long before Dan arrived back in Ireland and home to Termon. He entered his Dad's pub and was greeted by his Mother, who hugged him while Billy sat at the bar staring into a pint of Guinness.

'Welcome home, son. What happened to your face!'

'Thanks, Ma, I'm fine. Where's Sandy?'

'She's gone to Port Salon for a walk on the beach with young Naomi O'Brien.'

'I'd say they're gone to talk about babies, Dan,' laughed Billy as he gulped down a pint of Guinness.

'Is she OK? Is the baby OK, Mam?'

Dan dropped his bag, grabbed his Dad's car keys and drove hard and fast to Port Salon beach. The beach was deserted except for two tiny specs in the distance. Dan jumped from the car and ran in a fast sprint towards the two specs, which got closer.

'Sandy, Sandy!'

On hearing her name, Sandy turned and instantly realized it was Dan.

'Daniel!'

Sandy ran, well, more like fast walked, towards Dan. When the two finally met on the beach, they embraced in a loving and passionate kiss and hug.

'I will never leave you alone again, Sandy.'

'I hope not, Daniel.'

All three walked back to the car park and on to the hotel. Dan's mum phoned Barney and the guys, arranging a hooley night to celebrate Dan's return. Mickey greeted Dan in the pub, handing him a cold fresh pint of Guinness, which Dan drank in less than three gulps.

''Tis good to have you home. I've missed Ya,' said Mickey.

'Not as much as me,' responded Sandy as she hugged Dan.

That evening, Barney and the guys played with all their might as the locals danced the night away without a care in the world. Dan thought of how insulated his home was from the outside world, and he was thankful that he lived in Ireland with Sandy. He had received an honorable discharge from the U.S. Army, so he was free and ready to start his new life with Sandy and their yet-to-be-born child.

Sgt. O'Brien entered the pub and walked over to Dan with an angry look in his eyes. 'Is that troublemaking American... Robert Redmond with you, Dan?'

'No, Sgt. O'Brien, he isn't!'

'I have had him barred from entering Ireland. Immigration knows about him. If he ever tries to enter this country, I will have him arrested.'

The Sgt. turned and exited the bar without saying anything to Mickey or the other patrons in the bar. Billy sniggered away to himself at the bar while looking longingly at his glass of whiskey.

'What happened to the Sgt.... Billy?'

'A drop of whiskey and I will tell you, Dan.'

Dan walked behind the bar and placed a bottle of Jameson whiskey in front of Billy, who frothed at the mouth as Dan poured.

'Remember the night you left with Major Redmond?'

'Yes, I picked up Bob at the Police station.'

'That's right. Well, Betty found the Sgt. stripped naked and locked in a cell handcuffed to a bed. Sgt. O'Brien was very upset, especially when the Superintendent himself had to travel out from Letterkenny with the spare keys!'

'Oh, I see... Good old Major Bob Redmond!' laughed Bob.

Three months later....

'Push, push!' said the Nurse.

'You have a baby boy. Congratulations, Mr. and Mrs. Flynn.'

'We're not... married... but will you marry me, Sandy?' asked Dan.

'Yes Daniel, of course I will,' responded Sandy with her legs up in stirrups having just giving birth to a baby.

'Do you have a name for the baby?' said the Nurse as she placed the baby on Sandy's chest.

'Are you sure?' said Dan as Sandy nodded her head in agreement.

'Patrick... after my U.S. Army buddy Patrick Jelly O'Kelly.'

The End.

For 'Our Pal' – Billy Carrick 2015

THE LEGEND OF GARTEN CLAY

ↄℐ℘

I reland, my country, my home, is famous for its legends and folklore. It is a land possessing mystery and mysticism that contributes to its evergreen beauty. For generations, extending out from the period of the Great Famine of 1845-1852, Irish people have emigrated to the United States of America. Today there are over 40 million Americans who claim Irish descent.

The lengthy Atlantic crossing was rife with danger, a far cry from the eight-hour flight of the modern jet era. In times past there was no internet, Facebook, or mobile phones, and loneliness was a significant problem. Many Irish would socialize together, arranging dances and parties. Although America was welcoming, Ireland was still their home. The Irish found employment with the local police forces, fire departments, and in the medical profession. Many also joined the military and served with honor in the many conflicts faced by the Unites States. There are many Americans who claim Irish decent, most notably Presidents John F. Kennedy and Ronald Reagan. Others include Buffalo Bill Cody, Grace Kelly, and Conan O'Brien. At the famous Texan battle of the Alamo, ten Irish-born men died.

Ireland's legends span the globe, with intrigue and interest for young and old. One of these ancient legends is the story of the O'Friel of Gartan, in the townland of Termon, County Donegal, which is the most North Western county in the country, next to the Atlantic Ocean. It is written and passed down through the generations that in the year 521, Colmcille was born into the noble clan of Cinel Conall to his parents Eithne and Fedlimidh (Felim) in Gartan. Before the birth, his mother Eithne had a vision in which an Angel visited her and showed her a beautiful rose that floated over the land and sea. The vision was a foretelling that her son, yet to be born, would travel abroad, achieve great wonders, and bring honor to his name. Colmcille, or St Columba, is credited with spreading Christianity to Scotland. There are many churches and buildings throughout the world named in his honor, including even an Aer Lingus A330 Aircraft that is used on today's Irish North American transatlantic routes.

At the place of Colmcille's birth lies a great stone called Leac na Cumba (the stone of loneliness), which is supposed to have powers to cure loneliness and homesickness. The birth of Colmcille was difficult for Eithne, with a long labor. Some blood from the birth dripped onto the stone, which was covered by a kinsman named O'Friel. Eithne told the kinsmen not to hide the location of the birth as only he and the future male generations of the O'Friel clan would find the secret location. The location in which the blood fell turned into a white powder-like clay, and so began the legend of the Garten clay.

Folklore reveals that only a male member of the Friel family can collect the clay and pass it to another person. According to the legend, anybody who is given some of this clay by a Friel and keeps it on their person will come to no harm while travelling. Gartan clay will protect the holder from burning, drowning, sudden death, and related problems. However, it must be emphasized that the clay can only be gathered from the ground by a male member of the Friel family; otherwise it is useless. Some would claim that the O'Friel's are blood relatives of Colmcille.

Rose Friel, along with her sisters Nora and Ann of Termon, Donegal, emigrated and settled around the eastern coast of America, most notably Philadelphia and New York. However, Rose returned to Ireland and settled in Dublin before returning to her final resting place in St. Colmcille's Church, Termon, Donegal.

In writing this book, I remember all Irish Americans, whether living or passed on, and most notably Rose Friel and her sisters, who made the North Atlantic crossing to the United States of America and became American citizens, but who remained Irish at heart.

'Got a dream to take them there

They're coming to America'

Neil Diamond

Made in the USA
Charleston, SC
20 November 2016